A. J. FORD

A CROWN OF SOULS

Dedicated to my darling Anya,

Forever and a day.

CHAPTER 1

Phoenix

MY SOUL HAS BEEN CURSED SINCE THE DAY I WAS BORN. I came into the world on the winter solstice, the longest, darkest night of the year, with a crown of silver hair, bearing the wrath of an enchantress that fate couldn't save me from.

I sat at my window staring into the void of dawn, the moment between night and day when the world stands still. Watery daylight bled across the sky, as my kingdom slept. No harm had been done. No blood had been shed... yet.

My fireplace was a hollow hole in my chambers, not an ember in sight, and I exhaled slowly, the winter frost clouding my breath before me. I had been staring out of the window for so long I had lost sense of time.

Rooted to the spot, I was paralysed by an unknown enemy, one I couldn't see but knew was coming. I could feel it lurking in the shadows, waiting for its moment to strike.

From what my father had told me of the curse, it would strike when the moon was full.

1

I have always known of my doomed fate, of the curse placed upon the first-born daughter of the Devereaux king. I had been cursed to turn into a beast on my eighteenth birthday—and would remain so unless I could find someone I loved, and who loved me in turn, by my twenty-first birthday. I was the second first-born daughter, my ancestor Ember Devereaux was the first. She couldn't break the curse and remained in her beast form. She was eventually hunted down and killed by her own people.

Today was a day I had dreaded since I could remember. It should be a day for celebration, but this burden was a weight on my shoulders pushing me down into the depths of an abyss until I couldn't breathe. My kingdom had been on edge, waiting for my beast to emerge, but I at least had until the moon was high in the sky.

A Parakeet landed on the window ledge, its bright green feathers and rosy beak contrasted against the dull sky. It was said to be a bad omen to see a single bird. They had been in Endaria for over a thousand years, travelling in pairs. To see one meant that sorrow would follow, to see two foretold joy.

I scanned the horizon looking for the second bird, unease curling in my gut when no other appeared. Raising two fingers to my temple, I saluted the lone bird, a sign of respect in line with the superstition. I didn't need any more bad luck. I rose from my seat, my knees groaning in protest, stiff from the morning cold. Frozen. Unable to move. My chambers started to feel suffocating, so I made my way to the stables to get some air before the events of the day began. I had spent my entire life sheltered in the palace, often finding comfort in the isolation, but today, my comfort felt like a cage.

I approached the stables and couldn't hold back a smile as my gaze landed on Storm, her iridescent coat glistened as daylight crept higher over the horizon as if it could sneak upon us. Her silver mane mirrored my own and I tossed her an apple, strapping on the saddle as she crunched on the sweet fruit.

The stable boy Isaac was dragging bales of hay into the stall facing Storm's with one hand.

"Isaac?" My breath swirled in front of me as I turned to him. "What happened to your hand?" I asked, nodding to the shoddy bandage that was wrapped around his left hand.

He smiled a boyish grin at me. "It's nothing. I was cleaning the horse's hooves, my hand slipped, and I sliced my palm. It will be good as new in no time." His blue eyes shone before he looked away, returning to the bales of hay.

"Let me see it," I said, holding out my hand until he walked over reluctantly. I unravelled the bandage, revealing the sore red slice along the length of his palm, his fair, golden skin clashing with the darkness of mine. The edges of the wound had crusted and were red and angry and my jaw clenched as I studied the wound. Since our magick had been stolen by the enchantresses, wounds that would have been a simple fix were now trickier to manage. We had only what the mother provided naturally in the earth, our once-powerful runes rendered useless, leaving people like Isaac to suffer needlessly.

I looked out of the stables at the dull winter's day, not even summer's warmth could coax the lifelessness from the grounds. The very soul of the earth was broken.

"Why haven't you been to the palace healers? They will have a salve you can apply that will draw the infection out."

He shrugged his shoulders. "I didn't want to bother anyone, is all."

I wrapped the bandage back around his wound neatly and looked over to the heap of hay he needed to shift, he had at least twenty more bales to bring into the stables.

Isaac was a slight boy, at only sixteen he hadn't quite grown into his manhood yet, his frame was too slim for his height and his boyish charm only added to his youthfulness. He wiped his brow with his bandaged hand, his blonde curls falling back onto his face.

"Here," I said as I walked over to the pile of hay. I grabbed a bale by the strings and hauled it into the stables. "The quicker this is done the sooner you can get that hand healed."

"Phoenix," he hissed. "You can't be doing stable work!"

"Why not?"

He looked around to see if anyone could see us. "They'll have my head if they think I'm slacking," he whispered.

I sighed at his naivety. "Isaac, no one will do any such thing."

"But you're the crown princess, Phoenix."

I walked back to the pile of hay, picking up another bale. "I'm more than aware of who I am, Isaac, now do you want to help me bring them in or do you want to stand here conspiring all day?"

He shook his head, his blonde curls bouncing as he whispered under his breath, "Mother above."

Once the hay had been brought into the stables, I sent Isaac to the healer to get the salve for his hand. My back damp with sweat and the dull ache in my arms from the heavy lifting was a welcome distraction as I led

4

Storm out onto the grounds and mounted her. Dawn had broken across Mercea, the morning dew coating the grounds, sparkling in the light like tiny jewels sent from the mother.

Dawn was my favourite time of day, when the world was still asleep and the day was full of possibilities. It was the time when a new day casts away the shadows of a dark night and my mind raced as I thought about the events of today and the thought was a weight on my chest, stealing the breath from me. I was bound to this crown and the consequences that came with it.

I rode Storm over the grounds and away from the palace to the edge of Ivywood Forest. I paced Storm around the perimeter, not wanting to go into the trees just yet. My guard had created a plan for when my beast emerged—get to the forest and wait the night out. It was close enough to the palace for reinforcements should we need them. I had no idea what would happen to me once I turned, and I didn't know what my beast would be which only added to the uncertainty that boiled away in my stomach. I wondered if my beast would be the same as my ancestor, the cursed princess. She turned into an Amarok wolf on her eighteenth birthday, a vicious beast with poison fangs. I wondered if the fates would be so cruel as to give me the same hand as my ancestor.

I approached the edge of the forest and gazed up at the trees that stood wise and tall, like silent guardians of the land. I slowed Storm to a canter, the rich foliage of the forest grounds standing out against the grey light that filtered through the canopy of trees. Edging Storm in deeper I followed a path that had been forged over time. The forest was eerily silent, adding to my worry. No birds sang, not even the scuttle of small forest animals could be heard foraging for food among the fallen leaves.

The only sound was my mares' hooves crunching the ground beneath her feet and I couldn't shake the feeling that I was being watched.

The deeper I edged into the forest, the more I noticed the dull, hazy fog that drifted through the trees. The hair on the back of my neck stood up as I made out the faint sound of whispering. It came from the trees, as if they knew exactly who was among them.

Cursebreaker.

The soft voice sent goosebumps over my arms and Storm startled. I rubbed her neck as I tried to calm her. "Easy girl." I looked around to see if there was anything that had caught her attention, but there was only us. I pulled the reins, turning her around as the whispers of th

e forest echoed behind us.

On the ride back to the palace I pushed Storm to her fullest. We rode hard together, galloping over the Mercea terrain. The wind whipped at my braid as it pulled the strands loose, the brisk air bringing tears to my eyes, but I felt free. I felt so free and, for a moment, just a second, I left behind all thoughts of curses and beasts.

☐

CHAPTER 2

MY HANDMAIDEN HADN'T ARRIVED AT THE PALACE this morning and her absence unsettled me deeply. Guards were sent to her home to make sure she was okay, but the fact that she hadn't come to the palace on the day my beast would arrive filled me with dread. I pushed the feeling down and dressed quickly for training with my guard, pulling on leather pants that were lined with fur to keep out the winter chill, and a loose cotton shirt. I pulled my hair into a braid before wrapping a leather band around my waist which had holders for smaller weapons and squeezed my feet into my winter boots before making my way to breakfast.

I opened the door to my chambers and saw the captain of the king's guard waiting for me in the corridor. My guard had been assigned to me when I was eleven years old. They were an all-female unit of the most skilled warriors in Mercea—they struck their enemies down like it was second nature, often taking the eyes of the men they killed. Although they were a formidable force, I felt no fear towards them. They were my only friends in this cursed palace.

Ireland walked ahead while Esmeray fell into step beside me. Silver and Lex flanked our backs, they refused to leave me today which meant more than they would ever know.

"Good morning, Phoenix," Esmeray said. Her tone was neutral, and I knew better than to think she would give me an insight into her feelings about today. As the captain of the king's guard, she was a force to be reckoned with. I pulled my gaze away from Ireland's copper hair and turned to look at the captain, the edges of my mouth pulled into a tight smile. Her eyes told me they had seen things that still haunted her, things she would never speak about, they were old beyond her twenty-five years. She had been recruited from Mercea's west after convincing her father, the lord of the west, to allow her to enlist in the guard, and she was fiercely loyal to the Devereaux crown. To me.

We walked down the long corridor outside of my chambers, to the main stairs at the front of the palace. Grey light poured in through the high windows illuminating the family portraits that lined the walls. My chest tightened as I walked past my mother's portrait, her beauty illuminated by the winter light. I ducked my head, refusing to look at the portrait at the end of the row. It was of me and my father when I was seven years old, he stood behind me whilst I sat on a chair, grinning from ear to ear, our silver hair clashing against our dark skin.

Against my wishes, my father had called a Tithe. It was his last attempt to try and save me from a fate I didn't deserve. Members of the kingdom would present their offerings to my father, and if they could prove they had the means to break the curse they would be rewarded handsomely. Our magick had been suppressed for many years, the enchantresses had tipped the balance of nature over time and took every drop the mother poured into us until she simply stopped pouring. Our use of runes once gave us immense power, but were now nothing more than a reminder of what had been taken from us.

I made my way to the dining hall and took a seat as Esmeray stood guard at my back, facing the door, ready to intercept any possible threat. She would never know how much her presence comforted me.

Ireland and Silver stood guard outside the hall, while Lex did a patrol of the grounds. I wondered if they were protecting me from outsiders or protecting outsiders from me. As my eighteenth birthday drew closer, the people of Mercea had made their unease known and I wondered if anyone would be so bold as to attack the crown. Dread sat heavy in my stomach as I anticipated the day's events. By the end of the night, I would be a beast, unless someone could break this curse.

My father sat at the head of the table, not quite meeting my eye as I sat in my usual seat to his right. I didn't blame him for what was going to happen to me, although I knew he blamed himself. He had been so confident that his heir would be a son—there hadn't been a first-born daughter in three hundred years until I came into this world on a cold winter night with a crown of silver hair.

Once the king of the mightiest kingdom on the continent, he was now an angry shell of a man consumed by guilt and helplessness. As I sat down, my long silver braid fell over my shoulder and the loose strands that framed my face lifted with the release of a deep sigh.

"What time will the tithe be held?" I asked my father as I took in the food before me, my appetite non-existent.

He gripped his silver chalice so hard his deep brown knuckles turned white and I watched as he lifted it to take a drink of something I assumed burned his throat on the way down.

"The first offerings will begin at midday."

I picked up a roll and used a knife to spread the creamy salted butter over the freshly baked bread. It was still warm from the oven and the butter melted instantly.

The dining hall doors burst open and Lex's twin brother stalked into the room. My father put his chalice down and turned to face Axel who had closed the door behind him.

"General," my father said, "whatever it is, surely it can wait until after breakfast."

Axel clasped his hands before him not wavering under my father's stare.

"Your Majesty, we have received word that King Galven of the shadow kingdom has passed on to the other side."

My eyes widened as I turned to look at my father. King Galven was a tyrant ruler of the north and I wondered what this would mean for Endaria now his rule had ended.

My father clasped his hand over his face running it over his silver beard.

"King Galven's heir, Khaldon, will take the throne and is now the King of Sakaria."

A moment passed before my father spoke. "Thank you general."

Axel nodded before leaving us to our meal. I picked at my plate in an uncomfortable silence. Usually I didn't mind the quiet, I had grown used to it over the years, but today it seemed louder. It had grown overtime until it was merely an extension of our fractured relationship.

Until today I could have almost fooled myself into thinking this curse was just a figment of my imagination. The palace staff tried to act normal, but I could sense their edginess around me, from the way they were unnaturally quiet and stopped talking when I entered a room, or how they didn't dare get too close to me, as if I might bite their heads off there and then.

It had become a routine with my father. We ate every meal together, often in silence, then returned to our separate lives. The curse had created a wedge between us, and I didn't know how to have a relationship with him, often turning to my guard in my times of need, or my handmaid Chloris. I prayed to the mother that my father and I would find our way back to each other.

THE BLEAK MORNING AIR crashed against my skin like the blades in front of me. I had run laps of the courtyard with Lex to get my blood flowing and the remnants of my cool sweat clung to the inside of my clothing. I could watch my guard for hours, they were the most skilled recruits in Mercea. The dance of Silver and Lex was mesmerising, the clash of swords and daggers added another layer to their movements and the results were a complex symphony. Silver's obsidian sword clashed with the steel of Lex's weapon as Lex whirled around, swiping her leg low and taking out Silver's legs from underneath her. Metal flashed before me as Silver pulled a dagger from her thigh and had it aimed at Lex as she stood over Silver with the sword to her chest.

Lex reached out a hand and helped Silver to her feet. The women embraced and laughed it off and I felt a tug of something in my gut as I watched. I couldn't quite place the feeling—it was something between envy and yearning. They had been with me since I was eleven years old, they were only young women themselves when they came to be my protectors, but I couldn't help but feel like an outsider. It was me and them, them and me. I wasn't part of their sisterhood no matter how desperately I wanted to be. I was the crown princess, and they were the women that had sworn their lives to protect me. I wondered if I was destined to be alone, as if that were my punishment for some unknown crime my soul had committed.

"You're deadly with the kicks, Lex." Silver laughed as she walked over to the bench that had an array of weapons laid out. She poured herself a glass of water and started her stretches.

It was Esmeray and I that would duel each other next. Each member of my guard were formidable, but there was a certain edge to Esmeray's skills. I had grown used to not having my magick to rely on, I hadn't used it for so long the muscle of it had deteriorated until there was nothing left, and I needed to make sure I could defend myself physically. My guard had been training me since I turned sixteen, after incessantly asking my father to allow me to wield a weapon, he eventually gave in. After two years of training with Esmeray, I knew she wouldn't go easy on me today, even though it was my birthday.

The sky was hidden under a cloak of grey clouds and I longed to feel the sun pouring into me, its heat was nothing more than a distant summer's memory. I gripped my sword tighter as I took a few deep breaths to steady myself.

Without warning, Esmeray unleashed herself at me. I barely had enough time to bring my sword in front of my face as the brutal force of her weapon clashed against mine, forcing me to take a step back. I dug my boots into the ground to steady my balance as she pointed her sword in my direction, the daylight dancing off the blade. I looked higher to where her hand was gripped around the obsidian covered hilt, decorated with a single black diamond, such fine details that proved how carefully this weapon had been crafted. Her sword was one of only four in Mercea, created only for the highest-ranking members of the royal guard. You would expect nothing less for my father's warriors.

We danced around each other, and I kept her pace. Sweat crept down my back and my legs burned with the effort to match the captain's speed, but I kept going. I read between the lines of her silence and with every thrust of her sword I knew what she was saying to me. Never give in, never yield.

I took inspiration from Lex and swooped my legs low, kicking up some dust and stones which I hoped would cloud Esmeray's vision so I could get an advantage.

She spun around the cloud of dust slamming the hilt of her sword into my ribs and knocking the breath out of me. I keeled over as she swung her foot behind her, taking my legs out from underneath me and I crashed to the ground. She leaned over me, her hazel eyes watery from the dust and her sword inches away from my heart.

13

"A true Queen fights with honour," Esmeray said as she stood towering over me. I raised my hands to shield my eyes from the cloud of dust that was slowly sinking to the ground as she stepped over me to make her way to the weapons bench. I looked over to where Lex and Silver were watching, their faces were grim, and I knew I had pissed her off.

Lex walked over and helped me up.

"She goes so hard on you because she cares, you know that don't you?" Lex said, in an attempt to buffer my humiliation.

I dusted the dirt off my leather trousers as I looked back at the captain of the king's guard as she stood over the weapons table sharpening a dagger. "I know she cares." I bit out.

I made my way back to my chambers to get ready for the Tithe. The absence of my handmaiden echoed throughout my room, I missed her constant chatter and fussing—she was the only mother figure I had ever had.

My body was stiff and sore after training so I soaked in a bath of rose water for longer than necessary to soothe my ribs, which I'm sure were bruised after I pissed Esmeray off. My head slipped under the water and I only came up for air when I thought my lungs were going to burst. I wondered how long I could stay in the watery bliss before I was dragged, kicking and screaming, to sit at my father's side before our people.

CHAPTER 3

I SLIPPED INTO THE THRONE ROOM from a door behind the dais. I didn't want to make a grand entrance like my father would, I wanted to shrink down to nothing so I could be carried away on the wind where I could be free. Untethered. I had become used to hiding in the shadows where I could be invisible. I stepped onto the dais and ran my gaze over the room, my skin prickling with the attention of my people. I couldn't meet their eyes, fear wouldn't let me.

A turquoise rug had been placed at the foot of the dais that ran through the centre of the throne room, banners bearing the Deveraux crest with silver borders covered parts of the walls and members of the guard lined the perimeter of the room.

I had chosen an outfit that represented the crown and would show the people of Mercea that cursed or not, I was still the next in line to rule this kingdom and would one day be their Queen. My long silver curls were loose down my back, the aquamarine jewel hanging in the centre of the obsidian crown I had chosen glistened against my skin. The turquoise gown that had been custom made and brought in from the Darnassea kingdom was moulded to my body like a second skin and its silky train gathered on the floor around my feet, the long sleeves extended past my wrists and a silver loop hooked over my middle fingers to keep them in place.

The guard had changed into their uniforms for official events, they wore all black armour adorned with silver and matching masks that covered the lower part of their face so only their eyes were visible, their fierceness was striking. I eyed the dagger at Lex's hip and my hand itched for a blade.

I sat at my throne, the coolness of the obsidian marble seeping through my dress and coating my skin. I was always to my father's right. My hands gripped the arms of the seat as I tried to maintain my composure. Everyone in this room knew about my curse and I couldn't avoid the whispers and stares. My eyes flicked to Silver and she gave me a knowing look. If anyone tried to hurt me, she would unleash hell.

The doors to the throne room opened and my father walked in. Despite his lack of power, his presence demanded respect. His reputation preceded him, and he had the admiration of his kingdom. No one here knew how deep his troubles went, and I wondered if my kingdom could see through the façade of his strength.

I rose from my throne as a sign of respect and as my father approached the dais, bowed my head. He inclined his head towards me, which he wasn't required to do and the gesture almost brought me to tears. I knew he loved me dearly, but I wondered if his heart was completely frozen like mine, unable to bleed love freely.

The crowd quieted as my father's deep voice travelled across the room.

"We have gathered here today, on the Winter Solstice, to find the curse breaker for the torment the enchantress has placed upon my crown."

I kept my gaze neutral even as his words stung. I was the tormented one. The heat that flamed my cheeks was hidden by my dark skin, but I felt myself getting warmer and shifted slightly in my seat. I saw Esmeray in my peripheral vision edge a step closer to me and I subtly shook my head. I needed to stay, to see if this godforsaken curse could be broken.

My father's words garnered a response of disgust as murmurs rippled through the hall. I ran my eyes over the crowds and wondered who here had good intentions and who did not. My father offered a reward of a life changing amount of gold to whoever was successful.

The people of my kingdom were well looked after, and it was rare to see someone living in complete poverty, but the gold he offered was enough to create generational wealth.

My father motioned for the first offering to be brought forward.

Esmeray unsheathed the sword at her back, the metal sang as she brought it to her side. She was making a statement, daring someone to step out of line. An older gentleman bowed before me and my father and pulled a small vial of what looked to be water from his pocket. I noticed Ireland's hand shift to the dagger strapped to her thigh.

"Your majesty, if I may?" The man asked my father as he looked towards me, and I realised he was asking my father for permission to approach me. I gripped the arms of the throne tighter and stopped myself from shouting no.

My father looked to me and an invisible fist gripped my heart as I gave a nod. He held all the power over this kingdom, yet he still wanted to make sure I was okay. The man bowed again, and the throne room fell quiet. My entire life depended on this, I couldn't help but anticipate failure.

Esmeray's eyes didn't move from the man. He cautiously approached my throne and I looked to the small glass jar he held, noticing the slight tremor of his hands. He knelt before me and opened the vial. Immediately the smell of lavender and something stronger, maybe sandalwood, filled my senses. He sprinkled the water around my feet, closing his eyes as he drew runes in the liquid. I could feel the air in the throne room, rife with tension as I held my breath and waited for something to happen. The water started to bubble, and a cloud of smoke filled my vision. A few moments passed and nothing. I released the breath I had been holding. The man walked off sheepishly as the throne room murmured amongst themselves. If this was an indication of how the day was going to go, I would rather spare myself the torture.

A young woman approached the dais next, her skin was fair like a white rose and her dark wavy hair was stark against her skin. But her face was kind and I wondered what she would offer today.

"Your Majesty." The young woman bowed before me and my father, waiting for permission to step forward.

My father stretched out his hand and motioned for her to approach us.

I looked to my guard but they didn't seem concerned by the woman. In fact, she radiated light as though it was coming from within, casting an ethereal glow.

"What is your name?" I asked the young woman, who was only a year or so older than I was.

The woman smiled. "Quelin, princess."

I gave her a warm smile in return as she knelt before me. My guard had positioned themselves to intercept any threats.

I couldn't put my finger on it, but I felt no ill will from Quelin.

She knelt before me, pulling a small pouch from a concealed pocket in her dress and licking her finger before dipping it into the pouch. When she removed her finger, it was covered in some sort of shimmering dust. She edged closer towards me, holding her finger out in front of her, as she closed her eyes and drew runes into the air. Traces of glowing light lingered in mid-air in the spaces her fingers had moved and I looked on, fascinated.

Warmth sparked deep inside of me, ever so gently, and my eyes widened as the heat intensified and spread across my body.

Silver stepped towards me, but I shook my head. I wasn't in any pain. I felt as though the warmth was soothing me in a way I hadn't known that I needed.

The heat kept building, but it didn't burn. The feeling was familiar as it soothed my bones, like they had been craving the warmth of a flame for an eternity.

I looked to my father who was transfixed as the woman knelt before me. Air swirled around me gently as it lifted the edges of my skirts, and I felt my curls sway on the phantom breeze. Quelin was awakening something inside of me that had been asleep, the air in the throne room was thick and nobody dared move or even breathe too loudly. The sickening sound of bones snapping brought me back to reality.

My guard rushed to Quelin, who lay at an unnatural angle before my feet. Esmeray reached down, placing two fingers on the young woman's neck.

She looked to Ireland and shook her head. She was dead.

I gripped the edges of my throne, nausea churning in my gut. A woman had died at my feet trying to help me.

Lower ranking members of the guard rushed in and carried the woman out of the hall as shocked gasps rang out throughout the hall. Bile rose in my throat as I thought about Quelin losing her life trying to help me—she was someone's daughter, a sister maybe, and her life was gone.

My father called for a break, and I breathed a sigh of relief as I forced a watery smile onto my face. I stood from my throne and slipped away through the side door.

"Mother above, what was that?" Ireland asked as we sat in one of the lounging rooms overlooking the courtyard. The kitchen staff brought us some refreshments and I picked at the sandwiches and pastries, my appetite non-existent.

"She didn't wish me any harm," I said as I closed my eyes, the sound of Quelin's neck snapping rushing through my mind. "Whatever that was, it felt good—warm and light, before something snapped her neck."

Lex finished off one of the sandwiches, unbothered by the death that had just occurred. "Do you think it was a reaction from the curse? I mean, she was trying to help you and she looked like she was succeeding. What if the curse prevents anyone from helping you?" she said, dusting breadcrumbs from her fingers.

My father came in and I rose to greet him. His presence took up the whole room and I marvelled at the sight of him. He took off his crown holding it under his arm.

"Captain, may we have the room?" My father said as he waited for my guard to leave us. It was more of a demand than a request and my hands twisted in my lap as I tried to remain calm.

"I will reach out to Quelin's family and offer my condolences," he said as he walked over to the window, he placed his crown on the console table and clasped his hands together behind his back as he looked out of the window. My gaze flicked to the crown I would one day wear. Its obsidian and black diamond beauty glistened in the light that poured through the window.

I hesitated before I spoke. Our relationship was already fragile, held together by the threads of fate, I didn't want to damage it any further.

"Do you not feel this has been a waste of time?" I asked. "A woman has lost her life trying to help me."

My father turned to me, his silver hair illuminated by the light that seemed to gravitate towards him. "I will do anything I can to prevent you from enduring a fate you do not deserve, Phoenix."

I gave a shallow nod of my head.

A moment passed between us. The last two heirs of the Devereaux crown.

My father cleared his throat, breaking the silence. "I'll leave you to rest before we carry on for the afternoon."

I gave a small smile and watched as the mightiest king of our lands walked back into the throne hall.

I stared into space, flecks of dust floated by and I wondered whether my father's efforts were futile or did we stand a chance to break a three-hundred year-old curse? Thoughts of my future swarmed my mind, possible scenarios that ended with me being hunted down and killed like the cursed princess, or the alternative of ruling Mercea as its Queen.

The door opening broke my train of thought as Ireland's copper hair came into view.

"They're ready for you now, Phoenix."

I nodded as I wondered how my fate would come to be.

I resumed my seat on the throne. The tension in the room was suffocating as I gripped the obsidian seat, my nails clawing at its surface.

My father called for the next offering to be brought forward and nobody moved. A few murmurs echoed throughout the hall, and I looked to my guard who were scanning the room. Nobody stepped forward and I didn't blame them. No amount of gold was worth losing your life.

My father went to speak but stopped himself as the crowd parted. A frail woman made her way to the dais and something about her demeanour made me sit up straighter. She had a large, hooked nose laced with boils and her skin looked like it had been weathered by the sun and many storms. A black scarf covered her hair, but I could see grey wispy strands that had come loose.

My face remained impassive, but I couldn't ignore the feeling that I was in the presence of great magick. My guard felt it too, edging closer towards the dais and forming a wall between the crowd and me and my father. I peered over Lex's shoulder and met the woman's eyes. One was significantly larger than the other and her smile had a front tooth missing. She didn't fit in with the other people of Mercea and I wondered what land she was from.

"Your Majesty," the frail woman said as she bowed before my father. Her voice sounded like metal being dragged over stone and a chill went up my spine. "I believe I have the means to end the curse placed upon the crown princess."

She spoke with such conviction that it was hard not to take her seriously. I held back a sigh as I tried to not let my frustrations become evident. I wasn't sure that anyone here had the means to break it.

She stepped towards the dais and Ireland moved to stand in front of her. She was almost a foot taller than the frail woman and Ireland stared the woman down before stepping to the side. The woman approached the foot of the throne and knelt before me. She pulled a small needle from her sleeve and pricked the tip of her finger with it. A drop of blood dripped onto the dais and I felt disgust course through me—she was attempting blood magick, the kind that wasn't too different from the dark magick the enchantresses used.

She whispered in a tongue I wasn't familiar with as she drew runes with her bloodied finger and I shifted uncomfortably in my seat before she looked up at me, her eyes wholly black. I gasped as I shifted away from the woman, she opened her right hand and blew a powdered dust that covered my body. I started to choke as the dust clutched at my throat and made it hard to breathe. My eyes widened as I looked to my guard where Esmeray had her sword levelled at the woman.

I tried to stand before I staggered backwards and Silver rushed to my side. My breathing became laboured, and my body felt as if it were burning. This was different to how Quelin made me feel. This felt wrong.

My father's deep voice rang in my ears. "Explain yourself, witch."

Lex had joined Esmeray and had a sword levelled at the woman, she would be foolish to try to escape.

The woman laughed, the horrific sound escaping her mouth as she said, "Ravynne sends her regards."

My vision blurred as I saw Esmeray's sword come down on the woman's neck at the mention of the enchantress's name that had cursed me. The crowd gasped in shock as I heard more swords being drawn. The woman's blood splashed up the thrones as her head rolled down the steps onto the turquoise runner. The crimson droplets that splashed up the obsidian marble glistened like rubies.

That's when the pain came. My back arched violently, every bone in my body felt as if it were breaking. I heard Ireland scream at the lower ranking members of the guard to clear the room. Whispers of the curse rang in my ears as I realised what was happening. Claws ripped from my skin and a pained cry escaped me. Fangs filled my mouth and the coppery taste of blood coated my tongue as my arms twisted until the bones snapped. This was death itself. My beast was here.

CHAPTER 4

A RIPPLE OF FIRE TORE THROUGH ME as I took my new form. My vision was so sharp I could see the individual strands of gold in Esmeray's hair. My eyes snapped to a vein throbbing in Ireland's neck and her pulse pounded in my ears. My beast stood on four legs towering over the people in the throne room. I looked to my guard who stood steadfast, their weapons drawn, ready to counter any attacks.

Screams and shouts filled the hall, I made out the distinct whispers among my people. Amarok. Of all the beasts Ravynne could have chosen, she had picked the beast my people were most afraid of. The same beast my ancestor had turned into, costing the princess her life.

It was an ironic full circle moment, for the enchantress that had cursed me was the same person who had banished the wolves from the face of the earth.

I felt oddly in control of this new form, but the fear from the crowded room was overwhelming my senses. I needed to get out of the palace to the Ivywood forest.

The sound of an arrow flying made me move swiftly to the side, the arrow flew past me and grazed the edges of my fur. A growl reverberated in my throat and the people that hadn't yet fled, cowered. Cursed or not, I was still the crown princess, and my people were turning against me. A dagger flew across the room and embedded in the bowman's eye. I looked over and saw Lex reach for her sword, the dagger at her hip gone.

I ran out of the throne hall, jumping and dodging the cowering people on the floor. A high whistle sounded and I whirled around to see my guard following me. My father stood on the dais, his eyes widened as the blood drained from his face, I had never seen him look so grief stricken, as if he couldn't believe what his child had become.

I ignored the gasps and cries as I ran out of the palace, the scent of their fear overwhelmed my senses, I could feel it flowing through my cursed blood, igniting a hunting instinct. The strength that rushed through me was euphoric. My eyes adjusted to the darkness as I emerged outside and took off towards the woods at a run. My paws pounded the palace grounds until the woods came into view, hooves sounded in the far distance and I knew my guard would be with me soon. I ran through the trees, the beast's instincts connecting with mine. When I was sure I was away from any people, I slowed my pace and looked down at my paws. My fur was silver, the same shade as my hair. I stepped into a spot on the ground that was illuminated by the moon and looked up to see it swollen in the sky and I howled.

My ears pricked up as I heard hushed voices. I crouched low to the ground as their scent carried on the wind and torches came into view and I slowly edged backwards. Their forks and arrows cast shadows onto the forest floor, and I knew I was being hunted. The betrayal cut deep—they were trying to kill their future Queen. Although I had taken this beast's form, I still had a semblance of my humanity.

I could hardly blame the people. The Amarok wolves had terrorised the people of Endaria for many years before the enchantress rid the world of them with her dark magick, and although they had been banished, the fear still ran deep. People still told their children stories of wolves that were seven feet tall with poisonous fangs that roamed the forests.

I made to move off from my hiding place, when a sharp pain lanced through my back leg. The voices got louder and I reached back with my razor-sharp teeth, pulling the arrow from my leg as fury filled my vision. The plan to come to the forest wasn't known by many and they had gotten here too quickly for it to be coincidence. As if they were already waiting for me. There was a traitor in our midst.

The smell of copper filled my senses and I looked at my wounded leg, the crimson blood almost glowing in the moonlight.

The sound of arrows flying through the forest was all I could concentrate on as I ran. I had no idea where my beast was taking me, but I knew it was trying to keep us both alive. My hearing was sharp and the sound of branches snapping behind me brought me to a stop. I didn't want to hurt anyone, but I refused to be hunted down and killed like the cursed princess.

The branches that cracked under their feet stopped suddenly. Please don't make me do this. I whirled around to face them, my teeth bared in a snarl as venom dripped from my fangs.

Ireland came out from behind a tree with her hands in the air. My heart sank as my friend submitted to my anger and the creak of an arrow sounded from behind her. I growled as she dropped to the ground, spinning as she flung a dagger in the direction of the bowman, his head snapped back as the dagger embedded in his eye. Trying to kill me was bad enough, but my guard were protected under the crown and to kill one of them was to commit treason. Fury seethed in my blood at the thought of someone trying to bring harm to them too. I stalked over to Ireland and nuzzled my snout in her neck.

"I've got you Phoenix." She said as she ran her fingers through my fur.

The moment was cut short as men came from every angle as my guard surrounded me, I was swarmed as they fought off the hunting party. There were at least three men to each of them, we were outnumbered, and I couldn't see a way out.

A thick iron chain wrapped around my wounded leg and I howled in pain. Another was thrown towards me from the opposite direction, and I panted as the dull ache of the iron weighed me down. I pulled against the chains binding me to the ground but there was no give. The urge to kill them all rushed to the surface as smoke curled up my throat, choking me as I struggled to breathe. A dagger embedded in my fur, and I let out a cry. Esmeray reached me and ripped the dagger from my side.

"Stay with me Phoenix, we'll get you somewhere safe."

I strained against the chains until they cut into my beast's flesh, and I watched as bodies fell to the ground as my guard unleashed themselves on the hunting party.

I growled as a man stalked closer towards me. I was trapped with nowhere to go. The beast's instincts overpowered mine and flames erupted from my snarled mouth. I breathed the white-hot fire towards the man, keeping him at bay and letting the flames graze his skin. He howled as his skin charred instantly and stumbled backwards before breaking into a run through the trees.

Silver crept over towards me, low to the ground, and reached for the chains locked around my legs as she tried to free me. A man tackled her to the ground and her dagger flew from her hands. I watched helplessly as she wrestled with the man double her size. Unable to speak I whimpered, I wouldn't forgive myself if anything happened to her. The man was on top of her, reaching for the dagger she had dropped, when Silver used her elbows to break his nose and he rolled towards me. Without thinking, I sunk my fangs into his leg and felt the venom release into his blood, the rush that went through me was intoxicating.

Silver jumped up and tried again to release me from the chains just as an arrow whistled through the trees and embedded in my shoulder. The pain shot through me, and I collapsed to the ground panting. I was going to die. Ireland roared as she thrust her sword through a man's gut and Silver threw herself over my body. I dwarfed her in size, but she was willing to take the brunt of any weapon the hunting party threw at me, while I lay there with the metallic smell of my blood mixed with the fallen members of the hunting party, burning my nose. I saw more bodies fall before I gave in to the pain, closing my eyes as footsteps crunched over the forest floor towards me.

A SHARP PAIN SHOT UP MY LEG, rousing me from my sleep. My eyes were heavy, and I couldn't muster the strength to drag them open. I recognised the motion of a horse's movements and moved my fingers. Fingers. I was human again. I tried to lift my head when a dull pain throbbed in my neck, and I groaned in defeat.

"Phoenix?" I would recognise that voice anywhere. The horse stopped and a hand brushed my hair away from my face as the daylight stung my eyes. I looked down at Esmeray who was standing next to the horse. They didn't leave me.

A sob escaped my mouth. I will not cry, I will not cry, I will not cry. Nothing could have prepared me for what I experienced last night. Grim determination steeled my spine and I refused to let that happen to me again. I became aware that I wasn't wearing any clothes, my guard had covered my bloodied and bruised naked body with their tunics. The crisp morning air soothed my burning lungs as I adjusted to being human again. I had almost been killed, and I had to endure this every month until I found someone to truly love me.

I stayed in my position, laying on the horse to protect what shred of dignity I had left. I recognised my surroundings and knew we were approaching the palace.

Esmeray brought the horse to a stop, and I lifted my head slightly. My father stood at the foot of the palace surrounded by his guard. My handmaiden Chloris had returned and rushed over with a fur shawl to cover me.

I dismounted from the horse, my knees giving slightly as my feet touched the ground, Esmeray held me up as I steadied myself. Isaac approached me hesitantly, the look on his face was pure devastation. I didn't have the heart to put on a brave face or to pretend I wasn't broken so I walked past him as he took the horses reins from Esmeray. The gritty stone beneath my bare feet cut into my skin as I walked towards the palace doors. I couldn't meet my father's eye as I passed him, not wanting anyone's pity.

Lex's twin brother, Axel, stood beside my father, a muscle feathering in his jaw as he watched me enter the palace broken and bruised. I had to get behind closed doors. I couldn't fall apart in front of them. I made my way to my chambers, looking back as I climbed the stairs to see Esmeray talking with my father. There was a look of deadly violence in her eyes.

I opened the door to my chambers and closed it behind me before sinking to my knees and letting the tears fall. Last night had broken me and I didn't know if I would ever recover. The warmth of my pain fell down my cheeks and I crawled across the floor into my bed, my pillow turning damp as the tears poured out of me to no end. I pulled the quilts over my head and let the shadows consume me.

I WOKE TO A FIRE BURNING in the fireplace on the far side of my room. The embers cracked as they cast a warm glow through the darkness and I wondered how long I had slept for.

"No one enters the room until the princess has risen." Esmeray's voice travelled through the closed door and I sat up, my body stiff and sore as though I hadn't moved for a week. I glanced at the table at the side of my bed and saw a glass of water that I immediately reached for, quenching my thirst. My throat still raw from the flames I'd breathed on the full moon.

I tiptoed across my room to the fireplace, my muscles barking in protest at every step I took and put my hands over the flames. The warmth seeped into my skin and I reached my hand lower until my hand touched the fire. I expected the heat to bring a burning pain, but all it brought was comfort. I pulled my hand back as the door creaked open slightly, the candlelight from the halls glowing at Ireland's back.

Esmeray entered my room too, her eyebrows knitted together with concern as she took me in.

"How are you feeling?"

I rose from the fireplace and crawled back into bed as Ireland pulled the curtain open. A| sheet of snow was falling onto the palace grounds as I sank back onto my pillows, feeling impossibly heavy. My eyes were vacant as I stared into nothing, struggling to stay afloat. The thought of enduring this for the next three years was too much to bear.

"How long have I been out?" I asked, my voice thick with emotion.

Esmeray's gaze flicked to Ireland's then back to mine. Her mouth was a tight line as if she didn't want me to know the answer.

"Two days."

My breath hitched as I took in her response. I had lost two days of my life because of the curse. I rolled my neck, the stiffness throbbing down my spine.

"I can't live like this," I said to the open space before the window. "I need to find a cure before the next full moon. I can't go through this again." My voice trembled on the last few words, and I willed myself to be strong.

"There are people looking for answers as we speak," Ireland said as she came to stand closer to the bed.

My memory was a blur. Flashes of the tithe and Ivywood Forest flashed through my mind like a bad dream. My mind drifted to the cursed princess, Ember Devereaux, and my throat tightened with the realisation that I may end up with the same fate.

"Those who attacked you will be held accountable and punished as they should be." Esmeray's words should have provided me with some form of comfort, but they did the opposite.

"No."

My guard looked at each other, confused by my response.

"They have every reason to be scared. The Amarok's terrorised this land for too long, the fear has been bred into them. We can't punish them for that," I said, defeated.

"Phoenix, we can't let this behaviour go unchecked." Esmeray protested and I could feel the fury seeping out of her. "They attacked their future queen. Cursed or not, it can't be tolerated."

I knew she was right. I couldn't let the crown be seen as weak.

"There is a traitor in the palace," I said, my voice hoarse with exhaustion. "Only a few of us knew about the plans to hide out in the Ivywood Forest. They were already there waiting."

Ireland sat on the foot of my bed, the mattress dipping under her weight.

"Those responsible for your pain, Phoenix, will be held accountable."

"No more bloodshed." I managed to get out as memories of my beast flooded my mind. "Nobody else dies." I looked at my guard as I spoke. My word was final.

Someone knocked at my door but I had nothing left in me, not even the strength to call out and ask who was there. I lay in bed, frozen, watching the snow fall effortlessly to the ground.

Esmeray opened the door, and I heard hushed voices before Chloris entered.

My guard left me with my handmaiden and Chloris came over to my bedside to stroke my hair.

"Phoenix, how are you feeling?"

There were no words to explain the shame, the fear. I had been hunted down like a wild animal by my own people. How was I supposed to rule my kingdom one day when my people didn't even respect my life?

I stared into nothing as Chloris gave up waiting for a reply and instead went to my bathing chamber. The scent of vanilla and sage assaulted my senses as the tub filled up with the healing oils and Chloris came back to my bedside and coaxed me out of bed. I clutched my side where Esmeray had pulled out a dagger that had been embedded in my fur. My wounds would scar, and they would serve as a reminder of what I'd endured, and I would make sure it never happened to me again.

Chloris helped me into the tub, and I hissed as the water stung. My body was still battered and bruised, even after two days of rest. I lay back, letting the heat from the water seep into my skin and soothing me down to my aching bones. Chloris washed my hair gently and I listened to her cries from behind me. She was the only mother figure I'd ever had, and

I'd never seen her cry. I didn't have the energy or compassion to console her, a hardness settling over my heart like a steel cage that would always remind me of how cruel the world can be.

Once I was scrubbed clean, Chloris left me to soak in the bath and I watched her wipe her eyes as she left me in the bathing chamber. I slipped under the water and stayed there until my lungs burned. The desire to live was slipping away from me and I screamed as the water muffled my cries.

CHAPTER 5

M Y HANDS FLEXED AT MY SIDE as I walked to Esmeray's chambers. I had woken up restless and needed an outlet for the energy simmering under my skin.

I was up earlier than I needed to be, but after losing two days, I had to make the most of my time in this form.

I knocked on Esmeray's door and she answered almost immediately. Her hand went straight to the dagger at her hip when she saw me, and she stepped into the corridor her eyes flicking from side to side anticipating a threat.

"Can I come in?"

Concern clouded her face as she stepped aside so I could enter her room.

She closed the door behind us, and I looked around before taking a seat. I didn't spend a lot of time in her room, but I thought it reflected her personality perfectly. There were no frills—it was basic, functional. It also made me feel sad that she had no family trinkets that would make it feel more homely. Her entire life was the guard.

There were books and reports on the desk under the window, no doubt war strategies and royal correspondence, but her room was surprisingly light and airy and very well kept.

"What's on your mind, Phoenix?"

I turned my gaze towards her as she sat on the bed, strapping on her boots. Her bronze hair was unbound and fell in soft loose curls around her shoulders. I tried to picture her married with children, as some Lord's wife, as her father had wished.

Not knowing what had happened while I was recovering from my beast was eating away at me.

"What happened while I was gone?" I asked. I didn't know how else to put it—I had been unconscious for two days after my beast emerged. Two days lost forever.

Her eyebrows pulled together as she looked at me.

I carried on, "What happened in those two days after the full moon?"

She took a few moments before she answered.

"What exactly do you want to know?" Her tone was cautious, but I wouldn't back down.

I chewed my lip as I battled my mind, was ignorance bliss? Did I really need to know all the daunting details? I had been ambushed in the Ivywood forest and I couldn't rest knowing there was a traitor among us.

I took a deep breath before I replied. "I want to know everything. Please don't shelter me. I need to know it all."

Esmeray watched me for a moment, no doubt debating how much information she would share with me.

"There have been reports of a rebel group."

I couldn't hide my shock. I shook my head as I tried to process what Esmeray had said.

"The men that attacked you in the forest were likely working for them."

"A rebel group?" I asked.

Esmeray nodded, "As the only heir to the crown combined with the curse, a group of people have taken it among themselves to rebel."

I felt my kingdom slipping through my fingers. I owed it to my ancestors and to the cursed princess to fight for my crown.

"No one is alive to tell the tale of the cursed daughter, many believed it to be just that, a tale, a myth, but the people seeing your beast for themselves has created a wave of unrest throughout the kingdom."

"I'm to be their queen one day and they hate me?" I couldn't believe it. My father had tried everything he could to release me from this fate. "I suffer through no fault of my own—if they had just left me be, no one would have been killed." I winced as I remembered sinking my fangs into a member of the hunting party, and the release that ran through me as venom dripped from my fangs.

My thoughts were interrupted by a knock at the door. Esmeray walked over to open it and Ireland walked in, halting when she saw me. Her bright green eyes roved over me before she asked. "Is everything okay?" I noticed her hand shift the dagger strapped to her hip and I sighed as I closed my eyes. Maybe being unconscious for two days wasn't so bad. I wouldn't have to be so aware of the torment I caused my people.

Esmeray pulled on her tunic and strapped a range of weapons onto her body. I had never seen her without a blade, even when I'd burst into her room once after I had a nightmare. My instinct had guided me to her because even during a night terror, I knew she would protect me from the beasts my mind had convinced me were real. She'd jumped out of bed in her night clothes with a dagger in her hand that she had swiped from under her pillow.

"I was just filling Phoenix in on what happened after we returned to the palace after the full moon," Esmeray said as she rifled through the papers on her desk.

"Ahh," Ireland said as she sat down on the couch next to me. Esmeray leaned over handing a document to me.

"What is this?" My eyes scanned the paper before I looked back up.

"It's a list of people who we think may be part of the rebel group."

My eyes scanned the list of names again, and I breathed a sigh of relief when I realised I didn't recognise any of them.

I handed the paper back to Esmeray. "You were telling me about the men in the forest," I urged her to carry on.

She looked to Ireland and unspoken words went between them—they had the kind of bond that only those that had faced death together and lived to tell the tale could have.

Ireland turned to me as she said, "Once we knew you were well and recovering, we returned to the forest to identify the men that had attacked you." She stopped herself before looking to Esmeray. Fury flashed across her face before she spoke again, "when we arrived at the forest all of the bodies were gone."

"Leaving us with no leads," Esmeray bit out.

"Whoever is behind this knows what they're doing," Ireland confirmed.

There were rebels in the kingdom working against me and my father. The betrayal stung. My father was a just ruler, and although we were the largest kingdom in Endaria, my father treated the other kingdoms as though they were as mighty as Mercea—even the smallest of the seven kingdoms, Nadriah, my father treated with the same respect as those who matched us in size.

"What else?" I asked.

Dawn was breaking over the horizon and streaks of light filtered through the window as Ireland steeled herself before saying, "When we were ambushed in the forest, before I put my dagger through one of the traitors' heart..." She stopped herself and my heart beat frantically in my chest at what else could be revealed today. "He spoke in the old language."

I looked to Ez as I gathered my thoughts. "The old language? That hasn't been spoken in over five hundred years." It was the language of my ancestors and hadn't been used since the Battle of the Lost. It was a language of times long forgotten.

"What did he say?"

Ireland pushed her copper hair from her face. "It translated to the forgotten shall rise."

I looked to where Esmeray sat at her desk, her body tight with tension.

"Okay, so there is a rebel group that speak the old language and what? They wish to turn against their crown. What would they gain, it doesn't make any sense."

"It may not make sense right now, Phoenix, but we have to take these threats seriously."

I let loose a long breath as I processed what my guard had told me. Not only did I have to find a way to free myself from this curse I also had to worry about a rebel uprising.

I pushed myself up off the plush couch. "I need to work off some energy," I said as Ez and Ireland stood with me. "Do you care to join me in a sparring session?" I asked as I bowed deeply before them.

Esmeray rolled her eyes at my theatrics. "Are you sure you're up to it?"

I walked out of her room looking over my shoulder as I pointed a finger at her. "No holding back, Elordi."

Esmeray sheathed a sword at her back, with a wicked glint in her eye. "I never do."

ESMERAY WALKED OUT OF THE PALACE with me to the courtyard while Ireland was behind us, always guarding my back. I stopped to admire the Alba roses that bloomed at the south of the gardens, leaning over to breathe in their sweet scent, as I ran my fingers over the velvet soft petals. It was hard to pass a rose and not admire its beauty and the Alba roses bloomed even throughout the harshest winters. Resilient, just like I would need to learn to be.

We walked to the north of the courtyard, where the wind was knocked out of me. Esmeray slammed her arm out, stopping me in my tracks as she unsheathed her sword.

"Ez what on—" I gasped.

Ireland walked around us with her sword drawn and my eyes followed her path, landing on the twelve white shapes laid out before us.

41

The long narrow shapes had been individually wrapped in white cloth and tied with rope at either end to secure it. Horror unfolded in my stomach at what was inside.

Esmeray's arm was still across my chest, holding me back, so Ireland stalked forward and bent down. She sheathed her sword as she pulled a dagger from her hip and plunged it into the cloth, the material ripping with the force of her blade. She peered inside and stood up to face us.

"What is it?" My breathing was shallow, and I struggled to catch my breath.

Her eyes were full of thunder, the anger vibrating off her.

"It's one of the men from the hunting party."

Esmeray dropped her hand, going over to the bodies that had been left out in the palace.

It was a message—our people had turned against us.

"How did they get in?"

A muscle flicked in Esmeray's jaw. "The bodies must have been placed here after the last patrol. That means that someone knows our schedule."

Her eyes scanned the courtyard before she looked to Ireland, "Identify them. I want names, alliances, anything you can find, then dispose of them."

She turned to walk back into the palace, and I fell into step next to her. "Go to your chambers Phoenix, I'll station Silver and Lex outside. Do not leave until I tell you to."

I nodded as I hurried to my room. Esmeray was no doubt on her way to tell my father the palace had been infiltrated. They shouldn't have been able to get past the guard.

I opened the door to my chambers and quickly shut it behind me as I glimpsed Chloris fluffing my pillows.

"Would you like breakfast?" Chloris asked, her cheery nature was usually infectious, but my day was already off to a sombre start.

"No, thank you, I'm just going to lie down for a while." After what I had seen I couldn't stomach anything right now.

I jumped as there was a knock at my door. "Who is it?" I called weakly.

Silver walked in without replying and went straight to the windows, checking for any signs of threat. It troubled me that people would be going so far as to commit treason just to be rid of me.

Silver looked to Chloris, who seemed oblivious to the tension and potential threat around her, and waited for her to leave before she said, "You are the sole heir to the throne, Phoenix. You are also the first daughter to be cursed in three hundred years. Make no mistake, as loyal as your people are, there are those that are out for blood."

A chill ran through me as I looked into Silver's icy blue eyes. She was deadly serious and my blood ran cold. "If I died, there wouldn't be anyone to carry on the Devereaux crown which my family has ruled for a thousand years, my father would have to abdicate his throne." The words spilled out faster than I intended.

"Just breathe," Silver said as she came to stand in front of me rubbing my arms.

The pressure the fates had placed on me was immeasurable. The future of my kingdom had fallen into my hands whether I liked it or not. In that moment, I promised myself I would do whatever it took to save my crown.

I SAT AT THE TABLE to the left of my father. We often dined just the two of us and we had hardly spoken since my beast had emerged. My father busied himself with his royal duties in an attempt to avoid me, but I could tell the guilt was consuming him day by day.

We ate in silence, the tension becoming unbearable, there was no mention of the men that had been slain in their attempt to kill me.

"I've decided to host a ball in your honour," he said, finally breaking the silence. "It will give you a chance to meet some eligible men from across the kingdom."

My fork stopped mid-air. It was the last thing I would have expected him to say and drawing attention to myself and inviting strangers into the palace seemed like the last thing we should be doing right now.

"Oh." Was all I could get out. I couldn't force someone to love me. I cared deeply about my crown, but the idea of parading myself at a ball and hoping some pre-approved Lord's son would want to fall in love with me only filled me with dread.

"At least meet with the men, Phoenix, who's to say you won't meet someone and fall in love? If all goes well, the curse could be broken before three years."

I scoffed. "Or they will be repulsed as they watch me turn into the creature our people fear most, and I'm to stay in hopes of them looking past that. Our people are terrified of the wolves, Father. And I turn into the deadliest of them all."

I wiped my mouth with a napkin and threw it onto my plate. I hadn't finished my food but talking of the curse curbed my appetite. I excused myself and made my way to my chambers.

My balcony overlooked the grounds, and the crisp night air would be a relief from the shame that heated my very being. I wanted to scream. The hands of fate had dealt me a cruel hand and I was bound to it. I wrapped a fur shawl around my shoulders and sat under a sea of stars. I sighed, my breath misting in front of me as my frustration weighed me down. My hands tangled in my curls as I ran my hands through my hair wondering what I had done in a past life for my soul to be tangled up in such chaos. I believed everything happens for a reason, but I couldn't see to what end. My father choosing my mother, my mother losing her life hours after I was born. There was so much senseless pain that had been caused just for me to be in the world.

I heard the door to my chamber open but I didn't turn around, my gaze fixated on the delicate snowflakes falling before me. The cold was soothing, down to my aching bones.

My guard would be training. Probably running laps of the grounds in these conditions. I admired them endlessly.

I could hear Chloris humming to herself as she roused a fire, the melody as sweet as she was. I left my seat on the balcony and wandered into my room. The flames danced in the fireplace as I sank to my knees, the plush carpets of my rooms enveloping my skin as I leaned into the fire's warmth.

The flames entranced me. The warmth of the fire in my chambers reminded me of times long gone, and I prayed to the mother I would one day be able to summon a flame to tame the shadows again.

CHAPTER 6

I WOKE UP EARLY, feeling restless and agitated again. Since the full moon, I couldn't stay still. I felt as though every second I wasn't trying to find a way to save myself from the same fate as my ancestor was a second wasted. I bathed and made my way to the library— I needed a distraction from this restless energy simmering in my blood. There were records of all the Kingdoms and influential, powerful bloodlines. If I knew more of the enchantresses, or the cursed princess, I was sure I could find a way to beat this curse on my own terms.

I entered the library, closing the heavy wooden door behind and immediately felt comforted. Aside from being with Storm, this was my favourite place in the palace. There were rows and rows of ancient books dating back to the first King of Mercea.

Trysten emerged from one of the aisles, pushing a cart full of books. My heart warmed at the sight of him. He came from a family of scribes, that were responsible for the history of Mercea to be put into words so that the past wouldn't be forgotten. He had been one of the constants in my life and I walked over, taking the cart from him.

"Phoenix, what brings you here today?" he asked, and it was a simple enough question although I noticed his tone was laced with curiosity.

"I wanted to research the past Trysten." I said as I gestured to the rows of transcripts that contained knowledge of the last thousand years.

His eyes wrinkled in the corners as he smiled. "You have your mother's mind."

I smiled as an invisible fist gripped my heart at the mention of my mother.

"Do you need anything particular?"

I looked around the library at all the information it contained. "Anything that may help me beat this curse or help me understand what these rebels want, please."

He gave me a rueful smile, "I'll find what you need and bring them over to you."

I thanked him and made my way to a quiet part of the library, hidden away where I was sure I wouldn't be disturbed.

Trysten came over sooner than I expected and placed a pile of books in front of me.

"Sit with me?" I asked.

We sat in silence for a while flicking through the books but I was unable to retain anything I read. "What do you know of the enchantresses?" I asked breaking the silence.

He seemed troubled by my question, as if the topic was a sore one and I didn't press him further, giving him time to answer me.

"The enchantresses favoured the dark side of magick. When one dies, the power of that person is shared among the remaining members of the coven. Our power is given to us organically, passed down from generation to generation, channelled through runes, although the royal bloodline's powers are naturally greater than others."

I nodded as I waited for him to continue.

"Three hundred years ago, when Ravynne hadn't quite reached womanhood, she fell in love with one of your ancestors, King Etienne. While he was a prince, he sold her a dream of being his queen one day and she fell deeply in love with him. Whilst they were busy wrapped up in each other, the other kingdoms were plotting to banish the enchantresses due to their growing power. For the first time, they felt threatened, and so the Kings sought to eradicate them."

"How did Ravynne become so powerful?"

"They wanted to rid the world of them, so they massacred them. This didn't work as planned as the survivors of the clans only grew stronger with their sisters' magick. Ravynne is the last of her coven, and so she has more power than anyone should possess."

I listened eagerly as Trysten continued.

"Ravynne begged the young Prince to help save her coven, but he was just a prince and had no influence over his father. Her people were slaughtered, and any survivors were banished from Endaria. Ravynne somehow survived, taking on her slain sisters' power with every death."

"How did she survive that?" I asked.

"Only the mother knows. She could have killed the royal family and ended the bloodline, but she wanted to make Etienne pay. His first child was a daughter, Princess Ember, and so she cursed the first-born daughter of the king to turn into a beast on her eighteenth birthday. It's said he died of a broken heart as she was cursed to remain in her beast form forever."

I sat back as I exhaled a long sigh. I thought of what my ancestors had gone through all because of a young love and one person's pursuit of revenge.

"You are the only first-born daughter in nearly three hundred years," Trysten said, pulling my attention back to him. "All the heirs had been sons. I think our people had forgotten about the curse until you came into this world, Phoenix. Your father was beside himself when he took you in his arms, knowing you would suffer through no fault of your own. Your mother's death broke an already broken man."

The pain of never knowing my mother pushed to the surface and I blinked quickly to stop the tears from falling.

I heard the library doors open and close before Lex came around the corner. Snow dusted her braids, and she blew into her hands to warm them as she walked over to me.

"I'll leave you to your research Phoenix," Trysten said as he left me with Lex.

"I thought I might find you here," Lex whispered, sitting down in the seat across from me.

"You don't have to whisper, we're the only ones in here beside Trysten." I joked, trying to lighten my mood.

She looked around and nodded in agreement, "True, but I feel like I'm disturbing the ancestors by talking normally, the library is a sacred place." She said whispering the last few words.

I set aside the book I was reading and she pulled it across the table, her eyes scanning the page.

"You're researching the cursed princess?"

I leaned back in my chair. "I thought there might be something we've missed, something that we've overlooked that would help break the curse by the next full moon."

"Have you found anything?"

"Trysten told me some things I didn't know."

Lex stilled before continuing flicking through the book. "Your mother and father's bloodlines are both very powerful. You are a weapon in your own right and I truly believe you will beat this." She reached across the table placing her hand on top of mine. "I'm sure of it, Phoenix."

Her confidence in me was a beautiful thing. Here was one of the fiercest, skilled warriors in our kingdom telling me I would be the one to break the curse.

Trysten walked over to our table and placed a thick leatherbound book in the centre of the table. He leaned over to wipe the dust from its surface and Lex raised her eyebrows as he said, "I thought there might be something in here that can help you."

I pulled the book towards me reading the title, The Battle of the Lost.

"Ez told you about the rebels," Lex said as I flicked through the pages.

"They spoke in a language that hasn't been used in five hundred years." I replied. "It hasn't been spoken since the Kingdom of Monterrain fell, it can't be a coincidence."

I scanned the pages of the book, trying to find something that could point me in the right direction.

"I could ask Axel what he knows about the battle?" Lex suggested.

Her twin brother was the general of my father's armies, he knew every battle as much as he knew himself.

I pushed my hair off my face as I looked at the pile of books strewn about the table.

"Axel would be a great help right now."

"Okay, I'll be back." And before I could protest, Lex had left me alone in the library while she went to get the general.

All I could do was look at the books before me while I waited. A short while later Axel walked into the library, his fur shawl dusted with snow, and I marvelled at the sight of him. His muscled arms were covered in tattoos and battle scars and his body adorned with an array of weapons. I winced as I realised I had requested the presence of the general of the mightiest army in Endaria so that he could give me a history lesson.

Lex walked over to me and Axel followed, stopping at my side.

"Princess."

I smiled at the general while Lex picked up The Battle of the Lost, she pushed the book towards her brother and the table groaned as he leaned to read the title.

"I'm sorry if you were busy, I didn't realise Lex was going to get you straight away, we can do this another time."

"Don't be ridiculous! Axel would love nothing more than to educate us on the battles of Endaria." Lex said as she smiled innocently at her brother.

The corner of Axel's mouth pulled up into an almost smile. I was fascinated by their bond, they knew what the other was thinking, they finished each other's sentences, and I yearned to have a connection like that—to always have someone by your side from the moment you were born, to never be alone in the world.

Axel pulled a chair out next to Lex and sat down facing me.

51

"Is this about the rebels?" Axel questioned.

I looked at the general, his rich brown eyes bored into mine as I realised how kept in the dark I had been. If I hadn't asked Esmeray about what happened after the full moon, I doubt I would have been told. Everyone knew what was going on around me, while I blissfully buried my head in the sand.

"They spoke in the old-language that hasn't been spoken since the great battle. I figured if we knew everything about it, we might find out what the rebels want."

Lex looked to her brother. "Why did the lost kingdom fall?"

Axel clasped his large hands together on the table. "Monterrain was the smallest of the eight kingdoms on the eastern side of the continent, their king felt overshadowed by the other kingdoms, especially Mercea."

I looked to Lex as Axel continued. "The rulers of Mercea have always been fair and saw the other kingdoms as equal, but the ruler of Monterrain launched several attacks on Mercea, which King Aveyron was forced to counter. He didn't stand a chance against Mercea's armies, but he didn't back down. The other kingdoms offered the people of Monterrain refuge and those that wished Mercea no harm were protected. The people of Monterrain were eventually lost to the other kingdoms that they made their homes. The remaining people were killed in battle and once the king was killed, there wasn't a kingdom left."

"Why would the rebels speak the language now, it makes no sense?" Lex questioned.

My mind was still reeling from an entire kingdom being wiped out because of one man's quest for power.

"Although the people of Monterrain haven't lived on the land for five hundred years, there are still descendants among us that have ancestral ties to the lost kingdom," Axel reasoned "With the curse coming into effect and the earth being starved of magick the crown has never been weaker and there are those that believe now is the time to fight against us."

"What would they seek to gain from going against the crown? It doesn't make any sense." I questioned.

"We think that the rebels believe Mercea is responsible for the lost kingdom being wiped out, so given our vulnerability, it seems they want to destabilise us further, by eliminating the heir to the throne." Axel's gaze darkened as he looked at me.

Lex scoffed as she raised her eyebrows. "That is absurd, the lost kingdom fell five-hundred years ago and has nothing to with our kingdom in the present day."

"Absurd as it may be," Axel continued, "it's the reality we are facing."

I slumped forward as I listened to the twins discussing the lost kingdom between themselves. The danger to my kingdom was bigger than I could have ever imagined, and the enemy was still unknown, threatening to steal my birthright from me.

CHAPTER 7

A KNOCK AT THE DOOR dragged my attention from the book I was reading. I pulled my legs from underneath me and shook off the fur blanket that had been keeping me warm and padded over to the door, my bare feet sinking into my plush carpets. I opened the door to see Lex stationed outside. Stood next to her was Corbin Hemlock, one of my father's councillors, holding a scroll of papers tied with an onyx ribbon. He was a small man with beady eyes and a hooked nose like a bird's beak.

He cleared his throat. "Good afternoon, princess, I have your schedule of royal duties."

I groaned inwardly, wishing I hadn't answered the door. Now I had reached my eighteenth year, I would be a working royal and would be required to travel across my kingdom as a representative for the crown.

Corbin spoke as he took a step forward. "Your fa—" He was cut off by Lex's arm slamming into him, knocking the breath from his lungs as he went to step into my room, her arm shot out blocking the doorway and he dropped the scroll as he stumbled backwards.

I looked down quickly so he wouldn't see me laugh. I regained my composure and looked up to see him fumbling with his glasses as he pushed them high up his nose. He bent down to pick up the scroll and I shot a look at Lex, her eyes crinkled at the corners.

"Right, yes, well here is your schedule princess," he gasped, still struggling to catch his breath, "if you have any questions, you know where to find me."

I took the scroll from him, "Thank you, Corbin."

He nodded before rushing off down the corridor.

I grabbed Lex's arm and pulled her into my room, shutting the door behind us.

"Must you always be so protective?" I asked as I unwrapped the silky black ribbon.

Lex stood near my window where I had been peacefully reading before Corbin had interrupted me.

She turned to look at me, an incredulous expression on her face.

"I mean, my father's advisor is hardly a threat." I said as I ran my eyes over the engagements I would be expected to attend.

"Threat or not," Lex started, "why he thought he could walk into the crown princesses' chambers is beyond me. He's lucky I didn't put him on his back."

I rolled my eyes but couldn't help a small smile. Lex came to sit opposite me as I scanned the pile of reports, not knowing where to start. I had been so focused on trying to figure a way out of the chains fate had bound me in that the thought of my responsibilities had completely slipped my mind. I looked over the schedule—I was to meet with Lord Orbarrow in the south to discuss plans to expand the southern ports, then we would travel west to visit Esmeray's father Lord Elordi, we would also visit the priestesses on the western coast. It was customary in Mercea to pay respects to the priestesses once you were a working royal. They had been loyal to the crown for a thousand years.

I wasn't looking forward to the meeting with Lord Elordi. Esmeray's father was a manipulative man who showed his daughter the minimal amount of respect that was required to be deemed decent. Although she had become captain of the king's guard at a young age and was one of the most respected members of our kingdom, he diminished her accomplishments at every opportunity.

"Follow me," I said to Lex as I grabbed the reports and made my way to the council room where the rest of my guard already were, going over security measures.

I burst into the room and dropped the pile of papers onto the desk and slumped into a chair putting my head in my hands.

No one spoke as they waited for me to explain.

I pushed my hair back. "I don't know where to start," I said as I gestured to the reports I had dropped on the table. "How am I supposed to find a way to break this curse if I'm travelling all over the kingdom discussing port expansions."

Ireland leaned over and picked up the reports. Her gaze roved over them before she sat back with a smile on her face.

"And what are you smiling at, McVay?" I asked as I raised my eyebrow to question her. She knew if I addressed her by her last name that I wasn't in a playful mood, and that I was deadly serious.

"I think we should disguise your first working tour as a means to scour the kingdom one last time." she said confidently, as if it were the most reasonable thing in the world.

I looked to Esmeray and could see the cogs of her brain working to come up with a plan.

"Let me see those," she asked and Ireland passed the reports to her as she paced back and forth whilst she read them.

Silver sat back, her fair, slender fingers contrasted against the obsidian dagger she was using to pick her nails. Silver had a quiet but deadly confidence—she was also an only child and favoured solitude. When she wasn't with the guard, she was almost invisible, only being seen when she wanted to be. She wasn't one to bore herself with the details, but once her skills were required to protect her crown, she was all in.

"We can visit the Seers in the south, they may have knowledge or be able to use their...gifts, to help," Ireland suggested.

"What about my beast?"

I looked at my guard as I waited for them to respond, my entire life centred around the full moon and my turning into a beast.

"The full moon is just over two weeks away," Esmeray said. "We should go as soon as possible so we're back before the moon is full.

I nodded as I dropped my head into my hands. The pain of the turn was torturous and I couldn't bear the thought of enduring that again, but really it was the hunt that had rattled me the most. I couldn't be hunted again, I didn't know if I would survive it.

☐

CHAPTER 8

W E WERE LEAVING for our travels today. Our journey to the South took four days by horse. The weather was slightly warmer in southern Mercea, and they relied heavily on the southern ports for trading. I couldn't wait to wander the markets and taste the delicious southern delicacies.

My father had arranged for us to stay with Lord Orbarrow at his Manor. To an outsider, it would be an official visit—the crown princess performing her royal duties by representing the crown. To the few on the inside, it was an attempt to free myself on my own terms.

Ireland had suggested starting with the locals in the markets, where we could visit the seers. The number of seers had diminished over the years but the few that remained chose to reside in the south, spending their days telling the locals their future for a silver coin or two.

Lord Orbarrow had his guard meet us at the southern border. As he was a representative of the crown, he had his own guard that protected him in the name of the king. I watched Esmeray dismount from her horse with a lethal grace and walk over to the head of the southern guard as my eyes ran over the unit. They bore the Devereaux crest on their uniforms and it brought me comfort, knowing I had people on my side. They fought in my father's name and Esmeray was the captain of them all.

Lord Orbarrow was waiting on the steps as we approached his home. His manor was in the lush hills and I admired the grounds as we approached the Lord.

"Greetings, princess," he said, smiling bright and wide before he looked to Esmeray and nodded. "Captain."

"Thank you for having us, Lord Orbarrow."

"Oh, please, it's no bother and we don't need formalities, call me Ramsey." He waved his hand in dismissal. "My wife is visiting her sister, but she will be back tomorrow, and she has arranged a dinner on your behalf."

"Oh, that isn't necessary. I don't want to be any trouble." I protested.

"I tried to talk her out of it, princess, but she insisted."

"Then I'll look forward to it." I said as I gave him my warmest smile.

We were shown to our rooms and I looked out of the window at the hills in the distance, the manor was surrounded by lush greenery and flowers of every kind. I made a note to visit the gardens so I could admire them.

I walked over to the luxurious mattress that was set on a golden bed frame and decided to rest my eyes for a moment. My breathing slowed, and I felt relaxed for the first time in days. I sighed as a knock at the door forced my eyes open.

I opened the door and a young woman no older than me bowed. Her skin was golden brown, no doubt from the glorious southern summers, which was offset by her warm brown hair.

"That won't be necessary but thank you."

She smiled sheepishly and I went to take the tray she was carrying from her.

"Oh no, please allow me." She came into the room and put the tray down on a side table.

I looked at the food she had brought, and my mouth watered. A shrimp salad had been prepared with a fresh lemon dressing, there was iced tea, fruit and some delicate pastries.

After four days of eating bread and cheese on our travels or whatever Lex could catch for us to roast, I was famished.

"What's your name?"

"Bryn." she said quietly. I noticed she was fidgeting with her hands and made small talk to try and calm her.

"Have you worked for Lord Orbarrow for long?" I asked, I hoped if I could get her talking, she would feel more comfortable. I needed allies while I was here in the south.

I noticed her eyes roving over me as if she was looking at a myth, something from fairy tales. I wondered if she thought my beast would erupt here and now.

"This is my second year at the manor, Your Highness."

"And do you enjoy it?"

"I do," Bryn said as she looked to the floor. My plan clearly wasn't working, she had warmed up to me no more than a blanket of snow would warm the winter ground.

"Well, I won't keep you any longer. Thank you for the food, it looks delicious."

Bryn gave me a small smile and curtsey before leaving me to my own thoughts.

I popped a shrimp into my mouth and closed my eyes at the taste. The flavours of the dressing burst into my mouth as the sweetness of the shrimp contrasted against the tart lemon. They had slightly different ways in the south compared to back home and I was enjoying the change.

A knock sounded at my door again and I would have sighed but I knew it would be a member of my guard checking on me.

"Come in," I shouted from my seat, I didn't have the energy to move.

Lex bounded in, slumping on the seat next to me. She popped a shrimp into her mouth and moaned at the taste.

"Gods I miss the south," she said and I couldn't help but laugh.

Ireland and Silver followed her inside and I noted them scanning the room, looking for exits and signs of traps or danger.

"I don't think we have anything to worry about," I said to no one in particular.

Ireland walked over to the window and looked out over the grounds. "You can never be too careful."

I looked at Esmeray who was the last to enter my room. "What do you have in mind for today?"

"We should wait to head into the markets later, it will give us some time to recharge after our journey. We keep our ear to the ground and try to see if we can get any leads."

I sighed without thinking.

"It's worth a try, Phoenix," Ireland said from where she was still standing next to the window.

I looked to Lex who had finished off the rest of the salad and had moved on to the pastries.

"We also need to be extra vigilant," Lex said as she wiped her fingers on a napkin.

Worry coursed through me as Lex spoke. "Now that your... beast... has made an appearance, people will be more wary of the crown and the threat that comes with it. The Amaroks terrorised our people for so long that they don't know anything but fear."

I winced as I took a sip of my iced tea and let the sweetness distract me from my thoughts.

"Although magick in this land has diminished significantly, we may find a seer or someone who practises the old ways that can give us answers." Ireland said.

"Okay, but first, I need to rest and bathe."

Esmeray nodded as they made to leave me in peace. She turned around at the door. "We leave for the city in a few hours."

I WORE A SCARF to cover my hair hoping it would give me some anonymity. Everyone in the land knew that the royal bloodline had rich dark skin and hair like Moonlight.

We wandered through the markets and the bustle and noise was a nice distraction. Although it was winter the weather in the south was warmer and there wasn't a drop of snow in sight. The market stalls were dotted around the edge of a cliff overlooking the ocean, some selling fresh fish caught from the southern sea, others filled with southern delicacies. I stopped at a stall selling scented body oils. The owner was a middle-aged woman who was busying in the back. She turned around and saw Esmeray and I waiting. She stumbled and held onto the counter to balance herself.

"Oh goodness, good afternoon. Is there anything I can help you with?"

"Just browsing, thank you," I said to the woman, who smiled before she turned her back to us and continued rearranging her shelves.

I ran my fingers over the glass bottles and chose one that was labelled, Lavender and Vanilla. I opened the glass jar and breathed the scent in, it reminded me of Chloris and I felt a stab of homesickness.

Another jar that was labelled lemon and blood orange caught my eye and I placed them on the counter of the stall.

I pulled a few gold coins from my pouch as the stall owner turned around and saw us waiting.

"The lemon and blood orange scent is my best seller," she stated proudly as she wrapped the jars in cloth.

I looked to Esmeray who was scanning the market, the rest of my guard were spread out among the crowd so as not to draw too much attention.

"That will be two silver coins." The woman said, pulling my attention away from my guard.

I placed three gold coins into her hand and her eyes widened.

"Oh no, no that is too much dear. I couldn't accept that."

Esmeray stepped forward. "We are here sourcing gifts for the King, it would be his honour to gift you this gold." Her voice was laced with authority.

The woman picked up the coins from the makeshift counter clutching the coins to her chest. "Thank you." She gushed and it warmed my heart to know that we had a made a difference to someone.

We walked further into the markets, the scent of freshly baked pastries making my mouth water, and I pulled Esmeray to a stall selling the most delicious, sweet treats. I decided on a spiced pear tart. I took a bite and moaned at the taste while Esmeray stifled a smile.

I had almost forgotten what the purpose of our trip to the markets was, instead enjoying the anonymity and not having the weight of the world on my shoulders.

I noticed a wooden hut with runes carved into it and tapped Esmeray's arm.

"Over there." I nodded towards the small hut where a sign had been placed outside.

The seers of Mercea weren't like the enchantresses or priestesses, they were unaffected by the tip of balance with the mother.

Ez scanned the crowd before nodding and I walked over to the hut, bending down to read the sign. I tried to decipher what the runes said when a husky voice came from inside, a small window had been fashioned from the wood and was covered by a piece of silk that moved as if by a phantom wind.

"Your future isn't out there, girl."

I looked to Esmeray who was clenching her jaw.

The voice sounded again, "Don't worry captain, she will be safe."

I looked to Esmeray as she unsheathed her sword.

"I'm right here, Phoenix, the moment you feel uncomfortable let me know."

I nodded as I pulled back the silk curtain in the makeshift doorway. I didn't know what to expect from the outside, but the wooden floorboards groaned under my weight as I stepped inside. The hut was small and had barely enough room for the two chairs and table. I felt my senses heighten and my mouth instantly went dry, the energy was heavy, and I felt alert like I was prey in the presence of a predator.

I looked across the table at the seer. She was a unique looking woman with a deep olive skin and dark eyes like burnt charcoal, with a wild mane of black hair. Her fingers were covered in gold rings, and she looked at me as if she knew all my secrets. It was an effort to hold her gaze, I felt as if I had been stripped bare.

My gaze flicked over her face before I dropped my eyes to the table and coughed to break the silence. I didn't feel that she would hurt me, but I felt afraid of what she was capable of.

I could feel the burn of her stare on my skin as if she had pressed a hot iron rod onto my body and my hands started to tremble slightly. I had no idea what was happening, but I could feel adrenaline pumping through my veins as if my body were preparing me for an attack. It took everything I had not to bolt out of the makeshift doorway.

I felt something awakening in my blood as if it were reacting to her presence. My magick was non-existent, I didn't even have an outlet to channel it, but I felt that it wanted to protect me as if I were in the presence of something sinister. I pulled my scarf around my face tighter as if it could protect me.

Out of nowhere she spoke.

"That scarf won't protect you from what's to come, *cursebreaker.*"

My breath hitched as I tried to maintain my breathing. She looked at me for a moment, time seemed to stand still, I imagined her picking my thoughts apart wondering which ones to reveal.

Her eyes roved over my body as if I had words written on my skin and she was reading my soul. Between the body heat of us both, the air in the hut was thick and remembering my dry mouth, I licked my lips.

"Bitch."

"Sorry?" I breathed. My instincts were screaming to get out, but my feet were bolted to the floor.

"Spirit doesn't like it when you lick your lips, that's why it called you a bitch, don't do it again." She explained while looking at me like a woman possessed. It was as though someone else was looking at me through her eyes.

"Sorry" I managed to get out while my heart thrummed in my chest.

"Don't apologise, don't say sorry for doing what you feel is ri— Bitch."

I had done it again. Without even realising I'd licked my lips. I needed some water and to get out of this enclosed space, I felt trapped like I was underground desperate for air, but her gaze was piercing into me pinning me to the spot.

She reached over to the ledge underneath the makeshift window and placed a wooden box onto the table. The box was covered in runes and I watched as the seer drew over the markings with her finger and the lid flew open. I tried to make sense of what they said but I was too focused on my dry mouth and the adrenaline coursing through my veins. She pulled out a deck of black cards that were engraved with gold.

My palms were slick with sweat, the air in the hut almost non-existent.

She picked up the deck and held it to her mouth as she whispered something over it. She tapped it three times with her knuckles and started shuffling the cards.

"What is your name?" I blurted out, my father had once told me that to know the name is to know the person, so much could be revealed about a person just from their name.

The seer stopped shuffling and lifted her gaze to meet mine. I couldn't place her expression, it was something between surprise and caution.

"Amaris," she replied, her voice hoarse as if she had spent a lifetime screaming.

I willed myself to hold her gaze even though my skin prickled with adrenaline. Amaris returned to shuffling the deck and three cards flew onto the table face down.

She slowly turned them over and my eyes focused on the writing on each card.

I looked to the first card, where a gold embossed skull with two swords crossed underneath sat in the centre and the word Death was written at the top.

I sucked in a breath and fought the urge to wet my lips again.

Amaris smirked at me. "Death doesn't mean you have to die, *cursebreaker*."

She turned over the remaining cards. The Magician and The World.

I looked up at her waiting for her to explain. She closed her eyes, tilting her head slightly as if someone stood behind her, whispering in her ear.

"The cave you fear to enter holds the treasure you seek."

My mind raced as I tried to make sense of what the seer was telling me. Amaris must have read my mind because her eyes snapped open as she said, "You are the cave."

I forced a watery smile onto my face and nodded.

"Do you understand, *cursebreaker*?"

I met the seer's black eyes, they were riddled with anticipation as though she couldn't wait to spill the secrets of the spirit.

My voice croaked as I went to speak, fear had stripped my mouth of any moisture.

"I'm not sure what the cave could mean," I replied.

Amaris reached over and touched each card briefly, she looked at me as she said, "Each card on the table represents a major life event, the very fact that you have three means your life will change beyond recognition."

I swallowed, the sound louder than I'd intended in the silence.

"When you say change, is it good or bad?"

Amaris tilted her head, seemingly weighing her words before she spoke.

"Once these events happen, your life will never be the same, it is up to you to decide whether that is good or bad."

I went to speak but thought better of it. I needed some air, and I felt that this had been a waste of time. I gave the seer a tight smile and asked how much I owed her. I left the coins on the table next to the tarot cards, constantly aware of her gaze burning into me as I pulled back the silk curtain and stepped outside. I lifted my head to the skies and took a deep breath to calm myself. The feeling was jarring, I didn't feel as though I was in any physical danger, although she gave me the impression she could melt my mind with one thought.

I felt a hand on my shoulder and knew it was Esmeray before I turned around.

"Are you okay?" She scanned me, checking for any signs of harm.

"I'm fine." I pulled my scarf tighter around my face. "I'm ready to go."

Esmeray frowned at me. "What did the seer say?"

A shiver ran through me, as I looked over my shoulder to Amaris's hut, "Nothing I could make sense of."

AFTER THE MARKETS, I needed to clear my head. Amaris had unnerved me more than I realised, and I shivered every time I thought about being in that small space surrounded by her whispers.

I walked to the barracks where I saw Esmeray clasp arms with a man from the guard.

Esmeray saw me approaching and said something quickly to the man before making her way towards me.

"Ride with me?" I asked.

Lands' end was an hour's ride from the Lord's manor, and I wanted to watch the sunset over the white cliffs that the south was known for. Anytime I watched a sunset or looked at the moon, it reminded me of how insignificant I was. How our time is borrowed and all we can do is make the most of it.

Lord Orbarrow provided us with the best horses he had and insisted members of his most skilled unit accompany us. They gave us enough space that we didn't feel suffocated but if anything were to happen, they would be close enough. I gave the rest of my guard the night off.

We rode for an hour in the evening chill before reaching lands' end. The most southern point of Mercea.

I dismounted the horse, patting its neck as Esmeray took the reins from me. I looked out over the cliffs and marvelled at the view. It was breathtaking. The sun covered the sky in pinks and oranges, the clear blue sea crashed against the cliffs. Birds flew overhead as the sea breeze caressed my exposed skin. I wore the royal uniform as I stood at the end of the land I would one day rule if I could break this curse that had burdened my bloodline for centuries. I looked over my shoulder as the wind whipped at my hair and Esmeray stood back, allowing me the space I needed. I looked out over the sea and the cliffs carved out by the ocean, beating against them relentlessly since the beginning of time, but the cliffs stood solid, like soldiers of the land. I fell to my knees and roared at the sea and its waves roared back. The threads of fate and decisions made long ago had brought me to this moment. There would be no more heirs. It was up to me to break this curse and protect the future of my kingdom.

CHAPTER 9

LORD ORBARROW'S WIFE had arranged a dinner for us as her guests. I excused Bryn from her duties as I didn't want to make her any more uncomfortable than I already had and chose one of the simpler gowns that had been provided for me. It was a long sleeved forest-green dress that had a slight silver shimmer through the chiffon fabric, which I thought would complement my hair perfectly. I dusted a metallic olive-green powder across my eyes and left my lips nude, before applying the lemon and blood orange scented oil to my lips to give my face some dimension. It was a trick Chloris had taught me and I pushed the uncomfortable feelings of missing home back down to the depths of my core, where they couldn't bubble over the surface. A range of crowns had been provided but I decided against one, instead braiding my hair into a crown across my head and leaving a few curls free to frame my face. I looked into the mirror and smiled. I could take care of myself.

I left my room and was met with my guard stationed in the corridor.

"You look beautiful, Phoenix," Silver said and I gave my friend a warm smile as we made our way to dinner.

Lord Orbarrow's wife, Lady Kerrin, rushed over to me as I entered the dining room, her long black hair flowing behind her like a trail of midnight.

"Princess." She wrapped me in a hug and then pulled back to admire the gown I had chosen. "The green looks divine on you."

She gestured to a man chatting to Lord Orbarrow in the corner that I hadn't noticed when I'd first stepped into the room.

The man turned around, his pale green eyes stopped me in my tracks.

"Frey?" I breathed as he walked over to me. "What are you doing here?"

We'd kissed once. Memories of summers long gone rushed through my mind as I took in the man before me. I was fifteen and thought he was my chance at real love. Frey and his father had spent some time at the palace during a blisteringly hot summer, he was two years older than me, and I fell for him hard and fast. I knew my father favoured the Lord's son to be my betrothed and I often spent my days imagining a life with him. Images of a marriage filled with love and laughter consumed my mind, ruling my kingdom with this handsome lord's son by my side. His sun golden skin was offset by his green eyes and his jaw looked like it had been carved by the Gods themselves. The first time we kissed, I was showing him Storm, and how fascinated I was that my hair matched her mane perfectly. He'd pulled me behind the stables and kissed me. It was the only time I had ever been kissed—I still remember the feel of his lips on mine as he explored my mouth gently before pulling away leaving us both breathless.

"Oh, did I forget to mention?" Kerrin gushed, bringing me out of my thoughts, as she clutched her hand to her chest. "Frey was in the south attending to business, so I invited him to dinner. I knew you two were old friends."

I felt ambushed and couldn't get my mouth to form the words I wanted it to, my cheeks heated slightly as I stuttered.

Esmeray stepped forward, saving me from the embarrassment. "Should we get seated my lady? We need to leave at dawn tomorrow."

"Ah yes, yes of course!" Kerrin flapped erratically before she clicked her fingers to get the attention of one of the servers standing in the corner waiting for his orders. I looked to Lord Orbarrow who winced slightly as his wife's shrill voice filled the room as she gave out orders and started telling people where to sit.

"Now, Phoenix, you can sit here," she said as her hand found my back and she guided me towards the table. I looked at the place card on the plate where my name had been intricately written in black ink. I looked to the name next to where I would sit, and my heart sank a little as I read Frey's name.

I sat down and placed a napkin on my lap. Lex, Ireland and Silver sat facing me and Esmeray sat to my left.

A server leaned over my shoulder and placed a bowl of seafood broth onto my plate, the smell rich and fragrant. I reached for a spoon and my hand brushed Frey's as he reached for his, a shock jolted through my skin and I pulled my hand back quickly, unsure if he felt the same thing.

The dinner went by in a blur. I smiled, laughed at the Lord's jokes and feigned excitement as Lady Kerrin told me about the latest ball she had hosted.

After dinner, Frey asked me to walk the gardens with him and I admired the flowers as we talked about small nothings with Esmeray and Ireland following us at a distance.

"It's good to see you, Phoenix," Frey said into the silence.

I looked up at him and he towered over me, he had grown so much since the last time I saw him.

"It's good to see you too," I said as I let the light from the manor illuminate his features. "You look well."

"I heard about what happened to you on your birthday, Phoenix." I stopped in my tracks as shame prickled the surface of my skin. "I'm sorry that happened to you."

We had barely seen each other since that summer many moons ago. Every time his father, Lord Finley, had come to the palace, I would wait eagerly on the palace steps as the horses pulled up with the lord, only to be met with disappointment that Frey wasn't coming. Eventually, I stopped waiting for him.

As I got older, I realised that what we'd had wasn't love. My obsession with him stemmed from the fact that I knew I was cursed and yet someone still wanted me. The fact that my beast had appeared proved my theory that he didn't truly love me, not in the way I loved him, or at least thought I did. I hadn't realised how hard my heart had become since I last saw him and I felt the ice encasing my chest slowly crack with each passing moment.

"I thought we were friends," I said into the open space between us, "maybe more."

Frey turned to look at me. "I'm sorry that I didn't visit you more often, Phoenix. Once I turned eighteen, I had to take on more responsibilities back home, I would have loved nothing more than to spend my summers with you."

He closed the distance between us as his fingers gently stroked my cheek. A lump formed in my throat as I thought back to the times I had waited for him, only for him to never show.

"It would have been nice for you to send word." I said resisting the urge to lean into his touch. "Your father visited the palace plenty of times, a note would have sufficed."

Frey recoiled at my words and placed his hands in his pockets as he stared at the ground. "I was young and selfish, and for that I am truly sorry. I never intended to hurt you in anyway."

I was torn between my heart and my pride. I wanted a love that was given freely, not something I had to coerce out of someone.

"I can't do this."

I gathered my skirts and turned back towards the palace. Esmeray and Ireland quickly fell into step around me, waiting until we were inside the manor to speak.

"Are you okay?" Ireland asked as she touched me shoulder.

I took a deep breath before looking out into the gardens. Frey was stood with his hands behind his back and his face raised to the night sky. I watched him for a few moments, my heart longing for his lips to find mine. The fact he didn't come after told me all I needed to know.

"I'm fine" I said, harsher than I'd intended. "I'm just tired."

"I'll walk you to your room," Esmeray said as I grabbed the long skirts of my dress and made my way upstairs, the longing for love an ache in my chest.

WE LEFT LORD ORBARROW'S manor at dawn and made our way west before we headed back to the palace, a strange tension sitting in the stiffness of Esmeray's shoulders.

We camped overnight near a shallow stream, the night sky clear with just the occasional star dotting the sky. Ireland and Silver were making a fire, and Lex had gone to hunt something for us to roast as Esmeray sat on a log next to me.

In all the years I had known Esmeray, I had never seen anything knock her off centre, she always remained indifferent, never letting things get the best of her. To see her anxious about going back to her home made me question how awful her father truly was.

"Are you worried about seeing your father?" I asked. I knew it was a sensitive subject, but I couldn't help but press the issue.

She continued to sharpen her dagger with a rock she had found in the shallow water that flowed next to us. Her movements became more aggressive with each stroke of the stone against the sharp metal.

"My father will never accept the path I chose for myself. There is no use in thinking he will change his mind, the sooner we are back at the palace the better."

Her tone didn't invite further discussion so I left her with the blade and made my way over to the fire that was now crackling a delicious warmth against the winter's cold. I reached my hand over the flames and sighed as the heat seeped into my bones. Lex returned with dinner and I watched as she skinned and roasted the rabbit for us to eat. My guard laughed as they told stories around the fire, I looked to Esmeray who was sat at the edge of the stream, lost in thought. I wanted to go over and comfort her but thought better of it, instead tucking myself into my bed roll as my guard's stories echoed around me.

After a broken night's sleep, we arrived in the west in the early hours of the morning. "We don't have to do this," I whispered to Esmeray. Her shoulders were squared, and I could see her jaw muscles flexing as she clenched them.

"It's fine."

Lord Erik Elordi roved his eyes over his daughter as she stood steadfast, her royal uniform adding to her fierceness. I turned to look at Esmeray, my friend, the captain of the king's guard. Her father looked at her with disdain, although he tried to hide it behind pleasantries.

He bowed deeply before me and it took everything I had not to roll my eyes to the heavens at his theatrics.

"It's my pleasure to have you in my home, princess."

I bit my tongue on a retort. He hadn't shown his own daughter a shred of the welcome he had given me, and I thanked the stars Esmeray had found a way to escape his manipulative ways.

Esmeray's older brothers, Blair and Gabriel appeared behind their father and I watched as her niece and nephew bounded down the steps towards her.

"Ray!" her niece shouted before Esmeray scooped her up and buried her face in her bronze curly hair. Awe struck me as the captain of the king's guard melted at the sight of her family.

Her brothers descended the steps and bowed before me. "It's an honour for you to be here, princess."

A smile spread across my face as I looked at Esmeray's oldest brother, Blair. He had the same bronze hair as Ez, but where her eyes were hazel, his were amber.

"Thank you for having me," I said as I turned to her other brother, Gabriel. "Will you both be at the meeting later?"

"We will," Gabriel said through a wide smile. "We'll let you freshen up before we get into politics."

I laughed as he offered his arm as he led me up the steps and into Esmeray's childhood home.

After a painful meeting with Esmeray's father that consisted of him cutting Esmeray off every chance he got and boasting about how successful his lordship of the west has been, she showed me to her old room.

"I would be happy to take one of the smaller rooms," I said as I looked around the room.

"Please, I can't think of anything worse than reliving my childhood in here." She laughed, but I noted the pain under her humour. "Besides, I'm bunking with Lex tonight."

"Okay, what time am I needed for the dinner?"

"An hour should be enough time to get ready."

A young woman appeared in the doorway and Esmeray turned around to face her. "Phoenix, this is Ceron. She will be looking after you while we're here."

I gave a warm smile to the handmaiden as she came in and drew my bath water.

I bathed and sat on the end of Esmeray's old bed. I tried to imagine her as young girl with her dream of being a soldier, play fighting with her brothers and their wooden swords.

Ceron laid out a soft lilac gown. "It's beautiful," I breathed.

She smiled as she motioned for me to stand. "Lord Elordi had it shipped in from Darnassea when he heard you would be visiting, I thought the colour would favour your hair and skin perfectly."

I was surprised at the thought that had gone into it.

She fastened me into the dress and piled my curls into an intricate bun on top of my head, adding jewelled silver clips.

"You look stunning, princess."

I thanked her and stepped into the hallway. Blair was laughing with Esmeray, but they both turned as they heard me approaching.

"Shall we?" Blair said as he held his arm out towards me. I linked my arm in his and descended the staircase.

We entered the dining room, and Esmeray's mother gasped.

"Princess, I'm sorry I missed you earlier. It's such an honour." She hurried over, pulling me into her arms. She smelled of something sweet and powdery, like the dusting bakers used on top of cakes.

"Guinevere, it's so good to see you." I said as she gave me a squeeze before letting me go.

"Please, take a seat, you will be at the head of the table tonight."

My eyes flashed to Esmeray. I really didn't want to make a fuss. The rest of my guard entered the dining room and took up their seats at either side of me. Lord Elordi sat at the opposite end of the table as servers filled the room. I sipped my wine to ease the tension I felt. Esmeray's father hadn't looked at her once and it infuriated me. I wondered what a kind, gentle soul like Guinevere saw in him. He was pretentious and power hungry and I watched as he bragged about his rule of the west again with Blair and Gabriel.

I fought the urge to roll my eyes as the servers brought the food to the table. One thing I couldn't fault the lord on was his menu. My mouth watered at the sweet, curried meat and fragrant jasmine rice that was presented before me. Esmeray pushed the food around her plate—I hated the effect her father had on her.

"Ray, I hear the south want to expand their ports." Gabriel said as he raised his glass towards her, I couldn't hear over the blood throbbing in my ears.

"News travels fast," she said, still not eating her food.

Lord Orbarrow had briefly mentioned a few days earlier wanting to expand the southern ports to trade across the world rather than just Endaria.

"That isn't something that would concern a captain, Gabe," her father said, his remark laced with disappointment.

I wanted to throw something at him but didn't recall that being in any of my dining etiquette lessons. I put my knife and fork down slowly, not willing to tolerate his treatment of Esmeray anymore.

"Actually, Erik." The room went silent as his head whipped towards me. I didn't use his title and I wasn't required to. I outranked him in every sense, and he would do well to remember it. "As the highest-ranking member of my father's guard, Esmeray serves as my council when I'm representing the crown. Aside from myself, she is the only person in this room that has any power or influence over this kingdom." I stopped myself as I looked him dead in the eye. "So I assure you, Lord Elordi, that is something that would most definitely concern a captain."

Esmeray's eyes betrayed the slightest hint of shock and I made a mental note that if I ever became Queen, I would strip him of his lordship immediately.

No one spoke as I wiped my mouth with a napkin, but my guard were all fighting the urge to smile. "Captain." I said as I turned to Esmeray, "will you escort me to my room? I would like to rest, it's been such a long day."

My guard rose with me. "Guinevere, thank you so much for this lovely dinner," I said as I left the dining room.

My guard filed into Esmeray's old room. "Phoenix, you didn't have to do that," she said as I pulled my shoes off.

"I know I didn't, but the way he dismisses you is unacceptable. Just because you chose not to follow the life he wanted for you, doesn't mean he can treat you the way he does."

"I know he's your father, Ez," Ireland said, "but I've never wanted to punch someone in the face more."

My guard burst into laughter and I sat on the bed and smiled at them, at their unbreakable bond.

"We'll leave you to get some rest," Silver said as they piled out of the room.

Esmeray paused in the doorway before glancing back at me. "We leave for the priestesses in the morning."

I nodded as she closed the door. The priestesses were my last hope of breaking this curse on my own terms, the alternative wasn't one I could bear thinking about.

IT WAS A SHORT RIDE to the temple of light. I stopped to look at it in the distance, set atop a hill overlooking the sea. I breathed in the clean sea air as the breeze washed over me. Although we were in the thick of winter, the morning sun cast us in a golden glow and despite the chill from the sea, the sight warmed me. We rode along the cliff's edge, overlooking the turquoise waters and lush greenery covering the cliff's surface, and the waves lapping against the rocks was soothing. There was an arched rock that had broken away from the cliff's surface at some point in time and stood solid in the ocean like a doorway to peace. The sun's rays shone through the doorway, and I marvelled at what the mother had created. I understood why the priestesses would want to be here, it was breath-taking.

Esmeray and I dismounted our horses, leaving them with her father's guard, and walked towards the temple in silence. This had to be the closest thing to the mother. It felt pure and good, and the beauty of it was magickal. The temple was modest, a nod to the priestesses and their simple ways, and the natural stone had been carved and shaped to build a fortress for the women. I walked up the few steps at the temple's entrance and turned to see Esmeray, still standing at the bottom with the rest of her father's guard in the distance.

"Aren't you coming with me?" I asked as she stood with her hand on her sword.

"The priestesses are the purest souls in the kingdom, Phoenix, and I have killed more men than I care to admit. I would not sully their temple with my bloodshed."

I understood. I gave a shallow nod as I walked up to the white wood doors that stretched up to the top of the temple, carved with runes. I traced my finger over the marks that had been etched into the wood and recognised some of them as protection spells. Most runes were deemed worthless now and I wondered if the priestesses had other ways to channel their power.

I looked back to Esmeray, who hadn't moved from where she had stationed herself at the foot of the temple, her sword drawn as she stood looking out over the cliffs.

I knocked twice as I waited nervously. The priestesses were revered throughout the kingdom, and I wasn't sure how they would receive me. The waves crashing against the cliffs and the sea birds were the only sound as I waited.

After a few moments the door opened slightly and a woman in a pale blue, hooded robe stepped into the gap. Her skin was a deep, rich brown that bordered on black and her eyes a piercing blue—shockingly bright against the long spill of her black hair around her shoulders.

She took me in for a moment before opening the door wider.

I went to speak but stopped when I saw what was behind her. The temple was deceiving from the outside. It was enormous, with sky high ceilings and solid pillars carved into the structure.

"Princess, we welcome you to the temple of light." Her accent was heavy and not like anything I had heard before, I wondered which part of the world she was from.

She gestured for me to enter and I moved inside, my body tingling as I stepped through the doorway. The priestess smiled as she noticed me shiver. "It's the runes, it stops anyone with bad intentions from entering."

Hope sparked in me at the thought of magick still existing here and I gave her a small smile. "Thank you for having me, what's your name?"

"Neytiri, princess." Her voice was soft and centred, easy, as though her existence were effortless.

I followed her through the temple and we passed priestesses mixing herbal mixtures into jars, others transcribing scripts into leather-bound books. The women were all occupied, but each one gave me a warm smile as I passed them.

We walked down a candle lit corridor before stopping at a door. Neytiri knocked and a voice came from the other side, telling us to enter.

The priestess stepped inside and bowed her head slightly.

"Dahlia, the princess is here to see you."

I looked at the high priestess, sat at a white stone desk. Behind her was a view of the ocean.

Dahlia looked to Neytiri. "Thank you."

Neytiri bowed before closing the door and leaving us.

"Thank you for coming to visit us, princess, it's an honour."

I smiled at the high priestess who radiated warmth and light. "The pleasure is mine." I said as I looked at her in awe.

"I can only offer you my condolences for the position fate has put you in."

I thanked the priestess and a comfortable silence sat between us, the need to ask for help was burning although my pride almost stopped me.

"I wondered if you had any knowledge of how to break the curse?"

Dahlia gave me a sympathetic smile.

"Your father asked us for help shortly after you were born. We didn't have the answers he needed at the time. Before the mother stopped pouring into us the priestesses were profound healers, we used what the mother provided naturally in the earth and combined with our power and skills, we could heal almost anything. I think that is why we were the first place your father sought out after your birth."

"I haven't had any luck either." I mused.

"I think there is a reason you came into the world, Phoenix, there hadn't been a first-born daughter for three hundred years. I think you will be the one to make sure no other daughters suffer the way you have."

I jolted, Lex had said the same thing and I wasn't sure how I could free myself when I had no outlet for my power.

"I wondered… the runes on the temple door, they still hold magick. How is that possible?"

"Those runes are a thousand years old, maybe even older," Dahlia said, standing from behind her desk and walking over to an alcove that had been carved into the stone wall and filled with books.

Dahlia carried on as she looked through the books, "The mother intended there to be balance in the world. Ravynne has been stealing power for centuries, no one should possess the amount that she has. The mother has stopped pouring into us all. Why gift us with magick, just for it to be stolen?"

She picked a beaten book from the alcove and brought it around to her desk.

"The legends say, our ancestors fell from the sky. That they were neither good, nor bad, they just were. Ancient beings who were highly skilled in magick—where that magick came from no one knows, we simply refer to the source as the mother," Dahlia said as she flicked through the pages of the weathered book. "The runes on our temple have been there since Endaria was forged at least a thousand years ago. I can't say why the mother allows them to still protect us."

Dahlia looked at me, her blue-grey eyes full of an emotion I couldn't place. She pushed the book across the desk towards me and my eyes scanned the pages, it spoke of our ancient power and how the runes came to be. I was aware of Dahlia watching me, but I was fascinated by the knowledge she had allowed me to see.

"The mother chose you to be the first-born daughter for a reason. The world needs your light, Phoenix."

I looked up at the priestess, unsure of how to voice my feelings.

"I feel as though fate hasn't favoured me, I've been hunted by my own people, and I am no closer to breaking this curse." I sighed as I listened to the waves crashing against the cliffs. "I want to break this curse on my own terms, not the enchantresses. I can't expect someone to love me when the only reason I require that love is to break the curse placed on my bloodline."

I closed the book and placed it back onto the desk.

"I don't condone the way the ancestors dealt with the enchantresses, it didn't have to be this way, but Ravynne is a monster of our own making." Dahlia said softly, her words stained with regret.

I looked out of the window behind her desk, two parakeets flew in circles above the cliffs and I gave a small weak laugh. Was the mother taunting me or would I come out the other side of this curse unscathed?

Dahlia stood up and made her way to the door. "I'll make us some tea."

I smiled as she passed me, closing the door behind her.

The sound of my heart tapping against my ribs was the only sound before Dahlia came back into the room carrying a tray of tea that she placed on the stone desk.

I spoke into the silence, "I wanted to come and pay my respects now that I am representing the crown, but I also came in the hopes that the priestesses could help me." I couldn't meet her gaze, I was all too used to the feeling of shame burning across my skin like a brand.

"Ravynne has taken too much, Phoenix, I wish we could help you, but she is too powerful. We wouldn't stand a chance against her."

Nausea roiled in the pit of my stomach, and I nodded as I realised I was out of options. I looked at the high priestess, daylight illuminated her from behind, her sandy hair was streaked with white, and I wondered if she reflected how the mother sees herself.

We sat in silence as I listened to the waves crashing behind the temple. No one was coming to save me.

"Do you mind if I stay for a while?" I asked, my voice was thick and a painful lump had formed in my throat. My heart was heavy, and I just needed some time, a moment of peace.

Dahlia smiled, the expression bittersweet. "Of course, princess, if you ever need somewhere to just be, you are always welcome here."

I thanked the priestess as I felt my resolve to fight for my crown slip away. I had nowhere else to turn, the only thing left for me to do was return to my kingdom and let fate rip me apart.

CHAPTER 10

THE DAY OF THE BALL my father had arranged was here. I had a few days until the full moon and I wasn't any closer to breaking the curse. After visiting the priestesses, all sense of hope had vanished.

The evening felt like a farce, but I had no other choice, even though I thought it was futile I had to show up for my father. And even if there were someone here who could truly love me, it wouldn't happen before my beast emerged. The love had to be genuine, whether I liked it or not I would be turning into my beast again in a matter of days.

The men that would be attending had been handpicked by my father's counsellors. The most eligible bachelors in the kingdom. The thought of loving someone with an ulterior motive was abhorrent and I hated every moment of it. To appease my father, I agreed to at least meet with them.

Chloris spent hours preening over me in the mirror making sure my hair was done to perfection, my gown was the most exquisite she could find, and my face was powdered until I almost didn't recognise myself.

I wore a long-sleeve gown of obsidian silk that was embellished in crystals from head to toe, my movements caused it to glisten like a starry night sky. My hair had been stretched with heat until it was silky straight and flowing down my back.

My hair, skin and the dress all clashed in the most perfect way, and I had to admit that Chloris had done an excellent job of putting me together for the ball. I gave my eyes a few more lashes of kohl before Chloris placed a jewelled obsidian crown on my head. I looked in the mirror, staring at my reflection as a future queen stared back at me.

I made my way to the ballroom where there was an array of the wealthiest people in Mercea. Small talk bored me, and I dreaded having to force conversation with people. My guard waited for me to enter the room then fell into step around me. I saw my father conversing with a merchant from the east that specialised in the trade of fine materials, they were shipped from overseas to the eastern ports and then distributed throughout Mercea and made my way over to join him.

My father turned to face me as I approached.

"Phoenix, you remember Lord Bardell from the east?" my father said, as he gestured towards the merchant.

I smiled politely as the merchant took my hand and bowed before me, kissing the back of my hand. "Princess, it's an honour to be here in your name."

I smiled at the Lord who was a long-time companion of my fathers. He looked over my shoulder, his eyes lighting up as he said. "Frey, come and greet the princess."

My heart sank as I gracefully stepped to the side, I turned around to look at Frey who approached with a wide smile on his face.

Frey bowed as he said, "It's a pleasure to see you again, Your Highness." His smooth deep voice was a pleasure to my senses, I shook off the feeling as I surveyed the room.

It was a surreal feeling to have these men vying for my affection. I wasn't naïve, I knew they thought an alliance with me would give them a political advantage. I would be queen one day, and they would rule by my side although I would be more than happy to rule this kingdom alone.

"Ahh your gown is made of the finest onyx silk from the Darnassea kingdom," Lord Bardell exclaimed.

"I'm impressed Lord Bardell, you have a very good eye indeed."

Esmeray shifted behind me, signalling to move on, and I was grateful for the reprieve. There was a whole crowd I had to mingle my way through, and the thought filled me with dread.

Frey held me back by my elbow and leaned down to whisper in my ear.

"Will you meet with me later?"

I flinched slightly as I looked up at Frey. I tilted my head further so I could look him in the eye, "Why are you here?"

He had been scarce over the last couple of years and now he was everywhere. I looked over his shoulder where my father was still talking with the Lord from the east.

Confusion flashed across Frey's face. "Why am I here?"

"This ball is my father's attempt at finding someone that can love me so the curse can be broken, so yes, why are you here?"

"Phoenix," Frey started.

I couldn't do this. This night was going to be a strain as it was.

"I have to go," I said as I walked away from him, I didn't have any more time to waste. Hurt flashed across his face as I walked away but I didn't know what he expected from me.

I mingled with the crowd. I chatted, I smiled, I laughed at people's jokes and the night went by in a blur. I had danced with five different men and hadn't felt a connection with any of them. I walked over to the refreshment stand and poured myself a glass of winter wine. The fruity wine was balanced with subtle spices, and the flavours rolled over my tongue. Out of the corner of my eye I saw a tall man stalking towards me. I turned to look at him, ready to feign interest and smile until my jaw ached.

He approached the table and poured himself a glass of wine. The wine was renowned throughout Endaria and was hard to come by.

He tipped the dark red contents back, smiling as he said, "The finest wine in the land."

I nodded my glass towards him in agreement.

He turned to look at me, as he held out his hand. "Would you care to dance, princess?"

I looked at his outstretched hand, "I would like to know the name of the man asking me to dance."

He laughed, a deep, rich sound escaping him.

"Ruane, your highness."

"Very well then, Ruane," I said as I placed my hand in his. "Lead the way."

The mysterious Ruane took my hand, leading me to the dance floor. He was the epitome of tall, dark and handsome.

One hand rested on my lower back while his other held mine up as we swayed to the music.

"Where are you from?" I asked.

He smiled a bright white grin and spun me around. I could sense other people in the crowd watching us.

"I'm from the north of Endaria," he said, anticipating my response.

I thought it was evasive, why hadn't he just said which kingdom he was from?

I held back my inquisition. A rule my father had taught me was to speak once and listen twice. He told me from a young age that if you let people talk for long enough, they will reveal their true thoughts and intentions.

Ruane took my silence as an invitation to carry on the conversation. He leaned in, whispering in my ear as he pulled my waist closer. His warm breath smelled of sweet wine and sent shivers across my skin as he said. "I'm not here to win your hand, I'm here to give you a message."

My back stiffened as I remembered what happened on the winter solstice. I tried to school my features into a calm indifference, the last thing I wanted was to make another scene.

"The shadow king has heard about your quest for a cure and would like you to visit Sakaria to meet with him."

My blood ran cold. The shadow king was a ruthless man with the reputation of a sadistic killer. My father's counsellors had tried to convince him to reach out to the former king, but he'd refused. After the death of the king, and his son taking the throne, I was being summoned by someone we didn't know anything about—just his name. If he was anything like his father, he was an evil force that plagued these lands.

I was speechless and Ruane leaned in again as the music was tapering off, preparing for the next song.

He looked down at me, his deep brown eyes boring into mine, almost pleading for me to accept his proposition.

"At least think about it," he said.

I nodded, unable to get my mouth to form words as he bowed before slinking off into the crowd.

I turned around to see Esmeray stalking towards me. "What was that about?" she asked, resting her hand on the hilt of her sword.

I released a long sigh as I tried to process what Ruane had told me. I looked behind me expecting to see him standing in the crowd, but he was gone.

"He said the shadow king has heard about my quest for a cure and wants to meet with me."

If I blinked, I would have missed the shock that flashed across her face before her features returned to normal.

"Absolutely not." At the age of twenty-five, she was too young to be my mother, but she often took on a mothering role without realising.

I wasn't in the mood to argue. "We will discuss this later," I said as I went to turn away.

Esmeray held me back by my arm. "There is nothing to discuss, do you know how ruthless they are in the north? They make Ravynne look juvenile." She was deadly serious, but I had to stand my ground.

"Meet me in the council room. I need to excuse myself from the ball," I said as I looked at the steely determination in her eyes.

She stalked off, gathering the rest of my guard.

I made my way to my father who was entertaining Lord Orbarrow from the south. I had danced with his nephew earlier and his eyes lit up as I walked towards them. I grimaced inwardly at the thought of leading him on.

I tapped my father on the arm and he turned around to face me. For a moment, there was no despair, no curse, no beast, nothing. For the briefest moment I saw happiness in his eyes, I saw his life without the burden of me.

I pushed the feeling down as I said, "I'm retiring to my chambers for the night. Thank you for a lovely evening, father."

He smiled as he leaned to kiss me on my cheek. I hoped he spent the rest of the night enjoying himself.

I left the ballroom to see Esmeray standing outside and we made our way to the council room in silence. I walked in to see the rest of my guard sitting around the large oval table. Silver sat back with her feet up, twirling a dagger in her fingers. I sat down as Esmeray pulled a map from a shelf and rolled it across the table, it was a detailed map of Endaria. She leaned over the map and placed two heavy paperweights to secure it at either side.

Rain lashed against the windows behind Lex and Ireland as they sat at the council table, deep in conversation. Esmeray's eyes flicked to me for a moment before returning to the map.

"What's going on Ez?" Silver asked as she sheathed her dagger.

Esmeray nodded towards me, "Phoenix why don't you explain?"

I pinched the bridge of my nose, I knew what she was doing, she wanted me to say my plan out loud so I could hear how ridiculous it sounded.

I clasped my hands together dramatically, "The tall, dark and handsome man I was just dancing with is from Sakaria. He said the shadow king has heard of my quest for a cure and wants to meet with me."

I rested my chin on my hand as I waited for the chaos to unfold but Lex just whistled in disbelief.

"So, we travel to the shadow king?" Silver said with that infectious grin on her face and I knew she would follow me to the ends of the earth.

Esmeray stood with her arms crossed. "First, we would have to head north to the Black Forest where we would need to meet with the bone witch to gain passage. The bone witch is as pleasant as she sounds."

I looked to Ireland who gave me a tight smile as she said. "The bone witch is said to have lived in Endaria for more than a thousand years, her people lived here before our ancestors, and when her species moved on to another realm, she refused to leave."

"Why doesn't the shadow king come to Mercea if he wants to meet with you?" Silver questioned.

She had a point. "He must have his reasons," I suggested but the truth was I had spent my life sheltered in my kingdom, I knew nothing of the world outside of it.

Lex asked Esmeray. "Is it possible?"

Esmeray's eyes roved over the map, and she took her time responding.

"We'll need bones," Esmeray said to no one in particular.

Lex's face lit up.

"Why would we need bones?" I asked.

Lex leaned forward. "The bone witch lives in the wall, they built it around her home, which has been there since before Endaria was forged by our ancestors. The wall is a hundred feet high, the only way to get to Sakaria is for her to allow us past. She is more spirit than flesh and her face is said to send people to their graves. She will expect bones as payment for allowing us to pass through the wall. Only the bravest—"

"—Or the most foolish." Ireland cut in.

Silver nodded in agreement as Lex protested her point. "Only the bravest, would dare ask her for passage. So yes, we will need bones."

I looked across to Silver and Ireland, "Is there another way?" I asked.

Esmeray scanned the map again, "No it's the only way."

I sighed as I kicked off my heeled pumps, the cool wooden floor soothing my sore feet. I rested my elbows on the table leaning forward. "We have to try."

Lex and Ireland stopped talking, we all held our breath waiting for Esmeray's response.

"By the time we have arranged the travels, it's likely the curse will be in effect whilst we are on our way to Sakaria."

The information pounded in my head as I thought about becoming my beast again. "Can we be ready in two days?" I asked.

Ireland's eyes widened as Esmeray looked at me. For the first time in my life, I think she was speechless.

I seized the opportunity and explained my reasoning. "The full moon is a few days away, if we leave the day after tomorrow we will be in the black forest when my beast arrives, no one would be that close to the border." I kept my tone level as my leg jittered under the table. I couldn't risk another attack.

Esmeray stared at the map for what felt like an eternity before she finally spoke. "No one besides the king can know of this plan."

My guard nodded in agreement and I pushed the thoughts of the last full moon to the back of my mind.

"If anyone asks, we are travelling to the south. Let's deter the rebels for now and hope the shadow king has the means to help us," Esmeray said.

Anticipation simmered in my bones at the thought of leaving my kingdom for the first time. Only time would tell if I was heading straight into enemy lands, or if I would find the very thing I had been searching for.

CHAPTER 11

I HAD TO INFORM MY FATHER of my plan. I knew he wouldn't be happy, but a deep part of me knew he wouldn't hold me back from freeing myself from this curse.

I asked my guard to give us some privacy during our evening meal and they stood guard outside of the dining hall.

Once dinner was served, I helped myself to the feast that was laid out before me. I piled meats roasted in honey, sweet potatoes that had been mashed to perfection with a garlic and herb butter and green vegetables onto my plate. For the first time in a long time, I was hopeful.

My father broke the silence first.

"I hear Frey Finley was quite taken with you, Phoenix."

My stomach dropped, my father was oblivious to my feelings about Frey, I had no intentions of coercing him or anyone else to fall in love with me. None.

"Actually father, I was hoping I could discuss something with you?"

He held his chalice swirling the deep red winter wine waiting for me to continue.

I took a deep breath. "King Khaldon has asked me to meet with him in the Shadow Kingdom, he has heard of my quest for a cure and would like to meet with me." My father stopped drinking and looked at me. A war of emotions flicked across his face while he gripped the chalice so hard, he left dents in it.

"Sakaria is a ruthless kingdom, Phoenix. I cannot send my only child into the pit of an enemy's lands."

"Father, I know the kingdom has been ruled by a tyrant, but the new king may not follow his father's ways. There must be a reason that he has summoned me."

My father said nothing, tapping his finger against his chalice while I simmered with the need to plead my case.

"Your mother would be proud of the woman you have become."

His pain was evident in the tone of his voice and his words caught me by surprise. My mother was rarely spoken about. My life had been painful from my first breath, and I often wondered if I was to blame for all of this.

"I wish I could remember her."

A muscle flicked in my father's jaw as he seemed to be in conflict of what to say next. He left his seat and walked out of the dining hall. I knew talking about my mother upset him deeply, so I tended to avoid the subject.

I pushed the food around my plate as my heart sank, I couldn't bring myself to eat anything, my grief turning sour in the pit of my stomach.

My father came back and held out an emerald-green velvet box. "Your mother asked me to give this to you when you were ready."

I took the box from him and opened the lid. The inside was lined with a jewel green silk and in the centre was a silver ring engraved with runes.

"Was this hers?" I asked.

"It was." His tone was heavy with regret.

My throat tightened as I ran my finger over the ring.

I coughed to clear my throat. "Thank you," I said as I looked at my father. I wished I could take his sorrow away.

My father resumed his meal and the mention of me leaving Mercea floated between us, neither me nor my father dared carry on. I poured the last of my winter wine down my throat, as unladylike as it was and turned to face my father.

"I have to try." I looked into my father's eyes, not breaking his stare. "I can't rely on expecting someone to fall in love with me which may never happen, and then I'd be cursed into my beast form forever. At least this way I can try to end the curse on my own terms."

After a few heartbeats had passed my father looked away from me.

"I have tried to protect you, Phoenix, I have tried to free you from the burden of this curse that you do not deserve and I'm sorry I failed you."

I reached out and placed my hand on top of my father's. "You have never failed me, not once, but I need to try. I will not be hunted again," I said with as much conviction in my voice as I could muster.

My father nodded before squeezing my hand. I excused myself from the table and as I reached the door I stopped "What did my mother mean, when I'm ready?"

His eyes of onyx met mine. "She said you will know."

I gave him a smile of sorrow and made my way to my chambers.

100

I knelt in front of the fire that Chloris had left burning so my rooms would be warm after dinner. I opened the velvet box and slipped my mother's ring onto the middle finger of my right hand. The metal band was cool against my warm skin and my blood tingled as if it were reacting to the ring. I flexed my hand and held it against the flames, letting the light from the fire reflect off the runes. After the tingling subsided, I climbed into bed and let the shadows pull me under.

I WAS FLOATING. I swayed gently as I looked up at the radiant sky, there wasn't a cloud in sight and the sun had streaked the sky with oranges and purples.

Waves lapped over me as I listened to the sound of the ocean beneath me. I wondered if I had died. Was this the mother? I had never felt so calm and at peace in my entire life. Instead of pulling me out to the depths of its seas, the current pulled me into the shore, until I felt soft sand beneath my hands and feet.

I walked along the stretch of beach before me, the soft white sand whispered underneath my feet. I was unsure of where I was, but I didn't feel afraid. I felt calm. The waves lapped against the shore as I walked alongside it, the sun was setting in the distance, and I watched in awe as it disappeared below the ocean.

I walked further down the beach unsure of where I was going but relying on an instinct that guided me to where I felt I should be. As if a thread were connected to my soul pulling me along the shore of this idyllic beach. I stopped at a white tent that was nestled along the trees that lined the shore. Laughter sounded from inside, and I pulled back the curtain to see a gathering of some sort. Everyone was wearing white and laughing and smiling amongst themselves. I entered the tent, walking through the crowd of people and felt a tap on my right shoulder. I whirled around and my world fell apart.

Stood in front of me was my mother. A lifetime worth of emotions poured out of me, and I threw myself into her arms.

"I've missed you, my love." Hearing my mother's voice for the first time in my life brought a fresh onslaught of tears and pain, and she held me while I sobbed into her shoulder. Her hand ran up and down my back as I tried to make sense of what was happening. I had to be dreaming.

I pulled back to look at her face. She hadn't aged a day. Her skin was soft to touch and her curls braided into a crown across her head. She didn't look much older than me.

My mother sat me down at a table covered in white cloth. Her smile was one of dreams. I took in every detail of her face, her beauty radiating throughout her very being.

"How am I here?" I asked in disbelief. I looked around at the people that were gathered, everyone looked happy and at peace. "Am I dead?" Panic rose in me as I thought about my father being left alone.

My mother just smiled. "I have been watching you your whole life, Phoenix. I am so proud of you, my love, and I'm so sorry that I left you."

Tears welled in my eyes and I blinked away the sting. The wave of emotion that was building inside of me threatened to crash all over us.

I reached out and held her hand across the table. "We miss you so much." My voice cracked and I couldn't control the emotion that poured out of me.

She lifted my chin so my eyes met hers.

"It was my time to go." I went to drop my head, so I didn't have to look at her while I cried. A strangled sob escaped me, and she lifted my chin again.

"Everything you need is inside of you, my love." Her voice soothed me in a way I had never felt before. "You have the light to guide the shadows and you must not be afraid."

She looked at my hand as I ran my thumb over the ring of runes.

"Your father knew now was the time."

I looked into her deep brown eyes, a few shades lighter than mine with flecks of gold.

"Father said I was ready. What does he mean?" I was the future queen of the mightiest kingdom and I felt as small as a child.

My mother went to speak but nothing came out as though she were battling some unseen force.

She gave me a sad smile. "You have to go now."

Panic rose as I thought about leaving her.

"I can't leave! I have so much to say. Please!" The desperation poured out of me. I would have given anything to stay with her.

She ran her thumb over my cheek. "We will see each other again, my love."

I put my hand over hers and leaned into her touch. The smell of lilacs and jasmine washed over me and I closed my eyes, wanting to stay in the moment a little longer.

I opened my eyes, and it was pitch black. A chill crept over me as I adjusted to my surroundings. I blinked the haziness away and saw the moon glowing outside of my bedroom window. It had been a dream. It had felt so real I could still hear the ocean caressing the shore in its lazy embrace. I could still feel my mother's warmth on my cheek. The tears burst out of me uncontrollably and I clasped my hand over my mouth to hide the sobs that escaped me.

I cried until I thought there could be no more. My eyes were raw and stung every time I blinked but sleep still evaded me. I waited until the shadows were gone, until daylight crept through the window, before I let myself go back to sleep.

CHAPTER 12

PPEASE THE BONE WITCH, we needed bones. Esmeray suggested human rather than animal and my fear crept to the surface at what kind of being we were dealing with.

I had convinced my guard to allow me to accompany Lex into the city while she retrieved the bones we would need.

I made my way to Chloris's chamber. She never stayed the night at the palace but would arrive first thing in the morning and would leave last thing at night. When I asked her wouldn't it be easier to live here, she would smile and say she had slept next to the same man for over twenty years and she couldn't sleep without him.

Her chamber door was open, but I knocked anyway. She was hunched over her desk stitching something with thread.

"Just a moment," she called from where she sat.

I stood patiently waiting for her to notice me as I peered my head into the open doorway and looked around her rooms, they hadn't changed since I was a child.

She finally put the clothing down she was trying to repair and jumped up when she saw me waiting.

"Phoenix! Is everything okay, what do you need?" she asked as she hurried over to me, eager to help me in any way she could.

I smiled at her generosity—she would give the clothes off her back if it meant helping someone.

"Yes Chloris, everything is fine. I was wondering if you could obtain something for me?"

She took my hand as she led me to sit on the made-up bed, the sheets were never disturbed, purely there for ornamental sake.

"Of course, What is it?"   I looked into her chestnut brown eyes, as familiar to me as my own.

"I need to temporarily dye my hair." Her face frowned in confusion. "Preferably black please."

Chloris shook her head in disbelief. "Your hair is the rarest in the kingdom Phoenix, mother knows why you would want to hide it."

My silver hair wasn't the kind that comes with age, it was the kind that looked unnatural to this world. It flowed like molten steel, as if the blades of my ancestors' swords had been forged into every strand. I needed some anonymity while I went with Lex to get the bones for the witch, and hiding the very thing I was known for would help me blend in among my people.

I stood up and turned to look at Chloris. "Will you get it for me?" I gave her a big grin that I knew she wouldn't be able to resist.

Chloris threw her hands in the air, "Alright, alright."

I leaned down to hug her and breathed in her scent of linen and lavender.

"Thank you Chloris." I grinned as I left her and made my way to training.

After an intense training session with Esmeray and working on some drills to steady my footing with a sword, I entered my chambers and saw Chloris at my dresser mixing something in a ceramic bowl. "You got the dye?" I asked excitedly.

She put the bowl down and ushered me to sit in front of the mirror.

"Now." Chloris started, I knew she was going to lecture me about disguising my most prized possession. "This will last until you wash it out and I suggest washing it out as soon as possible"

I agreed, fascinated as I watched her apply the black oil with a small brush to my hair.

My features seemed to change before me, blending into my mothers. I inherited my silver hair from my father but with black hair it was as if my mother sat before me.

I looked away from the mirror as a lump formed in my throat.

Chloris left me to get ready, and I squeezed the excess oil from my hair, braiding it off my face leaving a few face framing strands loose. I pulled the hood of the guard's uniform I had borrowed up over my head and looked in the mirror. I hoped no one would recognise me, I almost didn't recognise myself.

My guard were not happy with me accompanying Lex, but I had argued with them to the point they'd had no choice but to give in.

Esmeray told me to ride Blade, which I was honoured to do. He was a gift from my father for her twenty-first birthday, he was said to come from a rare breed of horses that were imbued with the old magick. I stroked his silky black mane as I waited for Lex to mount her steed.

"Let me do the talking and we should be okay," she said, as her wide grin lit up her face.

I rolled my eyes to the heavens. I could play the obedient guard member.

The mouth guard I wore kept the cold chill from freezing my lungs. All the guards wore them over their mouths in the winter. Esmeray said it was a way of keeping the chill from their airways while still allowing them to look their kill in the eye.

We came to a stone building on the outskirts of the city.

"What is this place?" I asked Lex.

"The city morgue," she replied. "I need to ask a favour of an old friend." She grinned as she dismounted her horse.

I flinched at the thought of being surrounded by so much death.

We entered the building by a side door and descended into the basement. The smell of death and decay swarmed my airways, and I held my breath. Lex opened the double doors and greeted a man working on a body.

He didn't look up as we entered, and I looked over to the wooden table where he was pulling the intestines out of the body that was half covered by a sheet.

"Poor thing didn't stand a chance," the man said as he pushed his glasses high up his nose.

My stomach churned as I looked around the room. There were metal tools strewn around and a wall at the back covered in small wooden doors.

The man finally looked up and his eyes lit up when he saw Lex.

"Lexa!" he exclaimed while limping over towards us.

I looked at Lex who was looking at the elderly man fondly.

"What can I do for you, Lexa?" he asked.

Everyone I knew called her by Lex, not even her twin brother called her by her birth name, but it was interesting that this man did.

"We need bones," Lex said casually. "The more the better."

He peered at Lex over the rim of his glasses, his eyes flicked to me narrowing slightly.

"Do I want to know why?" he asked.

Lex gave him a wide grin. "It's best you don't."

He rolled his eyes in jest as if they'd had many conversations like this.

I felt as though the stench of death was coating my skin and trying to find a way into my soul. The intestines slid off the table and landed on the stone floor, I retched, and Lex's eyes shot to mine, I nodded towards the door and rushed up the stairs two at a time desperate to feel fresh air in my lungs.

Lex emerged outside a few moments later.

"I'm sorry, I couldn't be in there any longer," I said as I braced my hands on my knees, taking deep breaths to try and push the wave of bile down that was pushing up my throat.

"Are you okay?" she asked as she placed a hand on my shoulder.

"Yes," I replied as I pushed the nausea down. "Anyway, how did you come to befriend a Diener?"

Lex waited for me to mount Blade before she mounted too. "When Axel and I were younger, we would sneak to the cemetery after dark and hide out."

My eyes widened as I imagined the general of our armies and one of the most senior members of the king's guard, hiding out in a cemetery for fun.

Lex laughed at my shock "We were strange children I know, but one night we came across a disturbance. We saw a group of men digging graves and hauling the fresh corpses onto the back of a wagon."

"What on mother's light would people want with dead bodies?" I asked in horror.

Lex shrugged. "The black market probably, people would buy organs, even hair, so that they could do dark magick."

I nudged Blade forward, so I was at Lex's side.

"We were barely past our twelfth year and as big as Axel is now, he was a late bloomer."

I laughed at the thought of the general being smaller than the mountain that he was now.

"We heard shouts and that's when we saw Waylon being attacked by the grave robbers, he was trying to stop them, but he was outnumbered. Axel and I hid behind a gravestone not wanting to be next, but we couldn't bear to watch the poor man being beaten to death, so we snuck over to their wagon and detached the horse's reins, so it was free. The horse ran off through the dead of the night and the thieves had to abandon the bodies they had been trying to steal. I stayed with Waylon while Axel went to get our father. We knew we would be in serious trouble, but he was at death's door. My father brought him home and our mother healed him—although he still walks with a limp, she couldn't set his bones in time."

Her courage was inspiring, even from a young age she had to do what was right and she wouldn't see a good person harmed for doing the right thing if she could help it.

"What did your parents say?"

Lex laughed. "We had to muck out the horse's stable for three months, and we were forbidden from going to the cemetery again."

"Well, that seems fair enough I guess."

Lex nodded in agreement as we edged out of the city.

"Wait, we haven't got any bones," I said as I pulled Blade to a stop.

Lex looked at me over her shoulder. "We're on our way to get them Phoenix, don't worry."

I furrowed my brow in confusion. "Then why did we need to go to the morgue?"

"I needed to know where I could find human bones that nobody would miss. Waylon told me of a mass grave where prisoners had been buried many moons ago." She turned to look at me. "The bones we will be taking will be remains of people that committed the most heinous crimes."

I swallowed as I realised what we were about to do. My thoughts swam through my mind as we edged out of the city. We passed Chloris's house on the way. She lived in a modest home with her two sons and husband that my father had gifted her when she became my handmaiden. I noticed her front door had been broken and scraps of wood were nailed across a gaping hole.

I brought Blade to a stop. "Lex, that's Chloris's home, what happened to her door?"

Lex dismounted her horse and tied him to the fence. She drew her sword and knocked on the broken door.

Chloris's husband, Martel opened the front door. His eyes widened as he took in Lex stood before him, with her sword drawn ready for battle. His eyes flicked to me and back to Lex again.

"H-how can I help you?" he stuttered.

"As the princess' handmaiden, Chloris Prior is protected under the crown." Lex leaned down to observe the damage before looking back at Martel, "Who did this to your home?"

"I-I don't know," he stammered.

The broken door stood out against the surrounding houses, with their thatched roofs and well-kept gardens, and I wondered if one of the neighbours had seen anything.

Martel stepped into the doorway as he tried to pull the door closed behind him. "I came back from the market and saw the door had been taken to with an axe of some sort."

Chloris' sons Morgan and Merle came to the door to see what the fuss was about and my heart warmed at the sight of them. Morgan had Chloris' chestnut brown eyes with a dusting of freckles over his nose, whereas Merle favoured his father with his sandy blonde hair and sea-green eyes. Morgan, the elder of the two boys, looked past Lex to where I waited on Esmeray's horse, he tilted his head while he gaped at me, something like awe flashed across his face then his eyes lit up with recognition. I quickly looked around to see if anyone was within earshot if he revealed who I was. I looked back to Lex where Martel was ushering the boys back into the house. I breathed a sigh of relief, although his excitement to see me

112

brought a smile to my face. I would make it up to him next time I saw him at the palace.

Lex said, "If you do remember, let a member of the guard know."

He thanked her and shut the door quickly.

Lex mounted her horse as my eyes flicked back to Chloris's door.

The ride to the grave site was relatively peaceful, and I almost forgot why I had ventured out of the palace today.

After riding for a few miles, we came to a field that was edged with trees. The thick trunks stood solid in the ground, the branches were bare as winter had encased my kingdom in its steel like grip, coaxing the life out of the land until spring would let it breathe again. "Here," Lex said as she jumped down from her horse and retrieved a shovel from the saddlebag.

She stood with her back to a tree, counting her steps as she walked north. She counted fifteen steps then slammed the shovel into the ground.

I dismounted Blade, tying his reins to a low tree branch. Lex whirled around to face me. "What do you think you're doing?"

I gestured to the hole she was digging. "I'm helping."

Lex scoffed. "Absolutely not, it was a push getting Ez to sign off on you accompanying me, and that is all you will be doing."

"But—"

"Phoenix, I cannot allow you to dig up a mass grave of prisoners, you shouldn't even be watching me do this."

I sensed the underlying thing she would never say, that she was required to do the dirty work so the crown's hands were always kept clean.

"Fine, but the ground is almost frozen, it will take you twice as long without my help," I said as I walked over to the horses. I stroked Blade as the sound of the shovel pounded the ground.

Just when I was about to complain of the cold, Lex walked over wiping her arm across her forehead. "If you would have let me help, it would have been done quicker." I teased.

She rolled her eyes as she pulled a sack from the saddle bag. "I'll be done soon, then we can get out of here."

I suppressed a shiver as she piled the bones into the sack before shovelling the soil back into the grave. The breeze that had gently blown when we left the palace had picked up and was whipping at my exposed skin relentlessly. Dusk was settling over the sky, and I couldn't wait to be back in my chambers in front of the fireplace.

The ride back to the palace was quiet, peaceful, it was nice to just be with my thoughts and not be of concern to anyone. I took in my kingdom as we moved towards to the palace grounds.

"Did Chloris' husband seem strange to you?" I asked Lex as we approached the palace.

Lex scanned the grounds either side of the path leading up to the palace but didn't answer my question.

"I wonder why she didn't mention anything of her home being vandalised?" I pushed but Lex stayed silent focusing on the gates before us. My gut churned with anxiety as we waited for the guards to open the gates.

I left Blade with Isaac as I slipped through the side door to the kitchens and made my way to my rooms. Chloris had prepared a bath for me and laid out a simple gown for my evening meal, but she was nowhere to be found.

I sank into the hot water as the escaping steam brushed against my skin. I slipped under, letting it seep into every part of my body.

I came up for air and saw the water had turned a murky black. The feeling of being out in the open, with nobody knowing who I was, to have some anonymity, was a breath of fresh air. Anyone I encountered today would have thought me to be a member of the guard, not a forsaken princess. I scrubbed my hair with an orange and neroli soap, until it was back to its natural silver state.

I ate dinner in the usual silence with my father. It was our last meal together before I left for the shadow kingdom.

My father unexpectedly struck up a conversation.

"I knew the former king when we were boys, you know."

I turned to look at my father, he rarely spoke about the past, usually keeping our conversations to a minimum.

"What was he like?"

My father poured himself some more wine and it pained me that he felt the need to numb himself from his troubles in such a way.

"Galven wasn't always the tyrant we knew him to be. He lost his way a   long time ago and never found his way back."

I was aware of Silver and Ireland stood behind my back like silent sentinels as the dining hall doors swung open, and Esmeray marched in with Chloris. Chloris had been crying, her hands were tied with rope and her knees slammed on the ground as Esmeray stopped.

I jumped up, my chair banging as it fell on the polished wooden floor.

"Get off her!" I screamed at Esmeray. "What in mother's name are you doing?" I ran over to Chloris and tried to untie the rope binding her wrists together.

"What is going on captain?" My father's deep voice rang across the hall and Esmeray stood straighter as she spoke.

"Your Majesty. It has come to our attention that Chloris has committed treason."

Lex came into the hall, her face was grave as she stood firm at Esmeray's side.

My hands were shaking as I tried to free the woman that had raised me since birth and I froze when Esmeray's words sunk in, my hands went slack as I let go of the rope.

"Treason?" I scoffed. "That's impossible, untie her now!"

I looked down at Chloris who was still on her knees as she choked out words in between sobs.

"I'm sorry, Phoenix, I had no choice," she said as she hung her head in shame.

I took a step back as my father stood in front of her.

"Explain yourself, Chloris." My father's voice was gentle but firm and he gave her his hand as he helped her stand.

Chloris was looking at me, her eyes red from crying, but I couldn't hear anything.

Pieces of what she was saying rang in my ears. Threatened, Morgan, Merle, Ivywood forest.

The realisation hit me like a sword to my gut.

"It was you," I breathed. "You told the hunting party where I would be. You allowed them to bring those bodies into the palace."

"Phoenix, please I had no choice! They were going to hurt my boys!"

I stepped backwards, shaking my head. This couldn't be true. She wouldn't do this to me.

My head swam with thoughts of her betrayal. She could have come to my father for help, instead of trying to get me killed. This pain was worse than my beast's appearance. I braced myself against the dining table taking deep breaths to steady my trembling body.

My father's voice sounded in my ears as he said, "Chloris, if this is true, I have no choice but to confine you to the cells."

As much as her betrayal was like taking a knife to my heart, I couldn't bear the thought of her alone in those cold cells. She had looked after me my entire life and had also told the very people that wanted me dead where I would be hiding to stay safe.

"No." My voice was calmer than the raging emotions inside of me. I walked over slowly to where Chloris stood in front of my guard, she had hung her head in shame and had stopped begging for forgiveness. I tried to imagine why she would do this. Her family could have lived in the palace, protected day and night by the king's guard. Instead, she betrayed the very person she had sworn to protect, so she could protect her children. I couldn't punish her for choosing them. The boys she had birthed into this world.

"Phoenix, we can't let this behaviour go unchecked," Esmeray said as I raised my hand to cut her off.

I turned to look at Chloris. "Look at me." I said as her hair hung over her face. "Look at me."

She slowly lifted her eyes to meet mine. My heart tightened in my chest as a lifetime worth of love and trust disappeared before me.

"Esmeray is going to take you to your room for questioning about the people that want me dead. When she is satisfied that she has all the information she needs—" I took a deep breath, once I said the words there was no going back.

"I want you to leave. Take your husband and your children and leave Mercea."

Lex looked to Esmeray, whose rage was pouring out of her. I knew she would want to see any traitor of the crown brought to justice, but I couldn't allow Chloris to be taken away from her children who had done nothing wrong. Who were just collateral damage in this forsaken curse.

No one spoke as they waited for me to carry on.

"You have until the end of tomorrow to leave Mercea, but as of this moment," I hesitated as the words caught in my throat. "You are no longer a part of my kingdom."

The words burned like hot ash in my mouth and Chloris choked a sob but nodded her head to say she understood.

"I want you gone by the end of tomorrow."

I turned to look at Esmeray. "Please escort her to her room."

I looked away as I blinked back the sting in my eyes that threatened to spill over.

CHAPTER 13

THE GROUNDS OF THE PALACE were peaceful, the sky was overcast, and the air smelled of winter. I had Storm by her reins while we walked and I patted her silky mane, its silver-grey hue mirroring the clouded sky.

The day had finally come where I could take control of my own fate. Cursed or not, I still had a say in how my life unfolded.

The wind wasn't as relentless as it had been the last few days, as if the mother had screamed across these lands until her lungs were empty.

I sighed as my breath mingled with the air surrounding me. The memory of Chloris' betrayal was a gaping wound in my chest, that may never heal. I understood she had to put her family first, but I also knew that if she had just come to me, instead of betraying me, we would have figured something out. Now I had to ignore the hollowness that had settled over my heart where her love used to be, ripped from me with no warning.

I looked up at the sound of footsteps approaching and Isaac walked over to where I looked out over the grounds.

"Will you be taking Storm?" Isaac asked.

I took a deep breath, pushing my feelings down as the crisp winter air swirled through my lungs.

"No." I said as I turned to look at him. "I don't know how long I will be gone so I need you to look after her for me. Can you do that?"

Isaac stood taller, reaching his full height as he towered over me.

He placed his hand on his chest. "I swear on my life, princess."

I smiled as I looked back out to the grounds.

"You're part of my guard now Isaac. Don't make me regret it."

He turned and dropped a knee bowing before me, and I smiled at his innocence and determination to prove himself.

I opened my fur cloak and retrieved a dagger that was sheathed at my thigh, I held out my hand and Isaac placed his hand on mine.

"Isaac Beaufort, do you vow to protect the Devereaux crown above everything else?"

"I swear." He said as his pale blue eyes met mine.

"Then I swear you in as a member of the royal guard."

I pricked his index finger with my dagger, as he held his hand over the ground, a splash of blood dropped onto the ground seeping into the soil, sealing the vow.

I turned as I heard footsteps approaching and saw the captain walking towards us and I handed the reins back to Isaac. "Look after her for me."

He took the reins and placed his hand over his heart. "On my life, princess."

I watched as he walked Storm towards the stables. Esmeray came to stand at my side. "Did I just see you create a blood vow with the stable boy?" she said as her eyes scanned the grounds.

I turned to face her as I smiled. "I did. He's a good soul and it would do him no harm to have a sense of belonging."

Esmeray smiled as she shook her head, her loose unbound curls bouncing with the movement.

"Your father wants to see you in his study."

I took a deep breath and sheathed the dagger at my thigh. I wondered if he would try and talk me out of going to the north. "Okay, let's go."

"Chloris and her family are being escorted to the eastern port."

My chest tightened at the mention of her name, and it took every ounce of strength I had not to crumble on the ground where I stood.

Esmeray looked at me, no doubt gauging my reaction. "She will make her way to the Navi kingdom, where she has distant family from her mother's side."

I gave a curt nod, not wanting to discuss it any further.

I entered my father's study. He stood looking out of the window occupied with his thoughts. I would spend time with my father when I was younger while he did his royal duties and read his royal reports—his study used to be a safe space for me, but the older I became the more distance settled itself between us. I knocked on the door quietly and my father turned to look at me, his expression a combination of love and sorrow.

"Nixie, my love, take a seat." The veins around my heart twisted as he used the name from my childhood. He gestured towards the armchair that was positioned in the corner of the room, the chair I had spent much of my childhood curled up in. I felt so small as I sat down with my hands twisted in my lap.

"The day has come where you find your own way, Phoenix."

I looked up at my father, something akin to grief and pride settled on his face and my stomach sank.

He took a step away from the window and leaned over the large wooden desk as he picked up a sword. I hadn't noticed it lay there until now. He unsheathed the blade and I marvelled at it. It was made from a pure obsidian that glistened in shades of green and purple from the light pouring through the window. It seemed too beautiful to be used for its purpose, it was exquisite.

I looked to my father as I wondered why he was showing this to me, when I noted his fond expression turn to sadness in his eyes.

"Father, no."

He walked over to where I sat and placed the sword in my hands.

"It pains me that I cannot come with you, but I cannot leave the kingdom defenceless."

"I understand," I whispered as I ran my fingers along the obsidian hilt of the sword.

"Why are you giving me this?"

My father sat at his desk, his eyes focused on the sword in my hands.

"That sword has been passed down through the generations of our family. I want you to know that on your journey you will never be alone, no matter what happens in the shadow kingdom you will have the power of your ancestors behind you."

My throat tightened as grief gripped my heart. Grief for the loss of a relationship we never got the chance to have.

I coughed to clear my throat. "Thank you." My voice came out hoarse as my emotions threatened to spill over.

Corbin knocked at the door, interrupting us.

"Your Majesty, sorry to interrupt. There is a matter that requires your urgent attention."

I rose from the chair, gripping the sword by the hilt, leaving my father and his advisor to their business.

I left my father's study and Esmeray fell into step beside me. I saw her glance at the sword, but she didn't say anything. We made our way to the council room in silence, and I knew the rest of my guard would be there going over the last security measures before we left for Sakaria.

Esmeray opened the door, holding it open while I stepped into the room and saw them gathered around the table. It brought me back to the night Ruane had asked me to meet with the Shadow King.

Silver's eyes went straight to the blade in my hand.

"Phoenix, why do you have your father's sword?" Her eyes widened as I placed it onto the table.

I pulled out one of the velvet lined chairs and sat down, the heavy feeling in my gut was hard to ignore.

"Is everything okay?" Esmeray asked as she closed the door behind her.

I didn't know where to begin, the realisation of what I was about to do had sunk in and I could feel doubt creeping through the cracks.

"Phoenix?"

I looked to the captain of the Kings guard "Yes, I just—"

I cut myself off as I looked at my friends, the only friends I had ever had.

"I just don't know if we're making a mistake." I said as I chewed the inside of my mouth.

"What do you mean? Going to Sakaria?" Ireland asked.

"I can't explain how I feel, I just have a feeling that if we go to Sakaria something terrible may happen."

"If you don't want to go just say the word. We'll call the journey off and if the shadow king wants to meet with you, he will have to come to Mercea." Esmeray said.

I felt as though I were fighting my head and my heart. The logical thing to do would be to stay in Mercea and find another way to break this curse but another part of me wanted to seize the opportunity to see somewhere other than my palace and this kingdom. Who knew what the shadow king's motives were?

I looked to Lex and I could see the conflict warring across her face, as though she didn't know whether she should speak her mind or not.

"Out with it, Cortana."

Lex's eyes flashed briefly to Esmeray before meeting mine.

"I understand you have your doubts, and rightly so, but what if the answers we seek are in the shadow kingdom?"

Ireland leaned forward and I glanced at Silver whose eyes were transfixed on my father's sword.

"What did the seer say when we were in the south?" Ireland asked, her bright green eyes searching mine.

I closed my eyes as I thought back to being in the hut with Amaris, a shiver crawled up my spine and I shook off the feeling.

"She said the cave I fear to enter holds the treasure I seek."

"What if going to Sakaria gives you everything we've been searching for?" Lex argued.

I had to agree, a part of me wanted to stay in the safety of my palace, but with my beast making an appearance and there being a traitor among us, I wasn't left with much choice.

My options were to either stay in my kingdom and be hunted down by rebels and killed like the cursed princess, or go to the north and see if the Shadow King could help me.

Esmeray spoke into the silence. "We are taking a risk by going, and we can only assume the new king has followed his father's footsteps."

"What if he hasn't?" Silver said, finally tearing her gaze away from my father's sword.

"That's a possibility. But people are often a product of their environment and if he was raised by a man such as King Galven, it would be a miracle that he didn't end up the same as his father."

"Sakaria has been impenetrable since your birth Phoenix, maybe with the former king dying and his heir taking the throne, he wants to form an alliance?"

I looked to Ireland, what she said made sense although we wouldn't know until we went to the northern kingdom.

"If you're having doubts, Phoenix, just say the word and we will stay and find another way to get you what you need."

I hesitated for a second before I made my decision.

"No. We go to Sakaria."

Esmeray walked over to the door, turning to face me. "Then we leave at midday."

WE RODE NORTH all day and night and when morning broke through the sky, we dismounted our horses, having to go the rest of the way on foot. We left the guard that came with us, they were sworn to secrecy and threatened with beheading by Esmeray if they spoke of where they had accompanied us, before returning to the palace with the horses.

The thick trees of the forest that lined the border between my kingdom and Sakaria were covered in green moss, the roots consuming everything in their path. This would be the last night before we made it to the bone witch, and it's the night my beast would make an appearance. I tried to push down the feelings of dread as I thought about my bones breaking to accommodate my new form.

No one had spoken for a while, and I couldn't bear putting my closest friends in danger as darkness closed in around us.

"Why do you stay?" I asked no one in particular. Each of them stopped in their tracks and looked at me. Ireland's gaze flicked between her comrades, and I asked again. "Why do you choose to stay? You stay with me even though I am damned. Loyal to the crown or not, why do you repeatedly risk your lives for me?"

"Because we swore an oath." I looked to where Silver stood, her dark hair was braided down her back and her icy blue eyes pierced into me. She spoke as if it was the most reasonable thing in the world, to swear an oath to someone else at the cost of your own life.

"My life isn't worth more than anyone else's." I argued.

"Phoenix, you are the only heir to the crown of Mercea, it's our honour to keep you safe," Lex said.

I nodded, not needing anything more from them.

The moon's glow appeared through the branches of the trees around us and my body temperature was rising despite the biting cold. It started as a dull ache deep in my bones that I tried to put off even though I had no control of my body. I flexed my fingers to take my mind off the ache that was slowly becoming a burn until I couldn't hold it in anymore and I screamed as fangs filled my mouth, the canines tore through me and I cried out as my mouth filled with blood.

My guard stood watching me helplessly.

"Phoenix, we're right here!" Esmeray shouted above my screams and I dropped to my knees as my spine snapped, my back legs twisting at an unnatural angle. My screams echoed through the forest and my guard looked on in horror as I became the beast again. I heard every bone break, the pain building until I thought I might die from it. Fur rippled across my body, and I stood seven-feet tall. Towering over my friends, I raised my head to the sky and howled at the moon.

THE LAST THING I REMEMBERED was standing watch while my guard took turns sleeping. I had woken naked, in my human form, surrounded by my guard with their backs to me, swords drawn.

At least I hadn't been hunted. At least my body wasn't battered and bruised.

We continued north and, after a few hours had passed, we came to the edge of the woods and Ireland held up her hand in a fist to let us know to halt. I stopped to take in the sight before me, a hundred-foot wall towered before us against the backdrop of the forest. The ground surrounding the wall was completely barren, as if life refused to grow on this soil. The witch's lair was in the centre of the wall, built to keep the people of Sakaria in and anyone else out. The entire shell of the cabin had been covered in bones. Human bones mainly.

As the captain of the guard, Esmeray approached the lair first and knocked on the beaten door. I noticed claw marks scratched on its surface before the door opened slowly, and a gust of stale air escaped. I retched as the smell of death and rotten flesh coated my lungs.

As I entered the bone witch's lair, I felt consumed by her presence. The air was thicker, and my instincts screamed at me as though I was in the presence of something sinister. I glanced at the frail woman before me, she barely reached the height of my shoulders and her back slightly curved over towards the top of her spine. She wore a black dress, her face covered by a thick black veil. The stories told me I didn't want to see her face, that it was something of nightmares.

The walls were covered in wooden shelves, with jars of hair and skulls displayed on them. A cauldron sat before the fireplace, I peered into it and saw a thick soup of some kind simmering away. The bone witch reached for one of the shelves, oblivious to my guard and I in her home, and picked up a jar of dark hair and teeth, she poured the contents into the soup and used her withered finger to stir it.

Lex stepped forward and dropped the sack of bones at the witches' feet, her braids falling over her shoulder, and fast as lightning the bone witch reached over to grab them. She brought the braids to her veil and inhaled deeply. Lex went deadly still and my mouth went dry as I tried not to let my fear be known. We stood no chance against a being that had lived for a thousand years and consumed life from the very bones of the dead.

I felt the tension in the room as my guard held their breath, the witch swiped her finger across Lex's hair and a single braid fell into her hand. She brought it to her veil and sniffed deeply before releasing Lex's braids. Silver stepped forward and Esmeray held out an arm to stop her. One of the things I admired most about Silver was how fearless she was, she would take on this creature without a second thought if it meant keeping us safe.

The bone witch turned to the shelves behind her and selected an empty jar, placing the single braid she had cut off Lex's head into it. I watched confused and horrified as she placed the jar slowly back onto the shelf as though it were the single most important thing in the world.

The soup of hair and teeth bubbled away as the witch reached down to peer into the sack Lex had dropped at her feet. She reached her frail hand inside and pulled out a large bone that could have been an arm or a leg. She lifted her veil, and I gasped as I caught a glimpse of her lower face. Her skin had melted from her bones, the skin covering her mouth had wasted away and her teeth were visible through the hole in her face. I stepped back as she brought the bone to her mouth and bit down. The crunch of her teeth turned my insides to liquid as she swallowed what was left of it. I fought the urge to vomit as Esmeray broke my focus.

"May we gain passage to Sakaria?" she said, her tone was formal and I noticed it was edged with respect. The kind of respect you had for the dead. This being seemed to reside in the place between life and death, living off human bones to fuel her existence.

The witch cocked her head to the side and although I couldn't see her face, I could feel her gaze burning into me. My body grew warmer as no one spoke, sweat gathered on my brow as I went to speak but my breath hitched in my throat.

Cursebreaker.

The voice came from inside my mind and my eyes widened as I realised it was the bone witch's voice.

Time seemed to stand still. I was frozen to where I stood. I looked to Esmeray on my left and she hadn't moved.

Who are you? I asked. My eyes were fixed on the being before me.

I cannot say, child. The voice appeared in my mind again. The bone witch could control time. I was frozen, as were my guard.

Can you help us?

The witch inclined her head, never making a sound. *I cannot interfere with what has already started.*

I held my breath as the air around us charged with intensity.

Is there another way I can free myself from this curse? I asked as I spoke to the witch in my mind. My hair stood up on the back of my neck as she inclined her head towards the red door on the other side of the cabin.

A sacrifice must be made.

Something deep inside of me whispered not to turn my back on the creature—she was neither bone nor flesh. She stood completely still, silently watching our every move, a sound never escaping her lips. She was death incarnate. Her withered hands were clasped together in front of her, patiently waiting. If I wanted to be rid of this curse, I needed to get to the shadow kingdom, and this was the only way.

CHAPTER 14

E SMERAY AND SILVER went through the door first, I went third and Ireland and Lex flanked my back. I stepped through and was met with members of the king's guard.

My guard had their swords drawn instantly and formed a protective barrier around me.

The men wore a grey uniform that was embossed with the Trevelyan crest. A tall member of the guard with deep olive skin was holding a scroll and raised his hands to show he wielded no weapon.

Esmeray spoke first. "We were summoned by King Khaldon." She said, her sword still drawn in front of her.

The man looked behind Esmeray to me. "State your name before the guard."

I stood taller. "I am Phoenix Devereaux of Mercea."

He bowed before me. "The king has sent us to meet you at the border and bring you to the palace. You may lower your weapons, we wish you no harm."

Looks were exchanged between the women who had sworn their lives to protect me and one by one they lowered their swords.

He reached a hand towards Esmeray. "I'm assuming you're the captain?"

Esmeray didn't move for a moment before she accepted the offering and shook his hand.

"Yes, Esmeray Elordi, captain of the Devereaux guard."

"Pleased to meet you, my men and I will escort you to the king." I took him to be the person in charge. "We will be at the palace by sundown."

We walked through the lush forest, following the men, with Esmeray and Silver at my front while Lex and Ireland kept to my back. My guard were on edge, although they tried not to show it. Every so often Esmeray would turn to look at me to make sure I was okay.

We emerged out of the forest and the views before me were breathtaking. The landscape was full of lush green rolling hills and the smell of pine trees was a relief after encountering the bone witch.

I stood at the top of the hill just taking in the view.

"It's stunning," I breathed into the crisp air.

The head guard turned to look at me. "Sakaria has some of the best views in Endaria."

I looked towards the distance where a vibrant city buzzed with life a few miles away. As we made our way down the long stretch of road, I pulled my scarf over my hair.

"I hope we never have to encounter that creature again." Silver said as she shook off a shiver.

"I second that," Lex said as she pushed her braids off her face, as though she could rid them of the remnants of the witch.

The head guard stopped to face us. "Only the bravest would dare encounter the bone witch."

"Thank you," Lex said, her face beaming.

Another guard spoke up. "You couldn't pay me a thousand gold coins to step inside the bone witch's lair."

A guard that hadn't spoken the entire time whirled around to face his comrade. "Dominik Sinclair, why doesn't that surprise me." He laughed.

I waited a moment before speaking. "Did anyone hear a voice in the cottage?"

My guard halted and turned to look at me. "What do you mean?" Esmeray asked.

I chewed my lip as I contemplated telling them what had happened. "The bone witch spoke to me."

Ireland's eyes widened slightly as she came to stand next to me.

"What do you mean she spoke to you? I didn't hear a sound from her while we were in there."

I turned to look at Ireland, her piercing green eyes bore into mine.

"Her voice appeared in my mind."

"What did she say?" Silver asked as they all moved closer towards me.

"She called me cursebreaker. I've heard her voice before I just didn't know who it belonged to."

"What do you mean you've heard her voice before?" Lex questioned.

"On the winter solstice, before my beast came, I rode Storm to the Ivywood forest and heard a voice whisper cursebreaker. I thought it was my mind playing tricks on me."

Esmeray's eyes flicked between mine.

Silver stood closer. "What else did she say?"

"I realised that she controls time, maybe even life itself. While she was speaking to me, we were all frozen, like statues."

I could feel the stares of the king's guard as I spoke. "I couldn't see her face, but I felt her gaze burning into me, literally burning me."

"Mother above." Silver breathed.

"I asked if she could help break the curse," I blurted out.

Esmeray's head whipped towards me, I couldn't tell whether it was panic or anger or a mixture that vibrated off her.

"You asked the bone witch for help?"

"She didn't seem to want to harm us, she didn't have to let us gain passage, but she did, so I thought she may have the power to give us an advantage. We have been summoned to a foreign land with no knowledge of what we will face."

I struggled to catch my breath after the words spilled out of me.

The head guard edged forward slightly. "We have been told to assure you that no harm will come to you or your guard while you are in Sakaria princess."

Esmeray placed her hands on my shoulders as she looked at me, she was so close I could see the flecks of green scattered through the hazel of her eyes.

"Phoenix, what exactly did she say when you asked for her help?"

"She said that she cannot interfere with what has already been set in motion."

Esmeray released my shoulders. "Is that all?"

"I asked if there is another way to release myself." I took a deep breath, "she said there must be a sacrifice."

Ireland's mouth dropped in shock as Esmeray pinched the bridge of her nose.

"What does she mean by a sacrifice?" Ireland asked.

"Only the mother knows what she meant." I said.

Esmeray looked behind us, as though she were ready to go back and ask the witch to explain herself, while I looked towards the city in the distance that could have the very answers I needed.

CHAPTER 15

W E ENTERED A TAVERN through the thick wooden front door and were welcomed by aromas of roasted meats and the sound of laughter. A man behind the bar was busy pouring drinks but managed to acknowledge us with a nod of his head.

I had pulled my scarf over my hair to give myself some anonymity but I wondered how many people here knew of my curse. The former shadow king, Galven, had isolated his kingdom after my birth and people from Sakaria rarely left the north.

We had travelled for so long that I yearned for a hot meal and a bed for the night. The plan was to get some rest, then carry on to the Shadow Palace.

The initial silence that enveloped the tavern when we first walked in had subsided and people were talking among themselves again. We found a booth at the back and I slid into the seat as Lex and Ireland sat either side of me. Two members of the king's guard sat at the table next to us and I watched as Esmeray and Silver followed the others over to the bar. I glanced around the tavern and noticed people cautiously looking at my guard, but I kept my head down as I tried to get a look at my surroundings. The people here seemed jovial enough after the reign of King Galven. His reputation preceded him, and the kingdom was known to be one of brutality although as I looked around the tavern, the people here didn't look like they had been treated brutally for decades.

A couple sat by the window, the young woman on her lover's lap laughing and whispering in his ear as his hands roamed her thighs. Something inside my chest tightened and I wondered if I would ever have that, a love that was reciprocated. They looked in love and carefree, something I had yet to experience, and couldn't guarantee I ever would.

Esmeray and Silver put four pitchers of ale down on the table, the frothy amber liquid spilling over the sides of the metal mugs.

"I'm starving, I hope they have a good stew." Silver sighed as two women brought trays of food over. A bowl of steaming hot stew was placed in front of me, and I almost wept at the smell. My mouth watered as I reached for my fork. A plate of warm bread, fresh out of the oven was put on the table and the women left. They didn't pay much attention to us which I was grateful for.

I finished off the bread and stew quickly and stood up from my seat.

"I need some air."

Lex looked to Esmeray before standing with me, I looked to the king's guard who were drinking ale and Dominik gave me a nod as I passed him.

The fresh air was a relief to my senses, I pulled my scarf tight around my chin and breathed deeply. I looked around as the people of the shadow kingdom went about their day. Dusk was creeping in, and the world was tinged in a blue shadow. I raised my face to the sky and took a deep breath.

A noise distracted me from my thoughts, and I looked to my right down the dimly lit street and saw a girl stumbling. Two men approached her from the shadows.

"We just want to talk. Don't resist and you won't get hurt." One of the men said as he tried to coerce the girl to cooperate with him.

The girl was around my age, her long golden hair fell across her face like a curtain of silk as she tried to get away from the men. There weren't many people on the street, and I looked around to see if anyone had noticed.

One of the men gripped a hand tightly around her arm while his other hand covered her mouth, and she stumbled as she tried to pull away. He reached across her shoulder and pulled the strap of her dress down. Whoever they were, she clearly didn't want to go with them, but she was too intoxicated to fight them off.

I stepped towards the girl without thinking. "Let her go," I demanded.

Lex was next to me in an instant with her sword drawn.

The man with his hand around the girl's arm looked at me and spat on the ground. "This doesn't concern you, bitch."

The girls' eyes were wide with terror as she stumbled on the cobbles.

"Let her go now or—"

The sound of a dagger flying past my head cut me off and embedded in the man's eye. The force of it threw him back onto the cobbles, killing him instantly.

I whirled round to face Lex.

"Lex! We've been in Sakaria for less than a day and you've killed someone already."

The other man tried to slink away but Lex had her sword levelled at him.

"Forgive me, princess, for wanting to keep you safe," she said as she looked down at the man on the ground. "Besides he was the type of person the world would be better off without."

I looked at the shivering girl—she had on a satin red dress, and shoes that looked painful to stand in.

"Are you okay?"

Her lip trembled. "I'm—I'm fi—" she managed to get out before she bent over and vomited.

Lex's eyes widened as she kept the sword levelled at the man who was breathing frantically, anticipating that his death would be next.

"It's probably the shock," I said as I looked back at the girl.

"What did you want with her?" Lex asked the man and I watched as her hand slipped to the dagger strapped to her hip.

"W-we just wanted to talk," he stuttered.

"She clearly said no," I said as I peeled off my cloak and put it around the girls' shoulders.

Lex cocked her head. "You were trying to take her, weren't you?" Dark stubble dotted the man's face, and he wore clothes that suggested he didn't have much to his name.

Before he could blink Lex's dagger was at his throat and he was against the wall. I didn't know what kind of kingdom this was, but this would never be tolerated in Mercea.

Her dagger pressed against the skin of his neck, and she pushed it deeper, blood welling around the blade. The man's eyes widened as he tried to speak, I heard dripping on the ground and didn't have to look to know he had soiled himself.

"Why were you trying to take her?" I asked and Lex put more pressure on the blade as the man rushed to explain himself.

"We were told that there was a ransom to capture the girl, a thousand gold coins! We were told that no harm would come to her." His gaze flicked to his slain accomplice laying on the ground with Lex's dagger embedded in his eye.

I looked to the girl who was shaking and rubbed her shoulder to try and comfort her. I wasn't familiar with the rules of the north, and I didn't want to aggravate the king before I had even met him, not for this lowlife.

"What's your name?" I asked the girl, between almost being kidnapped, the cold and seeing her attacker killed, her whole body was trembling.

"Khayna."

I looked to my left as the tavern door swung open. Esmeray, Ireland and Silver stalked towards us followed by the king's guard.

They had their swords drawn instantly and closed the distance between us.

I wasn't sure what to do with the girl, we were in a foreign kingdom with different customs, and she was in no state to be left alone.

The head guard who I now knew to be Orion stormed towards the girl.

I instinctively took a protective stance in front of her as he said, "Princess, what in mother's name are you doing in the city? Where are your guards?"

I looked at Khayna in shock, she was the shadow princess.

Khayna mumbled something I couldn't understand when the sound of thunder cracked along the ground. I looked to the sky but couldn't see any flashes of lightning or a storm approaching, the sky was clear, except for the distant light of stars. Khayna bent over and hurled her guts up again, the stench of the vomit swayed me, and I clasped my hand over my mouth to stop myself from retching.

Shadows swirled towards us as if a storm was confined to the ground and couldn't quite reach the sky. I reached for my dagger when a man so beautiful it should be a sin stepped out of the shadows. His inky black hair contrasted against his fair skin, his face was like thunder and his eyes were a stormy grey like the shadows surrounding him.

The man's eyes flicked to where I was rubbing Khayna's back as she bent over retching, trying to rid her stomach of the last of its contents. I glanced behind him and frowned at the two figures waiting in the shadows.

My guard took a protective stance around me as I realised who stood before me. He closed his eyes, taking a few breaths as though he were steadying himself and I noticed a grey hue slowly disappearing from his skin.

A few moments passed before he stalked towards us. "How many times are we going to go through this Khayna?"

Khayna took a deep breath before she stood up and wiped the back of her hand across her mouth.

"Oh, so you do care. Well thanks for your consideration Khaldon."

A muscle flicked in his jaw as the tension rose. The king looked in my direction as his gaze pricked my skin but when his eyes met mine, I held his stare.

Orion stepped forward. "Your majesty, we have been escorting the princess to the palace as you requested."

I pulled my scarf down and let my loose braid fall over my shoulder. His eyes widened for just a second at the realisation of who I was.

"She's the person that stopped a traitor of the crown from kidnapping me," Khayna bit out.

His gaze found mine again as I held my head high. "I am Phoenix Devereaux of Mercea."

I knew he was the king, but he looked so normal. Two men slinked from the shadows, and I recognised one of them as the mysterious Ruane who bowed before me.

"Pleased to make your acquaintance again, princess." Ruane spoke smoothly, his deep voice like an unsung melody.

The other man stood slightly taller than Ruane, keeping to the shadows.

I needed to make sure Khayna was safe before I left her. "Are you okay with them taking you?"

"Yes," she said with distaste. "He's my brother unfortunately".

I choked a laugh and stopped myself from smiling.

Her brother, the king of shadows, clearly wasn't amused, and I got the feeling our time in Sakaria was going to be very interesting.

☐

CHAPTER 16

THE TREVELYAN PALACE was nothing like I had imagined. It was bright and light, the entire palace was crafted with bricks of iridescent moonstone.

My guard and I were given rooms in the west wing of the palace. I assumed we would buy supplies in the kingdom, so I was shocked to find the king had provided me with a full wardrobe of evening gowns, training gear and my guard had access to weapons and the Devereaux Guard uniform.

I sat on the edge of the king-size bed, unsure what to do with myself. I had prepared to meet with a ruthless king, but instead I was met with a ruler of this kingdom that seemed thoughtful and rational.

I had left the door open, Orion and Dominik were stationed outside at the request of the king and I waited for my guard to come and check in with me. The chamber I had been provided with was every bit luxurious as my own back home, and a four-poster bed took up a large portion of the room, adorned with fur throws and thick fluffy pillows. I walked over to the closet and wondered how long the shadow king presumed we would be in Sakaria. I ran my fingers over the gowns, marvelling at the silks, furs and jewel encrusted fabrics. On the back wall of the closet was a jewellery case, filled with the most stunning jewels that my breath caught when I saw an exquisite obsidian crown on the middle shelf. I opened the glass case and reached for it. I didn't know much about the young king, but he knew enough of me to make sure I had familiarities from my own kingdom. I picked up the crown, the black diamonds glistening in the candlelight.

I walked over to the window that looked over the palace grounds and the hairs on the back of my neck stood up. I felt him before I saw him. The energy in the room shifted and I turned around to see the King of Shadows standing in the doorway.

"I hope your rooms are to your liking." His voice was like sin and silk.

"They're perfect, thank you."

He placed his hands in his trouser pockets and looked up at me through thick, dark eyelashes.

"I wanted to thank you for what you did for Khayna."

When I stopped Khayna from being attacked, she said the man was a traitor of the crown. I wondered if the rumours of the shadow king were true. If people were so bold as to attack the princess, was this kingdom as ruthless as we had all been led to believe?

"Anyone would have done the same," I replied.

He gave me a smile that didn't quite meet his eyes. "I'll leave you to get settled."

A. J. FORD

He turned to leave, and I panicked. I needed answers. I needed to know why I was here. I was expecting to meet with a ruthless king and was met by a man only a few years older than me that seemed to have the weight of the world on his shoulders.

"Why am I here?" I asked. The not-knowing was eating away at me.

He stepped into the room and closed the door behind him.

My heart was a wild horse in my chest as I tried to steady my breathing.

"I asked you to come to my kingdom in the hopes that we could help each other." I jolted at his response. "Why bring me up to the north? Why not come to my kingdom?" I questioned. The north had been secluded since my birth, it was strange that the new king had summoned me.

"I will let you and your guard get settled before I explain everything."

My eyes narrowed as he spoke.

"I swear on my Kingdom, I wish you no harm, Phoenix. I will explain everything I promise."

My father once told me a promise was a comfort to a fool. I had no reason to trust him, his reputation made sure of that, and promise as he may, I wasn't letting my guard down.

"Please treat the palace as you would your own. I may be scarce the next few days."

I nodded as he turned to leave, frowning as I felt his energy leave the room. I wasn't sure why I was so aware of him, and I ignored the emptiness I felt as I stood in this foreign palace alone.

I wasn't alone for long, my guard piled into the room, dismissing Khaldon's men as Ireland closed the door behind her.

146

I looked at the women who stood before me, who would lay their lives down for me without hesitation.

"What do you think?" I asked.

Lex spoke first. "We've done perimeter checks; we've scoped out the grounds and the palace. I can't see anything amiss."

Ireland nodded. "I don't get the impression the king summoned you here with negative intentions."

I looked to Ireland. "Why do you say that?"

She clasped her hands behind her back before speaking. "We have been treated with nothing but respect and kindness since we stepped foot in Sakaria, sure it could be under false pretences but—" She looked around the room as she gestured to the luxury of it. "He's treating you like a queen. It doesn't make sense that he would drag you up to the north just to cause you harm."

Silver agreed. "He couldn't bear the force of the six kingdoms that would come down on him, so I agree with Ireland. I don't think we are here for him to cause you harm."

Esmeray pulled me out of my thoughts. "I saw him leave your room."

Of course she saw him leave, she didn't miss anything. Her gaze was intent, probing, as though she was trying to peer into the depths of my mind and see the interaction for herself.

"He came to thank me for helping his sister."

Esmeray's eyebrows lifted a fraction which was the only indicator that she was surprised by what I had said.

"I asked him why he brought me here, and he said he hoped that we could help each other."

No one spoke.

147

"He could only be referring to your curse, Phoenix," Lex said breaking the silence, "but how does he expect you to help him?"

"I'm sure we'll find out."

CHAPTER 17

W E HAD BEEN at the Trevelyan palace for a week, and I had hardly seen the king. Khayna had scarcely left her chambers, but I felt comfortable and the palace staff had made me feel at home. I had sent word to my father that I had arrived safely and Ruane was always around, he had surprisingly made me feel at ease in this foreign place.

I tossed and turned in the luxurious bed as sleep evaded me, as I lay surrounded by thick fur throws and too many pillows to count. I couldn't get my mind to switch off. Khaldon had told me to treat the palace like it was mine and I craved some sweet tea or chamomile milk, something that would soothe my mind.

My stomach twinged and grumbled slightly until, finally, I threw the covers off and made my way to the kitchen. I padded along the moonstone corridors, taking in its beauty. I heard a door click shut behind me as I descended the stairs and walked into the kitchen expecting no one to be there, but the cook was marinating a lamb presumably for tomorrow's dinner.

"That smells delicious," I said as the scent of rosemary and honey drifted towards me.

The cook jolted and turned around to face me. "Princess, I didn't see you there."

I smiled at him, as he wiped his hands on his apron and walked towards me.

"What can I do for you?"

I looked into his warm brown eyes and instantly felt like I was in the company of a friend, his bushy eyebrows raised in anticipation of my request.

"I don't want to be any trouble. I just wanted some sweet tea or chamomile milk, if you show me where to find it, I can brew some myself."

"Don't be ridiculous! You are our guest of honour. Please, take a seat."

He pulled a high stool from under the counter, clearly offended that I had offered to make my own tea and motioned for me to sit.

I watched as he walked over to a pantry, stocked with glass jars full of herbs, teas and dried flowers.

"Having trouble sleeping?" He called from where his head was buried as he sifted through jars.

His question caught me off guard and a glint of steel caught my eye as it passed the doorway. Esmeray was outside the kitchen standing guard. She would always give me my freedom, but I would never be completely free.

I thought about what to say before responding. "A little, this is the furthest I've ever been from home. It's unsettling me more than I anticipated."

"Aha!" he called as he lifted two jars from the shelves. "Chamomile and lavender milk will put you straight to sleep."

"That sounds great, thank you."

"So, it's your first time leaving Mercea?" he asked.

I watched as he busied himself warming up the milk on the stove. I was unsure of how much information to give in case I found myself trapped because of what I had revealed.

"Sorry, I've forgotten my manners. What is your name?"

"Phelan, Your Majesty."

"It's a pleasure to meet you, Phelan."

He gave me a warm smile before returning his attention to the milk.

"Given my circumstances, I haven't been to any of the other kingdoms. My visit here is my first time out of Mercea."

"Ahh but Mercea is the largest kingdom in Endaria princess, you could never leave if you didn't have to and still see the wonders of the world."

"Do you know much of my kingdom?"

His expression darkened slightly, and I felt I had overstepped somehow.

"The last king was a harsh ruler and those of the north were forbidden to leave, for fear we would see what the world has to offer and abandon Sakaria."

"So, our experiences aren't so different I guess."

Phelan gave me a tight smile and I watched as he added the lavender and chamomile to the warm milk before straining the mixture into a chalice. He drizzled some honey on top and left a stalk of lavender floating in the mixture.

151

I brought the drink to my mouth inhaling the sweet earthy scent. It tasted heavenly.

"Wow, I've never tasted anything like this. It's delicious."

Phelan beamed before he turned his attention back to the food he was preparing. He seemed passionate about his craft, and I watched as he focused on tending to the lamb.

I was unsure whether he wanted me to leave, but I didn't want to go back to bed yet.

"Khaldon wants a different future for our kingdom. Although he is young, I believe he can bring Sakaria to greatness."

I swirled the milk in the chalice and brought it to my mouth when a voice stopped me in my tracks.

"Captain."

I looked to the doorway where the king of shadows stood. He walked into the kitchen casually, making his way over to Phelan who was putting the finishing touches to the lamb.

He clasped his hands on the cook's shoulders, "Phe's famous lamb roast, you're spoiling us."

I sipped my warm milk. It relaxed me immediately and gave me something to focus on.

"Should my ears be burning Phelan?"

Phelan laughed, the sound deep and heartfelt. "I was just getting the princess up to speed."

Khaldon must have felt my gaze burning into his back, he turned around to face me, only now deigning to acknowledge my presence.

"Princess."

I levelled a stare at the king of shadows. "Your Majesty."

A moment passed between us, and I felt the world slow around me as if only the king before me existed.

Phelan finished off the lamb, putting it to roast overnight, leaving me alone with the king.

I put the chalice down unsure of what to do with myself. Khaldon pulled another stool out before taking a seat opposite me.

"Is something on your mind?" he asked, tilting his head as he waited for me to reply.

I took in his appearance while I thought about what to say. He had loose pyjama bottoms on and a white linen shirt, his hair was slightly dishevelled, and he smiled at me lazily, patiently waiting.

Something about his presence unnerved me. He reminded me of my father, a force to be reckoned with but defeated at the same time.

He looked up and his hair fell across his eyes. He was beautiful without even trying. Our eyes met, making my stomach flip over, he looked at me so intently I felt stripped bare as we sat in silence, the words caught in my throat.

"I've been curious since I heard about your quest to break the curse." Khaldon probed. "The stories tell of a princess with no magick but is it you can't practise magick, or you won't?"

I was thrown off by his question. I didn't think he would be interested in me personally and I was more than aware of Esmeray stood just outside of the kitchen listening to every word.

"Both." I replied. My tone was curter than I intended it to be, and I looked to him to see if he had taken offence.

"Could you do magick if you tried?" he asked.

153

I hesitated and thought carefully about my reply because I wasn't sure. I hadn't practised magick since I was child, the flames that shone brightly within me had reduced to embers.

"My magick has no outlet now our runes have been rendered almost useless." I stopped myself not trusting my emotions to not overwhelm me and I couldn't be seen as weak in front of a potential enemy. Khaldon watched me silently, not pressuring me to continue if I didn't want to.

"I haven't used magick since I was a child and you know if you don't use it, it deteriorates so who knows." I picked up the chalice swirling what was left of the honeyed milk, so I had something to do whilst I felt the stare of Khaldon burning into me.

"Some say the royal bloodlines don't need runes to channel their power." He said confirming what I already knew. I thought back to being a child and having a tantrum which ended in my chambers being burnt to ash, and on the winter solstice breathing white-hot flames.

"And what of your magick?" I asked into the silence.

"My magick is a gift and a curse, Phoenix."

"In what way?"

"There must be balance in the world, it's the way the mother intended it. It can't all be light and good. We appreciate the sun because of nightfall— if the sun shone on us relentlessly, we would surely tire of its light. My magick is the darker side of what is good."

I listened to what he said. Here I sat in the palace kitchens of a king that had a ruthless reputation drinking chamomile milk and discussing what's good in the world.

"So, your father's reputation? Do you follow his ways?" I asked.

My eyes dropped to his throat as it bobbed while he swallowed.

"My father was a troubled man; he lost his way and became the tyrant Endaria knew him to be. I want to rule this kingdom with a different approach."

"I see." I wasn't sure what else I could say, it would take him an age to undo the damage his father had done to Sakaria's reputation.

"I could help you."

I froze, lowering the chalice slowly. I wasn't sure if he was referring to why he had summoned me to the north or if he meant my magick. The thought of practising hadn't crossed my mind until now, that part of me was dead as far as I was concerned.

Khaldon pressed further. "I could show you a simple rune, something you would have used as a child. You can sense how your body responds to it. And if you don't feel comfortable you can stop."

I couldn't see Esmeray, but I knew she was there, out of sight. I wanted to ask her what I should do, but I already knew the answer. He made it seem so simple. I felt like practising magick would rip my heart wide open. I had shut myself off from that part of me to detach but if I was honest with myself, I would love to follow in my mother's footsteps and practice. She brought joy and light to so many people.

"The enchantresses tipped the balance of nature, runes have no merit anymore."

"How did your magick manifest?" Khaldon said, completely ignoring me.

I thought back to being a child with fire dancing at my fingertips.

"Flames."

His eyes flicked to mine, he looked at me as though he were searching for something in my eyes.

"All you can do is try, Phoenix."

Before I knew what I was doing the word flew out. "Okay."

My head and heart were fighting each other all while I tried to stay calm and composed like my entire identity wasn't about to come crashing down. My hand was being forced and no matter how long I had tried to outrun it, the need had caught up to me.

"Are you sure?" Khaldon asked. "We don't have to, I just suggested it as I know what a beautiful thing magick is when used as it should be."

"I want to." I said as I smiled the sincerest smile I could manage but it felt forced. For some reason I found myself trusting him.

"Wait here," he said as he left me sitting in the kitchen. As I sat alone, I felt my guard dropping. We had been in Sakaria for over a week and had come to no harm. My guard had taken to training with the best of Khaldon's men. If he were going to harm us, surely, he would have done it by now?

Khaldon came back into the kitchen with a cushion under his arm, interrupting my thoughts as the candlelight danced in the shadows around us. He grabbed a knife from a chopping block and plunged it into the cushion. He tore the fabric and pulled out a goose feather. The dim candlelight made his fair skin glow in the darkness. He placed the feather on the counter as I watched his every movement.

My eyes wouldn't leave him as he walked to the pantry and retrieved a jar containing a white powder.

"Flour," he said as he sprinkled the powder onto the counter's surface.

He looked at me. "Now watch what I do. There are no spells, no words, your magick is already within you. It just needs an outlet—you need to channel it through the rune."

The king drew a symbol into the flour with his finger and I craned my neck to make sense of it. I recognised parts of it as the symbol for air, but it was different to what we used back home.

He placed his hand over the rune, and I watched as the feather floated higher and higher off the counter until it was in front of my eyes. I felt my heart warm slightly. He was showing me a trick my father had taught me many moons ago.

"Okay, now I want you to try."

My eyes flicked to his as the feather sank slowly back to the counter.

I wanted to do this. I wanted to at least try. It was now or never.

Khaldon was staring at me with concern, and it felt nice that he cared. I scooped some of the flour in my hand and sprinkled it over the counter, using my finger to carve the symbol Khaldon had drawn into the powder. Once I was sure I had done it correctly I held my hand over the rune.

I was too aware of Khaldon's gaze, I could feel his stare imprinting itself on my skin, and suddenly felt very self-conscious, my cheeks started to heat, and I felt foolish.

"This isn't going to work." I sighed.

"Don't be so hard on yourself. Your magick has been dormant for a long time. You need to have faith in yourself, it may not happen right away."

I placed my hand back over the rune until it trembled with the effort. I closed my eyes, so I wasn't distracted by Khaldon's gaze. I felt a small ember of hope lighting within me, I hadn't let myself feel like this in so long. My arm was starting to shake, and my head was pounding at my temples. I was pushing myself too hard but with each heartbeat I could feel the essence of my magick again.

"Phoenix." Khaldon warned. His voice was an echo in my mind. The ember was slowly lighting up more of my core and I felt a bead of sweat roll down the side of my face. I could feel the magick inside of me, building, but there was no outlet for its release.

"Phoenix. You're pushing yourself too hard." The concern in his voice shocked me and my eyes opened. The feather hadn't moved at all, and my disappointment was a dull thump aching in my head.

I looked to the door as Esmeray burst into the kitchen and her eyes flicked to the blood I could feel dripping from my nose.

She stood there, dagger drawn, her chest panting as if she could save me from myself.

I won't cry, I told myself as I pushed back the sting of tears and the prickle of humiliation that roved across my skin.

What I felt was surreal. My magick was there but there was a block. I started to cool down and Khaldon leaned over the counter pressing a cloth under my nose. He pulled it away and I saw the blood seeping through.

"Your nose is bleeding."

Esmeray reached over and took the cloth from Khaldon. "Phoenix, what were you thinking?"

Esmeray's voice was gentle, my throat tightened as tears formed threatening to spill over and announce my defeat. I expected her to chastise me, but her gentleness bothered me more.

"It was my fault, captain." Khaldon said, his eyes were full of concern that unsettled me. He had no reason to care.

"My magick is there, but buried so deep I don't know how I will ever free it."

I turned to look at my friend and there was understanding in her eyes.

"I'm going back to bed," I said to the king and my captain as I held the cloth to my bloody nose.

Khaldon passed me a glass of water. "That's a good idea, you might have a headache in the morning."

I walked to my chambers with Esmeray at my side, frustrated and defeated.

CHAPTER 18

Khaldon

THE ARRIVAL OF THE PRINCESS had set my nerves on edge. Each moment I spent with her ignited something within me, as if there was a familiarity between us although we hadn't met until recently. My father had eyes and ears throughout the seven kingdoms, his paranoia often clouding his judgement, and I was aware of the troubles Phoenix had gone through, especially those on the winter solstice. The fact that she came gave me hope, and I paced my study as I waited for Aeden and Ruane to join me.

Aeden arrived first. "Khal."

I nodded as Aeden sat in one of the chairs. I sat at my desk, the silence a comfort as my mind raced.

Ruane arrived next, his larger-than-life persona hard to resist. He shut the door behind him and sat next to Aeden. They both waited for me to speak as I sat back in my chair and crossed my hands before me.

"Any update?" I asked the men before me who I would trust with my life.

Ruane spoke first. "It's more than likely to be true."

Aeden leaned forward in his seat. "The translation is as clear as we could get it, but everything we have gathered leads us to the land of souls."

I nodded as I processed the information, this could change everything.

"And what of the princess, do you think she will do it?"

The mention of Phoenix snapped my attention to Aeden. I felt a primal instinct towards her, from the moment I laid eyes on her outside the tavern in the city. She didn't know who my sister was, but she still protected her, nonetheless. I shook off the feeling.

"We all have something to gain from her co-operation," I said.

"Agreed," Aeden chipped in. "She is in a foreign kingdom that has a distinct reputation for being ruthless, we need her to see what our goals are for the future. That you are nothing like your father."

"I know," I bit out. If she didn't cooperate, I wasn't sure I would have a kingdom left to rule.

☐

CHAPTER 19

Phoenix

KHALDON HAD PROVIDED ME with a handmaiden, I told him it wouldn't be necessary, but he had insisted. The wound of Chloris' betrayal was still raw, tender, as if her actions had bled my heart dry. I had barely seen him since the night in the kitchen, which had been almost a week ago, but he made sure I was well looked after.

I knelt in front of the fireplace, the ashes from last night's fire were thick and had settled in the centre. I carved runes into the ash and held my hand over the empty chamber. Excitement churned away in my gut, as I concentrated on summoning a flame. Khaldon sparked a desire that I didn't know I had. Possessing magick was a dream I never thought I would be a reality.

My hand trembled as I held it over the ash, pain shot across my head as I felt blood dripping from my nose. A sigh escaped me as I swept the ash and runes across the floor in a fit of frustration and wiped the blood from my face. My dream was short lived, and I was certain magick wasn't going to be a part of my future.

Serafina knocked on my door as I finished dressing. I opened the heavy wooden door which was covered in delicate runes although I couldn't decipher their meanings.

She came into my room and placed a tray filled with breakfast onto the table in my suite. She bowed once she had put the tray down and I grimaced. She looked up at me and I quickly schooled my features into a pleasant smile.

"King Khaldon has requested your presence at dinner this evening."

I was busy eyeing the delicious breakfast she had brought me to eat when my eyes snapped to hers.

"Will there be others at the dinner?" I asked, my nerves jittered as I thought about being alone with the shadow king again.

"He has only requested your presence, princess," Serafina replied.

Her eyes dropped to the ash on the floor and embarrassment heated my face. My eyes flicked between Serafina and the mess I had made when I noticed I had left a rune visible in the fireplace.

"I left the window open last night, I'm sorry." I rushed to explain as I bent down to clear the ash and erase the rune. I didn't need any evidence of my failure.

Serafina gently touched my arm. "It's okay princess, I'll have one of the maids attend to it."

I left my chambers as the anticipation boiled away in my stomach at why the king would request a dinner with just the two of us as I made my way to the gardens. I drank some of Phelan's famous honeyed milk as I sat outside and relished the sun pouring into me. Its heat was non-existent, but the light warmed my soul. Those with magick tended to harvest the moon, but I preferred the sun. The moon's power was more understated, its power subtle. The sun forced people to acknowledge its power and it would burn the world to ash before it dimmed itself for anyone. I listened to the river flowing beside the moonstone palace and a feeling of peace settled over me, as though I was exactly where I was meant to be. Somehow my life had ended up here and I hoped magick would be a part of my future, I was ready to give it up for good until Khaldon encouraged me. I found myself smiling at the thought of him before I stopped myself and came to my senses.

My guard were training with Khaldon's men, so I sat alone in the winter sun. Khayna approached me, and I smiled as she sat down. The sun illuminated her golden hair and while Khaldon's skin was fair, hers was golden as if the sun gravitated towards her.

"I hope I'm not interrupting," Khayna said as she sat down.

"No, not at all," I replied.

"I wanted to thank you for what you did at the tavern. I've been—" She looked out towards the gardens as she hesitated to carry on, "I've been struggling since my father's death."

I looked at the girl next to me, I had barely seen her since I arrived in Sakaria, she seemed to favour solitude. She was close to me in age and struggling with grief, but our troubles seemed worlds apart.

"You don't have to explain yourself to me." I said as she looked out over the gardens.

"My father was a troubled man and his death took us by surprise, I don't think Khaldon ever expected to be king so young. I know my father wasn't the most loved man and his ways were often deemed excessive, but I miss my father dearly and I cope the only way I know how."

I placed my hand over hers. "I understand your grief Khayna, more than you may realise."

She held on to my hand as she said, "My mother fled Sakaria when I was a child, my father was power hungry, and he changed as a person the more power and control he sought to gain. I dread to think what would have become of our kingdoms if he were still alive."

My father's counsellors had asked him to reach out to the former king of shadows and my father had refused. He had said King Galven was too ruthless and couldn't be trusted. Now, as I looked at his daughter, I wondered how bad he must have been for her mother to have fled these lands.

"Did you not want to go with your mother?" I asked.

Khayna let go of my hand and her warmth disappeared instantly, as she pulled her shawl tighter around her shoulders.

"I begged my mother to take me with her. I had to be pried from her legs. She told me I would be safe in Sakaria, and she couldn't take me where she was going. My father would have ripped the world apart to find me." She gave me a sad smile as she looked over my shoulder.

"I'll leave you to enjoy the rest of your morning," Khayna said as she gathered her fur shawl and made her way back inside the palace.

I watched her walk away. Her world had been torn apart. Her mother had left the kingdom when she was a child and now her father was gone. As ruthless of a ruler as he may have been, she'd loved him dearly. Now Khaldon was king, responsible for an entire kingdom.

Esmeray came to sit beside me and I noticed a thin sheen of sweat on her skin and wondered how hard Khaldon's guard had pushed her. We had been in the moonstone palace for some time now and my guard were finally warming up to Sakaria.

I broke the silence first. "Khaldon has invited me to a private dinner tonight."

One of Esmeray's eyebrows lifted as she said, "Maybe he will finally explain why we're here."

"I think we were wrong about Sakaria. The rumours of this kingdom don't make sense. The people here have been nothing but kind to us."

"Except for the traitor of the crown that attacked the princess," Esmeray said, matter of fact.

She was right, it didn't make sense that people around the world feared this kingdom, but its own people were bold enough to attack the royal family. I watched as Khaldon trained with Aeden on the other side of the courtyard. By the end of the night, I would finally know why we were here.

CHAPTER 20

SERAFINA CAME TO MY ROOMS to dress me for dinner. Khaldon had asked that my guard not accompany me so we could have privacy but Esmeray insisted on standing guard outside.

I had been provided with clothing fit for a queen. I looked in the mirror as Serafina finished my hair, the off-shoulder silk gown she had chosen clung to every curve on my body and a silver beaded cuff was placed on my upper left arm. As I crossed my legs, a split in the fabric revealed my thigh, my skin glistening with an ointment Serafina had suggested I use. My hair was a cascade of silver curls down my back with one side swept up and held in place with a moonstone comb shaped like a crescent moon that reflected in the light.

Serafina took me to Khaldon's quarters as Esmeray followed behind. The only sound in the light and airy corridor was my silk dress grazing the marble floor as our footsteps echoed off the moonstone pillars guiding our way. The palace seemed quieter, as if its people had been told to make themselves scarce. So much was riding on us being in Sakaria, I was almost out of options. If the shadow king couldn't help, I would be forced to live the rest of my days as a beast or entice someone to fall in love with me. Both options made me nauseous.

Serafina stopped outside a chamber, knocking on the door. Khaldon answered and she bowed before leaving me alone with the king.

Khaldon stepped away from the doorway and beckoned for me to follow him, nodding to Esmeray as he shut the door. We walked through the lounging suite, which was imbued with white and silver, and a white fur rug lay in front of the fireplace. My mind thought back to my beast, it would be a full moon in a matter of days and my stomach tensed with unease.

Khaldon walked us through a set of double doors and onto the balcony. Candles covered every surface and a firepit had been lit, providing us with much needed warmth.

I shivered as he pulled my chair out for me and I sat down in the cold winter air. Khaldon came behind me and placed a fur shawl around my shoulders.

The table had been filled with delicious food, and the smells coming from the spread that had been prepared made my mouth water. I looked at the feast laid out before me, there was roasted lamb in a mint sauce, roasted truffles with creamed winter greens potatoes and a lemon and chestnut whip for dessert.

There were more candles on the table illuminating the spread as he sat facing me, the sharp lines of his face lit up by the candlelight, and my breath hitched. His beauty was that of devastation. The rumours of a ruthless king seemed far-fetched but I knew better than to let my guard down. This was politics. I ran my gaze over his attire, he wore a dove grey shirt with silver buttons, smart fitted black trousers and a black jacket to finish the look. I met his gaze over the candlelight and noted that Serafina had chosen a dress for me that complimented his outfit perfectly.

He was the complete opposite to me. His skin was creamy white, his inky black hair the opposite of my silver curls and his eyes were light grey, countering my eyes of onyx.

"Thank you for meeting with me, Phoenix." His voice was deep and smooth.

I reached for a glass of wine and took a sip. Winter wine. Another comfort from my home, and I fought the urge to smile knowing he had done his research.

"You said you thought we could help each other; in what way did you mean?" I asked. I tried not to let the thoughtfulness sway my opinion of him. Although I had realised he wished us no harm, I still didn't know why he had summoned me to his kingdom. My nerves were jittery and I took another sip of wine, the hint of fruit and spices warmed my chest as I tried to maintain an uninterested demeanour.

He swirled his wine before taking a sip. His throat bobbed as he swallowed while he held my gaze the entire time he drank.

"I hope my approach wasn't deemed excessive. I have certain limits when it comes to leaving my kingdom."

I noted the evasiveness in his statement and thought back to Ruane dancing with me, asking me to meet with the young king. Khaldon couldn't have been more than a few years older than me, but he seemed

169

tired and weary. As if the weight of the world had been set upon his shoulders.

He carried on, "Whispers of your curse have spread throughout our kingdoms over the years and under my father's reign, I can understand why your father wouldn't ask for assistance. But I was hoping I could help."

His response surprised me although I tried not to let it show. "Why would you want to help?" I asked. Why did he allow himself to be portrayed as ruthless then summon me to his kingdom to help me?

"I have my reasons."

His gaze met mine and darkness clouded his eyes. I took in the man before me, burdened with a crown he may not have been ready for.

"You said you would explain everything once my guard and I were settled. We have been here for weeks now, and I still am none the wiser of why a potential enemy summoned me to the north."

Khaldon flexed his hands and my eyes drifted to the moonstone ring on the middle finger of his right hand. I ran my finger over my ring of runes and waited to see what the king had to say for himself.

"Ravynne is in a cell below the palace."

I blinked. He'd had the enchantress that was responsible for my curse in his dungeons this entire time. I spoke slowly as my mouth caught up with my racing mind. "You have her captured below the palace?"

His stormy eyes pinned me to where I sat. "I do."

My eyes flicked between his frantically, "If she's captured, we could bargain with her to reverse my curse!" I shouted across the table.

The king laughed, the sound rich and dark. "She would do no such thing. She would probably kill you given the chance." I blinked slowly as

I processed what Khaldon was saying. "She wasn't so evil as to kill a babe but now that you're an adult, Phoenix, she would see nothing wrong with ending the Deveraux bloodline."

My mind reeled at this information.

"Why did you ask me to come to Sakaria? You say you wanted to help me, but why? What would you gain from it?"

A muscle ticked in his jaw as he thought about his response.

"Ravynne approached me after the death of my father and sought to catch me in what she thought would be my weakest moment. I had no desire to be king at this age. She had struck a deal with my father and after his death she felt that I should honour it. She found me in my chambers catching me off- guard. She bound me to my land and siphoned the magick I inherited from my father which she had gifted him in order to give him an advantage over the other kingdoms. It shouldn't have even been possible and I had no way to retaliate."

I picked up my chalice and noticing it was empty placed it back onto the table.

Khaldon rose from his seat and refilled my winter wine. "Thank you." I said as I tipped my glass towards him. The wine was soothing my frayed nerves and I knew I needed to be mindful not to lose my inhibitions around the king.

I ran my finger around the rim of the chalice, "what deal did your father strike with the enchantress?"

Khaldon watched me intently before answering. "My father had agreed to retrieve a powerful relic for her on the condition that she granted him the power he should rightfully have. With runes not being viable, my father was hell bent on gaining an advantage over the other kingdoms but died shortly after she gifted him the power, it may have been too much for him to bear. His power transferred to me as the heir to the throne and that was when Ravynne approached me, while I was grieving my father. I refused to work with her and she bound me to my land in the hopes that I wouldn't retrieve the relic and use it against her, I assume. The fact that the other kingdoms stayed away from Sakaria must have given her reason to believe that I would be helpless until I agreed to help her."

"How did you manage to capture her if she took most of your power." I asked.

"Ruane managed to get the shackles onto her that nullify her magick and she has been in the cells below the palace since. If I were to remove those shackles, she would kill us all. She weakened me to the point that I only have a sliver of power and my father's reputation to keep my kingdom safe. People haven't attacked yet because they think me to be evil, like my father, and the wall my father created at your birth keeps Sakaria safe. I would love nothing more than to live in peace with the other kingdoms, but she has bound me to my land and I cannot leave. That's why I sent Ruane to meet with you."

My body stiffened at this. The ruthless shadow king had no more power than I did. I cocked my head to the side, folding my hands in front of me. The only reason I'd come is because I thought the almighty king of shadows had powers strong enough to free me of my curse.

"You can't help me," I said as I pushed my chair back and moved to leave. Khaldon reached over and grabbed my wrist, his touch gentle but firm. A shock jolted through my blood at the contact, and I looked to where his skin met mine. His grip was like a brand, searing into my soul. His eyes widened as if he felt it too.

"Please, Phoenix, just hear me out."

I looked down to where he was holding my wrist and he let go. The warmth of him slipping away. I sat back down, well and truly defeated. He was my last hope and he had just shattered any chance I had of ending my curse on my own terms. Now I would have to force myself to make someone fall in love with me, if that was even possible at all.

"The reason I asked you to come to my kingdom is because there is a way, I believe, that we can end our burdens."

I narrowed my eyes as I waited for him to carry on.

"The relic is hidden in the land of souls, it can only be wielded by someone of one of the seven royal bloodlines that forged it and if you would retrieve it, we could use the ancient power to rid of us the enchantress for good, it is the only thing that could kill her and stop her reign of madness. No one should have the amount of power she has."

I took in the king before me, unsure of how what he had revealed would help me. "As appealing as killing the enchantress seems, I'm not sure how your plan helps me."

"It helps you by giving you the chance to free yourself on your own terms."

I had read stories of the land of souls as a child, it was more myth than truth.

"The land of souls is merely a myth. I can't waste any more time on a fool's mission," I said as I looked out into the night sky.

Khaldon pulled at his shirt cuffs. "I assure you that the land of souls is real, Phoenix."

His gaze pinned me to the spot, his eyes were like a storm at sea, and I forced myself to look away.

173

I reached for the fur shawl on the back of my seat and pulled it around my shoulders, the warmth that coated me was comforting and I rose to stand and look out over the moonstone balcony. I was aware of Khaldon's gaze never leaving me.

"I have been nothing but surprised since I arrived in your kingdom." I admitted as I looked over my shoulder and caught Khaldon's eyes roving over my body.

He rose to join me, and we both looked out over the palace grounds.

"Pleasantly surprised, I hope."

"Well, after I was summoned."

Khaldon laughed and the tension between us eased as my eyes instinctively found his mouth.

"I was expecting to arrive in a kingdom of death and despair, but that hasn't been the case."

He turned to look at me as I watched his guards doing their rounds of patrols below.

"That's fair, I suppose, given the circumstances," he said.

I noticed the tone of regret that laced his words.

"What do you truly want? For yourself, for your kingdom?" I asked the king.

"In a perfect world, Phoenix, I wouldn't be bearing the weight of this cursed crown," he said as he loosed a breath. "It will take a long time for the damage my father has done to be reversed and for my people to see me as a just ruler."

I could tell he cared deeply about his people and his kingdom. He turned to face me, edging slightly closer as his arm leaned on the balcony edge.

"And what do you truly want, Phoenix?" the king asked.

"I want an all-consuming love." I breathed and his full lips parted slightly, I imagined how they would feel against mine before pushing the thought away. "I want a love so deep the oceans would envy it."

He stood solid as his eyes took in every inch of me. "I do not want a love for convenience or to break a curse." I said as I held his gaze.

The sound of feathers came towards us as a Parakeet landed on the balcony's edge followed by another.

"Two for joy." Khaldon mused.

I couldn't see any joy in my future, I couldn't see past this curse.

"My beast will be here soon. I will have to leave before the moon is full, I can't risk causing your people any harm or bloodshed," I said as I shivered, the cold winter air was clawing at me, and I looked over to the fire pit that had reduced to cinders.

Something I couldn't quite place flashed across Khaldon's gaze. "Let's go inside."

Khaldon pulled a chair next to the fireplace where a delicious warmth was burning and sat down across from me.

"I can't imagine what you must go through on a full moon, Phoenix," he said as he handed me another glass of wine.

He looked at me so intently I felt stripped bare, like he could see all my fears and secrets. I struggled to hold his gaze as his eyes burned into me so I sipped my wine as the heat from the fire seeped into me.

"It isn't something I would wish on anyone."

"What if I could offer you a reprieve from your torment?" Khaldon said.

"In what way?" I asked. The wine had turned to acid in my stomach, and I swallowed as I tried to push the feeling away.

"The same shackles that allow me to hold Ravynne captive can be used on you, they will nullify any magick in your blood until you take them off. The curse won't be able to work during the full moon."

I took in the man before me. He was offering me a lifeline, a reprieve from my cursed torment.

My heart leapt at the idea of not having to endure the turn as my beast took over my body. "Are you sure it would work?"

"I'm sure, Ravynne has been in the cells since the day after my father died."

"Okay." I breathed, my heart thrummed in my chest at the realisation of what he was doing for me. "I'll use the shackles."

Khaldon simply nodded.

Hours passed and the night went by in a blur. I found myself revealing things that only my guard knew. Khaldon and I had similar upbringings, although the circumstances were wildly different, but it was nice to be understood by someone that had lived a similar life.

I left Khaldon's chambers after midnight as Esmeray escorted me to my room, I didn't say anything about the evening only that I had enjoyed it and would explain what the king wanted in the morning. I climbed into bed as memories of the evening flashed through my mind, until sleep overcame me.

CHAPTER 21

Khaldon

I SAT AT THE DINING TABLE waiting for the princess while my closest men talked around me. I ran my thumb over the moonstone ring on my middle finger, the very fact that the princess had agreed to see me at dinner was progress.

The feelings I felt towards her were irrational, we had been alone together a handful of times, but I couldn't ignore the closeness I felt towards her, as though there was a thread of fate binding us together. I felt it last night when she tried to leave, as I grabbed her wrist. I'm not sure if she felt it too but the moment my skin touched hers, I felt something snap inside of me.

"A coin for your thoughts?"

I looked up and saw Ruane watching me, my mind was somewhere else completely, back on the balcony of my chambers with the princess of Mercea.

"My mind isn't a place you would want to be," I replied.

He frowned slightly before returning to his breakfast. He knew better than to try and coax me out of my sombre mood.

My thoughts drifted back to Phoenix and I groaned inwardly, the point of her visit to Sakaria was to gain an alliance. We had been isolated in the north with the other rulers fearing my father, like a rabid animal, better to stay away than risk getting bitten.

I ran my hand down my face as I tried to focus on what Aeden was saying to Ruane. I needed to repair the damage my father had done and gain the trust of one kingdom at a time. Mercea was the only kingdom that shared a border with Sakaria, so it was logical to start there.

I hadn't expected to feel such a pull towards the princess. We had spoken for hours after dinner, and I was surprised at how many similarities there were between us and I knew in the very depths of my soul that she would be my undoing.

☐

CHAPTER 22

Phoenix

THE NEXT MORNING, I made my way to the dining hall. The light, airy corridors led the way as my guard fell into step around me.

I spoke quietly, knowing that Esmeray would hear every word. "The king has offered me a temporary solution to my curse." I didn't mention him wanting me to go to the land of souls to retrieve an ancient relic for him, or the fact that Ravynne was in the cells below the palace, she would probably take his head off the moment I told her.

Esmeray pulled my arm gently, and I halted my steps.

"What do you mean?" She asked, her eyes flicking between mine.

"He has the means to nullify any magick in my blood, so the curse won't work during the full moon."

I had been exhausted after my dinner with Khaldon and hadn't had a chance to inform my guard of any updates, I thought I should tell them now before we met with the king.

She straightened herself as we carried on walking. I descended the steps and saw Aeden waiting at the bottom of the stairs. He kept himself to the shadows and I only now noticed his eyes were two different colours. His left eye was a deep blue that reminded me of the ocean, while his right eye was the same shade as an emerald jewel. He sketched a low bow, and we followed him into the hall.

I entered the dining hall and was met by Khaldon at the head of the table, lost in his thoughts. Ruane was next to him, and his bright smile lit up his face as he saw me.

"Good morning, Phoenix, did you sleep well?" His deep voice boomed across the room.

"I did, thank you," I said as I sat in the seat at the opposite end of the table, my guard sat at either side.

I looked up at Khaldon whose eyes were fixed on me. His grey eyes met mine and the world stilled. My senses centred on the man sitting before me and I shifted in my seat as something stirred inside of me deep in my core.

My thoughts were interrupted by Khayna walking into the room, her golden blonde hair was braided in a crown and loose pieces of hair framed her face. Her gown was a blush pink that was offset by her golden skin.

"Is everyone excited for the ball tonight?" She asked as she sat down, filling her plate with fruit and pastries.

She had been around a lot more recently, seemingly out of her self-imposed isolation. It was nice to see her smiling, although Khaldon hadn't mentioned a ball, my eyes shot to his as Khayna looked between us.

"Khaldon! You didn't invite our guests to my birthday ball?" She sighed as she rolled her eyes at her brother before turning to me.

"Phoenix, you and your guard are more than welcome to join us tonight. I really hope you will celebrate with us."

I smiled at her generosity. "I would love to celebrate with you Khayna, happy birthday."

After a day spent worrying about the ball it was time to get ready. The gown Serafina had chosen for Khayna's ball was exquisite. A fitted bodice covered in rose gold detailing that looked like liquid gold covered my upper body, leaving my arms bare, whilst the nude chiffon skirts flowed to the ground where they pooled around my feet. My hair had been left loose with small sections intricately braided. Serafina looked in the mirror as she met my gaze. She smiled at her work as she finished applying a bronze powder to my cheekbones. I had to admit, the look was breathtaking. Serafina fussing over me made me think of Chloris. I couldn't bear thinking about choosing another handmaiden since her betrayal. Letting someone else get close to me wasn't something I was willing to do.

"Now you just need a crown," Serafina said as she walked into the closet.

I jumped up gathering the skirts of the gown to stop myself from tripping. "Oh, that won't be necessary, the gown will be enough, thank you," I said, not wanting to sound ungrateful.

Serafina emerged from the closet holding a rose gold crown. The gold had been shaped like the branches of a tree and it was covered in rose quartz crystals. It complimented the gown perfectly.

Serafina was practically giddy with excitement as I nodded.

"Fine, I'll wear the crown," I said reluctantly.

She all but squealed as I sat in front of the mirror whilst she fastened the crown into my hair.

She stepped back to admire her work and clasped her hands over her mouth.

"You look beautiful."

I met her eyes in the mirror and smiled.

I opened the door, unsure of what to expect from the evening, Khaldon hadn't mentioned the ball despite me being with him last night. He didn't owe me anything, I knew I was here for political reasons. It was naïve of me to think he wanted anything more than my help to defeat a common enemy.

I pushed the feeling down as I stepped outside of my rooms and found my guard waiting for me.

We made our way to the courtyard where it had been transformed into a wonderland. A large marquee had been set up to shelter guests from the winter chill and candles had been placed around the courtyard for the few guests who mingled outside. I wouldn't know anyone, except my guard and Khaldon's closest people.

I closed my eyes as I took a deep breath, my guard a solid presence at my back. I pulled back the curtain and stepped into the marquee, I saw Khayna dancing in the centre of the crowd. A group of musicians were set up on a stage towards the back of the makeshift ballroom, an upbeat melody coming from their instruments. Lex and Ireland stepped in front of me while Silver and Esmeray guarded my back, they formed an impenetrable wall around me, and I felt my body relaxing. We moved as one as I made my way to a corner where I would be hidden.

A server carrying a silver tray of what looked to be sparkling honey wine walked past, and I reached and grabbed a glass. I poured the contents down my throat and laughed as Esmeray watched me with wide eyes. The drink hit my bloodstream almost instantly as the bubbles danced across my tongue and my head started to feel lighter. I felt the tension easing out of me as I watched Khayna dancing away.

A deep voice cut into my thoughts as I turned to see Ruane approaching us with a drink in his hand.

"Phoenix, aren't you a sight for sore eyes," he said, and I laughed at his shameful attempt at flattery.

"I could say the same about you Ruane." He threw his head back as he laughed, the sound rich and dark. He held his hand out towards me. "Would you do me the honour of dancing with me?"

I panicked as I tried to think of an excuse not to dance with him, I wanted to stay in the shadows where I could be invisible.

Silver tapped my arm as she took the empty glass from me. "Go on, Phoenix," she said as she nodded towards where the guests were dancing. "You deserve some fun."

My chest warmed at her thoughtfulness and I took Ruane's hand as he guided me to a space among the crowd. My eyes instinctively scanned the room and I caught Khaldon's gaze on the far side as Ruane spun me around. We glided effortlessly through the crowd, keeping up with the music. I felt giddy with laughter and the sweet wine had gone to my head,

I couldn't remember the last time I felt this free. I couldn't remember the last time I had had fun.

I danced two songs with Ruane before a man approached us. He had bronze hair that was neither red nor brown, but in between. His eyes were amber gold and he held out his hand towards me as he asked, "May I?"

I looked to Ruane, a muscle feathered in his jaw. I sensed tension in the way Ruane's eyes darkened before he looked to me.

"Of course," he said as the man took my hand, placing a kiss on the back of it.

Ruane gave me a tight smile before walking back into the shadows surrounding the edge of the Marquee.

"And to what pleasure do we owe Mercea for bringing us its crown princess?" He asked.

Something about his presence unnerved me and the way Ruane had stiffened at the sight of him made him feel like a snake poised to strike.

"You have me at a disadvantage," I said as his hand slipped lower down my back. "You know of me, but I don't know your name."

He spun me around dramatically, tilting me back so I bent over his arms, I saw his eyes rove across my body before he lifted me back up, pulling me flush to his chest. I glanced over his shoulder and saw Khaldon in the shadows, his face like thunder.

"My name is Xander, princess." The way he was charming me reminded me of a predator luring its prey before it went in for the kill.

"And are you close with the king and his sister?" I asked.

He gave me a smile that didn't quite meet his eyes. "I'm an old friend."

His gaze drifted above my head and his expression changed at whoever was behind me, then I heard the deep smooth voice of the king.

"I'll take it from here," Khaldon said from behind me. I turned around to look at him. His grey eyes were stormy, and the hardened lines of his jaw were set as if he were clenching it so hard it might break. I wondered what the history was between them.

Xander took my hand again kissing the back before bowing and leaving me with the shadow king. Khaldon took my hand as the other one found my lower back, the music had changed to a softer melody perfect for me to catch my breath.

"Is that how you treat all of your friends?" I asked as we swayed to the tune of a string quartet.

Khaldon scoffed. "Xander is no friend of mine, Phoenix."

I looked up at the young king, he wore a silver crown adorned with moonstone, his inky black hair falling onto his face.

"Did you not want me here?" I asked, I cursed myself as soon as the words left my mouth. I shouldn't care whether he wanted to invite me or not.

He looked down at me as the music filled the marquee with a sweet melody. "My apologies, I wasn't sure if you would be up to meeting my court." He looked around the room and then smiled at me. "You look beautiful Phoenix."

I was at a loss for words, the song came to a finish and Khayna rushed over, interrupting the moment.

"Phoenix, you came!" She said as she wrapped me in a hug. Khaldon stepped away slightly as I was enveloped by his younger sister.

"The ball is amazing, did you come up with the theme yourself?" I asked as she swiped a glass of sweet wine from a passing server, she brought the glass to her lips before Khaldon took it from her.

"I think that's enough wine for you."

Khayna rolled her eyes. "You need to loosen up a little Khaldon, it's a party." Khaldon stood steadfast and raised his eyebrows as if he was daring her to push him.

"Ugh, you are insufferable!" Khayna said as she threw her hands in the air. "Fine," she said as she turned to me. "Don't let this old grump dampen your fun, Phoenix." She winked at me as she stalked off to mingle with the other guests.

Khaldon smiled as he shook his head. "She knows you're only looking out for her," I said, their relationship caused a yearning I felt anytime I was around Lex and Axel. I had no siblings and often wondered what my life would have been like if my father had remarried and had children.

His expression turned sombre as he walked away from the crowd, his hand against my lower back guiding me to a quiet area in eyesight of my guard.

He put the glass of wine down before turning to me. "I know she's been struggling since our father's death." He looked to where Khayna was laughing with some of the guests. "I worry she isn't dealing with her grief, turning to distractions instead that will only end up hurting her more."

I thought back to her stumbling out of the tavern about to be taken by those vile monsters.

I took the wine from where Khaldon had set it down and downed the honey gold liquid, as I felt the effects instantly. I could see why Khayna buried her grief with drink. It provided a temporary relief, where nothing else in the world mattered but this moment.

The music slowed and Khaldon's hands wrapped around my waist as my hands clasped behind his neck, the melody was beautiful. We rocked softly and I leaned my head against his chest. The scent of the sea and storms washed over me, and I breathed it in deeply, wishing I could stay in the moment forever, hidden in the shadows, safe, where nothing could hurt me.

CHAPTER 23

A KNOCK AT MY DOOR roused me from a deep sleep. I peeled my eyes open and tried to swallow but my mouth was as dry as the hay in the horses' stables. A dull thump pounded the top of my head and I cursed myself as I felt the aftermath of drinking too much sweet wine at Khayna's birthday ball.

I couldn't muster the strength to get out of bed, I flopped back on to the plush down pillows as I called out, "Who is it?" I instantly regretted it as the throbbing in my head became sharper and I winced in pain.

"It's me." Esmeray's voice came from the other side of the door.

I knew if I whispered, she wouldn't be able to hear me, and I had around five more seconds before she kicked the door down.

I threw the covers back and stood up. I swayed slightly as I steadied myself, tiptoeing over to unlock the door.

I opened the door and Esmeray raised her eyebrows at the sight of me. I climbed back into the king-size bed and groaned.

"Too much honey wine?" she asked, the corner of her mouth pulled up into a smile and I groaned again pulling the covers over my head.

"As much as I would love to let you stay in bed all day recovering, the king has requested your presence."

I rolled my eyes to the heavens, could he not just give me this day to rest?

Esmeray pulled the covers back and I winced as grey daylight poured in from the windows where she had kindly opened the heavy velvet drapes.

"Damn you, Elordi," I said as I blinked away the sting.

Esmeray laughed to herself shaking her head as she made to leave my chambers. "You have thirty minutes to be ready."

Serafina knocked shortly after Esmeray had left with a tray of breakfast, there was water, sweet fruit juice, that made me nauseous just looking at it, plus, apple and cinnamon oatmeal and a small glass jar that looked like it contained a healing tonic of some sort.

I lifted the glass jar to the light examining its contents, it was a dark green that looked like it contained a herbal remedy.

"Serafina, what is this?" I gestured to the glass vial as she looked up from where she was fluffing the pillows.

"The king thought you may need a healing remedy after the ball last night."

My stomach flipped at his thoughtfulness again and I frowned as I focused on the tonic.

Serafina came over to me, taking it gently from my hands.

"It's an old recipe but it's said to heal the stomach and mind from any toxins." She smiled before carrying on, "Including honey wine."

"So, I just drink it and I'll feel, okay?" I asked cautiously.

She had moved to the bathing chamber and I heard water filling the bathtub and the scent of something sickly sweet filled my airways.

I covered my mouth as I retched grabbing the tonic at the same time. Twisting the jar open and I sniffed its contents. It smelled of mint and bad choices. I threw the contents back and swallowed it down, grimacing as the bitter taste travelled down my throat.

I bathed and dressed, conscious of the time. The incessant thumping in my head had softened to a slight tapping and the nausea had almost disappeared. I opened the door and stopped short as Esmeray stood with her hand raised about to knock. Her eyes roved over me, and she smiled to herself again. We fell into step as I followed her to meet with Khaldon.

We walked into the dining hall where no one was eating. I felt his eyes burning into me, and I willed myself to look at everyone but him.

Khaldon's voice travelled across the room, wrapping around my senses as my body became more aware of him day by day.

"I have offered Phoenix a reprieve from the torment she faces on a full moon."

I winced as everyone's attention went to me. I lifted my chin higher to disguise my discomfort as Khaldon continued.

"I have the means to nullify any magick in Phoenix's blood."

Esmeray turned to face the king. "You've had the means to help the Devereaux crown all this time and you didn't think to volunteer this information sooner?"

I kept my gaze neutral as Esmeray questioned Khaldon, he had explained to me why he couldn't visit Mercea at our intimate dinner, but I wasn't sure if he wanted to share this information with my guard. I hadn't told Esmeray Ravynne was captured and I dreaded the aftermath of her finding out.

Khaldon's lips pressed together in a slight grimace. "I assure you captain, I had my reasons."

I noted his evasiveness, so he wasn't willing to share this information with just anyone, but he shared it with me. I made a mental note of this as I tucked my hands together on the table.

"Ravynne is imprisoned in the cells below the palace, so we will take turns in keeping watch on Phoenix's cell." His voice laced with authority.

Esmeray jumped up her hand going straight to the dagger she always had sheathed at her right hip. "The enchantress is in the palace?" She asked, her voice was dripping with rage.

I tapped my fingers against the grand dining table, I found the movements to be soothing, but Ireland's gaze flicked to my hand then back to me and I stopped the tapping. Not wanting my discomfort to be known.

Khaldon looked to me, his eyebrow raising slightly before he turned to Esmeray. "Yes captain she is. She is locked in a cell with no access to her power.

Esmeray looked to me as my guard sat in silence and I winced. She slammed her dagger into the dining table and I watched as the hilt shook with the force.

"Before you agree to spend the night in the cells, I think it would be wise to see Ravynne for yourself," Khaldon said as his eyes met mine.

My eyes darted to the door as I wondered if I could run out of the dining hall and lock myself in my chambers before Esmeray caught me.

"Let's get this over with," I said as I rose from my seat.

The thought of coming face to face with the person that had cursed my bloodline for the last three-hundred years unnerved me. I flexed my hands as we followed Khaldon to the cells. The dimly lit stairs spiralled downwards, and I placed my hand against the cool stone to steady myself. Water dripped somewhere along the staircase, the sound echoing through the hollow passageway.

We came to a corridor that had oil burners along the walls, the stone walls   lined with iron doors with a square hole carved out and iron bars covering the empty space. It was known that iron affected those with magick, it reacted to something in our blood, rendering us weak. I peered into one of the cells as we passed and saw a man looking back at me. His face crumbled with disgust before recognition flicked across his features.

"Is that—?"

Khaldon stopped and turned around to face me where I was still standing outside of the prisoner's cell.

I pointed to the door. "Is that the man that attacked Khayna?"

Khaldon tilted his head slightly as if pondering his response.

"Yes."

"What will happen to him?" I questioned.

"He will stand trial for his crimes," Khaldon replied.

I couldn't hide the shock on my face. I assumed if he had been caught, he would have been killed.

"You seem shocked, princess."

I stuttered over my words, the more time I spent with the king the more I was realising he wasn't the ruthless leader we had been led to believe.

We walked further down the corridor before Khaldon stopped in front of another cell. I noticed runes covered the cell door, and I felt the air thicken around me. My mouth dried as I anticipated seeing the enchantress that had cursed my bloodline, anger simmered beneath my skin as I thought of my ancestor being hunted down and killed through no fault of her own, and the thought that I might meet the same fate.

Esmeray and Silver stepped in front of me while Lex and Ireland guarded my back.

Khaldon pulled a ring of keys from his pocket before looking to me. "Are you sure you're ready?"

Every instinct in my body was screaming no, I wanted to run out of the cells and out of the palace, feeling the winter air on my skin. The corridor suddenly felt too small, I swallowed before nodding.

Khaldon turned the key in the lock and the sound of chains scraping across the floor came from the cell. Nothing could have prepared me for what I was about to see.

I looked to the far side and noticed there weren't any windows. The smell of rust and iron, mixed with urine caused me to retch. The enchantress was crouched on the floor, she had backed herself into the corner and made no effort to look up when the thick iron door to the cell opened. Her hair was long, dark and straight and reached past her waist. I noticed she still wasn't looking up, but she was now snarling, the sound guttural and animal-like. Her dark hair fell across her face, hiding her features, but when I stepped into the cell her head shot up, deep brown eyes finding mine. My leg muscles tightened as my body prepared to flee the cells.

That's when I noticed the chains, there was an iron cuff clamped around her neck, a chain connected the neck piece to her wrists which had the same cuffs on which were also connected to her ankles. I could feel the magick pulsing from her with no outlet, the air seemed to beat with the pulse of her essence. She was enraged. Her nostrils flared as the anger trembled throughout her body.

I stepped back and caught the scent of her. Death. The enchantress smelled of pure death. The tarot reader Amaris came to mind, was this what she meant when she pulled the death card? Was this how I was going to die, at the hand of the enchantress before me?

"Gods above," Lex breathed as she took in the sight before us.

Ravynne crouched lower, banging her head against the cold stone floor until blood poured from an open wound above her eye, leaving smears dripping onto the concrete floor. The thick darkness dripped down her face and her tongue reached out to taste it.

I was frozen to the spot, my breaths became shallow as I grabbed onto Esmeray's arm, my fingers dug into her sleeve and if it weren't for her uniform, I'm sure my nails would have drawn blood.

I could feel Khaldon watching me the entire time, but I couldn't take my eyes off the scene before me.

Her eyes rolled back as she tasted her own blood, and I felt the bile rise in my throat. When her eyes found mine again, they were completely black. She cocked her head to the side and lunged.

The metal cuff that was clamped around her neck pulled her back as the chain ran out of length.

Esmeray stepped forward and slammed the hilt of her sword into Ravynne's head and she dropped to the floor in a heap.

"I need some air," I said as I pushed past Khaldon and my guard. The burn of bile was rising in my throat as last night's wine churned in my stomach. I ran up the spiral stairs desperate to feel fresh air in my lungs. I burst through the door at the top of the stairs and was met by Aeden. His eyes widened at the sight of me, and I noticed his muscles stiffen as though he were preparing to take on what I was running from.

I covered my mouth with my hand hoping I could save myself the embarrassment of vomiting in front of him. A thin sheen of sweat gathered on my forehead as I bolted out of the main doors. I bent over leaning on the cool moonstone as I emptied the contents of my stomach on the front steps of the Trevelyan palace.

Aeden came to stand beside me.

"What happened down there?" he asked.

I bent over holding onto my knees as I tried to catch my breath. I wiped my mouth with the back of my hand, my eyes watering from the retching.

"The madness has consumed her." I said, my voice hoarse. "Power like that shouldn't exist."

Aeden looked back through the palace doors. "She is a plague that is rotting the earth. Once she is gone, Endaria will know peace again."

I could only hope that was true.

CHAPTER 24

K HALDON ASKED ME to meet him in his council room. Serafina guided me, leaving me in front of the open doorway. I walked into the room and all eyes looked to me, I shrank under the scrutiny and stood beside Ireland and Silver.

Lay on the table were the same shackles I had seen Ravynne wearing. The thick iron cuffs imbedded with ancient runes to nullify any magick in the wearer's blood.

"My beast doesn't wait until the moon is visible to make its appearance," I said to no one in particular. "It's for the best that I put them on now."

Silvers flexed her hands into fists at her side.

"I've instructed Serafina to make the cell as comfortable as possible and your guard and my men will keep watch the entire time you are down there. You won't be alone," Khaldon said and my heart twisted at his thoughtfulness.

I smoothed my tunic as I tried to stay composed. Nobody spoke as we made our way to the cells, Aeden carried the chains that would bind me and the sound of the iron cuffs knocking against each other made my legs weak with nerves. I placed my hand against the wall to steady myself and before I knew, it we were at the cell I would be confined to until the sun rose.

I looked around the space and what Khaldon had said was true. Serafina had added touches to make me feel more comfortable, there was a plush white rug on the stone floor, a table and chair had been placed in the far corner, and on the table was a vase of white roses and a pile of books Serafina thought I might like. My heart twisted again at the kindness I had been shown since I arrived in this kingdom that I had been led to believe was under the reign of a cruel and vindictive ruler. I looked to Khaldon who was watching me intently, and his gaze softened, he was anything but cruel.

I cleared my throat as my emotions threatened to pour out of me.

"It's perfect, thank you," I said quietly. There was no guarantee this would work but I was out of options.

I put my wrists together and held them in front of me, ready to be bound.

Aeden stepped forward, his face was grave, and I willed my heart to beat slower.

"I'll do it," Khaldon said as he stepped towards me.

I didn't say anything as he took the chains from Aeden and motioned for me to sit on the cot.

Every time his fingers brushed my skin I felt as if he was branding my soul. I wondered if he felt it too or if it was just my imagination.

I breathed in deeply as I watched him kneeling before me as he secured the cuffs first around my ankles, then my wrists before finally, we were eye to eye as he fastened the last cuff around my neck.

The tension in the cell was thick and it felt as if everyone held their breath waiting for me to speak. I closed my eyes as I concentrated on my heartbeat. The cuffs were ice cold against my warm skin. They felt other. I opened my eyes and looked to Khaldon who was stood in front of me looking straight into my eyes.

"How does it feel?" he asked, and there may as well not have been anyone else in the room.

"It's okay," I replied, "a little uncomfortable but it's bearable."

His mouth was a tight line as he said, "If you need anything just ask."

The lump in my throat was growing with every passing second. Esmeray stepped towards me as she said, "I'll take the first watch."

I thought I might come apart there and then, but I clenched my fists, determined to keep it together.

Everyone filed out of the cell and Ireland, Lex and Silver each looked back at me before they left. The door shut and the sound of metal on metal clanked as Khaldon locked me inside this temporary prison.

"We're right here, Phoenix," Esmeray said through the door, and with that I came undone. I covered my sobs with my hand and lay on the cot with my back to the door. I didn't want anyone to see me like this. The anticipation was a different kind of torture, so I cried until the cell went dark.

I OPENED MY EYES as I stood in a clearing. The sun shone its rays on me and I relished in its warmth, the very essence of the mother seeping into my being, and I lifted my face to the sky as I smiled. The clearing was covered in flowers, the edges were surrounded by trees and the long grass came up to my hips as I leaned to breathe in the scent of the flowers. Leaves rustled and branches snapped, then I saw her. A wolf stalked out of the trees facing where I stood, its coat was a lighter silver than mine, almost iridescent, and it stood seven feet tall. I didn't feel afraid, I felt as though I had been waiting for this moment my entire life.

The wolf spoke, her voice was delicate like the phantom breeze that danced across my skin.

"I've been waiting to meet you, Phoenix." The wolf walked closer to me, and I was drowned by her size.

"It's an honour to meet you, Ember," I said as I bowed low before my ancestor, the cursed princess.

"I see fate has dealt us the same hand."

I nodded before looking around again at the clearing. There were no birds in the sky, not even insects in the grass.

"My wolf will be here at any moment; I'm trying to find a way to break this curse once and for all on my own terms but—" I cut myself off as I looked down.

The pain of who stood before me and what she'd had to endure slammed into me like a thousand knives. I had no way of knowing if I would meet the same fate as my ancestor.

Ember nudged her snout into my neck, and I reached up to run my fingers through her fur.

"Child, the fates have chosen you to do what I couldn't. You have the strength of your ancestors within you, and you will find a way."

I stepped back to look at her, the cursed princess.

"I will," I said, I owed it to her and to myself.

She edged backwards towards the trees and slowly turned to mist before the phantom breeze carried her away.

A pain shot through my skull bringing me to my knees, as though someone had shot an arrow through my head. I put my hand out in the long grass but instead felt cool stone beneath my fingers. I had been clenching my eyes shut so tightly I was seeing stars.

I opened my eyes and looked down at the ring of runes that had belonged to my mother. I didn't understand its power, but it seemed to give me a way to see my ancestors although I had no say in who I saw and when. The cursed princess had waited until now to visit me, and I wasn't sure why.

The heat came in waves, like the ocean lapping against the shore, it pulled back giving me temporary relief, only to slam into me at full force. It was a furnace raging over my body giving me brief moments of peace and I looked to the cell door, the heavy iron made sure that there was no way my beast could escape and I screamed.

The shackles that were cuffed around my neck, wrists and ankles, were ice cold, as if they were reacting to the curse flowing through me. Sweat gathered on my skin as I desperately tried to dampen the inferno building within me.

"Phoenix, we're right here!" Khaldon shouted through the door.

My breathing became laboured as I was consumed by the heat. I cried out as fangs ripped from my mouth before retracting again. I lay on the cool stone floor to relieve the discomfort. The pain was unbearable, constantly building with no release. My back arched and pain lanced through my spine, but it didn't break. I turned my face, so it was on the floor and let the cold seep into my skin. My head pounded and I prayed for a reprieve. A scream escaped my throat as pain shot through my skull. Khaldon appeared at the cell door, and I lay helplessly on the floor as he watched me suffering.

I held his gaze as I lay helpless, his stare was pained as though it physically caused him harm to see me like this. I pulled at the cuff around my neck, the ancient power was suffocating me, I was foolish to think I could ever escape my fate.

The pain eased slightly, and I brought myself to my knees, blood coated my tongue and I longed for ice-cold water to wash the taste from my mouth.

I sat with my back against the cell wall as I slowed my heart down. Each breath burned my lungs as if every breath I took were flames. Khaldon's face appeared at the hole in the door again.

"What do you need?" he asked as his grey eyes pierced into mine.

I was so weak, I barely had the strength to open my eyes. "More water please," I whispered, my voice hoarse from the screaming.

Khaldon's mouth was a tight line as he walked away, his footsteps echoed along the corridor.

"Devereaux."

My eyes snapped open as I heard the voice that sent ripples of fear along my skin. Esmeray's honey bronze hair flashed through the makeshift window in the door.

"Be quiet, witch," Esmeray spat, her tone like steel.

"Let her speak," I croaked, I needed to hear what she had to say, she couldn't hurt me anymore than she had. If I died at her hand, it would bring me nothing but peace, I would finally be free from the torment.

I heard the shuffle of Ez's boots against the stone floor before Ravynne's voice travelled across the corridor.

"You know I asked your ancestors for help once?" Ravynne called from her cell. She seemed more coherent than the last time I saw her, the madness seemed to have vanished.

"I know, and now I'm paying for the actions of someone that lived hundreds of years before I came into this world," I called back, the effort brought searing pain up my throat, and I coughed blood onto the white fur rug.

"I was promised your kingdom." She carried on, "I was promised to rule by Etienne's side. Instead, my sisters and I were hunted down like animals."

I had nothing to say. I couldn't make up for the deaths of her sisters, all I could do was survive this godforsaken curse. I closed my eyes as I sighed. I needed water desperately, my throat burned with every breath.

"The enchantresses were down to a hundred." Ravynne carried on. "There were thousands of us once. Now, I am the last known one. I asked your ancestor to stop this madness, to help our race survive. He was too weak to stand against his father, even though we were in love. I wanted him to burn. He knew I would become mad as I took on the power of my slain sisters, it is too much for any one person to bear. He knew and he did nothing."

I opened my mouth to speak when my attention went to the door. I heard the key turn in the lock before Khaldon came into view. He had a jug filled with water and a small glass on a metal tray. I tried to push myself off the floor but couldn't bring myself to leave the coolness that was keeping the burning pain at bay.

Khaldon rushed over to where I sat slumped against the stone wall.

I tried to push myself away from him. "You shouldn't be in here." I breathed. "Just leave it at the door please."

I could feel another wave of the pain building, threatening to drown me in agony and I didn't want him to see my bones break.

He put the tray on the table before leaning down and bringing the glass to my lips. I swallowed the cool water as Khaldon reached up, hesitating slightly before wiping a drop of water from my mouth.

My fangs ripped through the soft flesh of my mouth without any warning, and I cried out as a drop of venom dripped onto Khaldon's hand.

He hissed as he pulled his hand back, his skin blistered instantly, and I felt my heart break. Esmeray rushed into the cell, her eyes betraying nothing as I panted through the pain. My fangs retracted and I slumped to the ground. I lay my face against the cold floor as tears fell without any effort. Esmeray walked over and wiped my hair back from my face. The way she did when my beast first arrived, letting me know she would never leave me.

I closed my eyes, willing the strength to get through the night.

"Bring her to me," I said.

Although my eyes were closed, I knew they hadn't left the cell.

"Bring her to me now, please."

"Absolutely not," Esmeray replied.

I didn't have the energy to fight her on this. Who better to give me the answers I need than the person responsible for my torment.

"I won't argue with you captain. Bring. Her. To. Me."

I opened my eyes as I emphasised every syllable of each word that I spoke.

Khaldon turned to look at Esmeray before stepping away to leave the cell. Esmeray gripped his arm and I thought she may kill the king of shadows there and then.

Khaldon looked down at where her hand had his arm in a vice like grip.

"If anything happens to her, I will not hesitate to kill you, Your Majesty," Esmeray said, disdain lacing every ounce of her words.

Khaldon looked back at me before nodding and leaving us in the cell.

Esmeray rushed over, wiping the hair back that had stuck to my damp face.

"Phoenix what are you thinking? I can't stand here while you sit with the very reason for your suffering."

"I appreciate your concern, Ez, but I can't live like this." I lifted my wrists and her gaze landed on the metal cuffs.

"What better way to find a cure than from the source?" I said, hoping she would see reason.

Esmeray left to get the rest of my guard.

Khaldon returned with Aeden and Ruane, the three men all six foot and above made the cell feel more suffocating than it already was.

Aeden left to get Ravynne, a member of my guard stood in each corner of the cell, swords drawn. Aeden came in with Ravynne her dark hair covering her face.

She lifted her head and her gaze met mine, beneath the dirt and dried blood, I was surprised at how youthful she looked given she was over three-hundred years old.

I set my jaw as I stared down the enchantress. "I'm sorry for the loss of your sisters, I truly am, but I had nothing to do with the actions of my ancestors or the other kingdoms. So tell me, how can I break this curse, without coercing someone to fall in love with me, how can I be free?"

Ravynne studied me for a moment before she choked back a laugh.

"You will never be free as the daughter of a Devereaux king."

The sound of metal scraping over stone was the only sound in the cell as Ravynne pulled at the shackle around her neck. "Do you know how it feels to be so powerful it turns you to madness?" she asked as she eyed me thoughtfully. "All I wanted was the killing to stop. We could have come to an agreement and found a way to live in peace."

I didn't have anything to say to that, I almost found myself feeling sorry for her. I knew how it felt to be hunted and I pinched the bridge of my nose, frustration seeping out of me.

"I think we're done," I said as I looked to the king.

"Get her out of here," Khaldon barked at Aeden and Ruane.

I leaned back against the cell wall and slumped to a heap on the ground. I placed my head in my hands as I rocked back and forth.

"Phoenix," Ireland said gently.

I looked up to my guard, their presence brought me some comfort and I knew I wasn't in this alone.

I pushed my hair off my face as I loosed a breath. "I feel like I'm fighting a losing battle, I'm so tired."

Silver looked towards where I slumped on the floor. "The sun will be on the horizon in a few hours Phoenix, just hold on a little longer."

I closed my eyes as my guard stood, protecting me from myself. I just had to make it through the night.

CHAPTER 25

FTER THE NIGHT IN THE CELLS, Khaldon had carried me to my chambers as the morning light crept over the horizon. I vaguely remembered the scent of the sea and storms washing over me as he held me to his chest. While I was in his arms, it felt like nothing else in the world mattered. I had been so exhausted I had fallen asleep the moment he had laid me in bed. My guard informed me that I had slept for a full day, another day lost, but at least I hadn't been hunted.

I had gotten myself ready, Serafina had probably been told to make herself scarce while I rested. I stepped into the corridor to see Lex and Silver stationed outside.

Lex scanned me from head to toe checking for any signs of injury. "I'm fine Lex." I sighed.

"The king told Serafina to leave you to rest, do you need anything?" Silver asked.

"I need to see the king, do you know where he is?"

"He's in his study." Lex said as she gestured for me to follow her.

We made our way to the east wing of the palace and I halted as I heard voices travelling through the open door of Khaldon's study.

"Your father's ways kept the kingdom in line, excessive as they were, Sakaria was impenetrable." I recognised that voice, but I couldn't place where I knew it from.

I slipped between two moonstone pillars in the corridor. I wasn't sure whether I should come back later or wait for the king to finish his meeting.

"Phoenix what are you doing?" Silver asked, she had lowered her voice and looked at me with a humoured expression.

A palace staff member walked past holding fresh linens and I jumped to brush the moonstone pillar with my fingers as though I were just admiring its beauty.

Khaldon's voice travelled through the open door. "No. I will not rule my kingdom as my father did. You may have enjoyed killing on my father's behalf, but I assure you Xander, your services are no longer required."

Now I understood Khaldon's reaction to Xander at Khayna's ball.

I felt foolish loitering in the corridor with my guard stood around while I hid out of sight, so I stepped out of my hiding place and knocked on the open door. Khaldon looked up from the pile of papers on his desk. His gaze roved over me and once he was satisfied I wasn't harmed in any way, he dismissed Xander.

"Leave." His tone invited no further discussion.

Xander gave me a devilish smile as he left. I watched him stalking down the corridor and wondered how many men he had killed in

Khaldon's father's name and why he was trying to persuade him to follow in the same footsteps.

I turned to look at my guard and Lex nodded as I stepped into Khaldon's study.

"How are you feeling today?" he asked as I sat down facing him. It was a simple enough question after spending the night in the cells with Ravynne. I wasn't sure what was worse, the pain of turning into my beast or the relentless pain of the iron cuffs fighting against the curse. The shackles that were used made me feel nauseated, and I had the remnants of the splitting headache that came after they worked to nullify any magick in my blood.

"I'm as okay as I can be," I replied.

He took a small key from his pocket, unlocking a drawer in his desk before reaching into it and pulling out an old book, the pages worn and faded.

"What's this?" I asked as he handed it to me. I flicked through the pages, my hand stilling on an intricate drawing of a majestic sword and I traced my fingers over the image.

"That is the sword of Danann."

"Is this the relic your father agreed to retrieve for the enchantress?" I asked.

"It is."

My eyes skimmed over the words written in the book, it was in a language I didn't recognise.

"Which language is this?" I asked as I tried to decipher the symbols to make sense of them.

A look flashed across his eyes, as though he wasn't sure how much I knew, or how much he should reveal.

"It's the old language."

My hand stilled on the page, the old language had been forbidden after the battle of the lost and the language we speak today had been used ever since. I thought back to the rebels in my kingdom and their use of the language that hadn't been spoken in centuries.

I tried to push the feelings of panic down and remain calm.

"What do you know of the old language, Khaldon?" I asked the king.

"Not much more than I suppose you do."

"Why show me this?" I asked.

He stood from his desk and walked over to close the door. Goosebumps covered my skin as his scent washed over me. My body responded to him of its own accord, and I coughed to break the silence.

"I wanted to show you that the land of souls isn't merely a myth and what you would be retrieving for the sake of both of our kingdoms, for the sake of Endaria."

"How exactly does it work?" I asked.

Khaldon came to stand next to me. He leaned over my shoulder and pointed to the text on the page.

"The sword contains powerful magick from our ancestors, the sword holds this power until it is ready to be used. The magick of the sword was created before Ravynne came into this world and it is the only thing that could kill her." Khaldon said as he leaned over my shoulder, he was so close I could feel the heat radiating from him although we weren't touching.

"It can create or destroy, however the wielder sees fit. It is strong enough to overpower the magick of entire kingdoms, should the need arise."

I turned slightly to look up at him, our lips were inches apart as he looked down at me through thick ebony eyelashes.

I swallowed as I tore my eyes away from his gaze.

Khaldon carried on, "It was created as a way of controlling the kingdoms, in case one of the rulers became too power hungry."

"When was it created?"

"After the battle of the lost. One man's quest for power caused an entire kingdom to be wiped out. The sword was created to make sure that didn't happen again."

"And you're absolutely sure that this can defeat Ravynne?"

Khaldon walked around me and my gaze instinctively followed his movements as he leaned against the dark oak desk behind him.

He slid his hands into his pockets. "The magick in the sword can weaken Ravynne, even kill her. Weakening her is the only way to take back her power that she has stolen. Once her power is back in the earth, we can kill her."

The enchantress had taken so much from us, and caused my bloodline so much pain, I crossed my legs, leaning forward as I spoke. "If retrieving the sword and killing Ravynne is the only way for us to finally be free, then so be it."

His eyes widened slightly before he spoke as though he was surprised that I had agreed to it. "I dread to think what would have happened if my father would have retrieved the sword for her, there would have been no way to end her reign of madness."

"So, you summoned the cursed princess."

Khaldon laughed at the absurdity of our situations.

"It's funny how a mad woman's quest for power and revenge has led us to one another," he said as he stared down at me.

I turned my attention back to the book feeling my cheeks heat slightly. "Why have I never heard of this?" I asked. I had been taught about the Endaria's history during my royal tutoring. I had never heard of the sword of Danann and the power it held. If the wrong person got hold of it, they could bring kingdoms to their knees.

"I believe it was hidden from us with the hopes that it would never need to be used." Khaldon replied.

The air between us was thick with tension. I closed the book and placed it on his desk. The silence was palpable between us as I thought of what he was asking of me. I would do anything to be rid of this curse. If taking Ravynne's power was a way for me to be free, then I really didn't have another choice.

WE MET OVER DINNER to inform everyone of the plans. Khaldon sat in his usual seat at the head of the table, and I sat facing him at the opposite end. I wasn't sure I would be able to convince my guard.

Khaldon leaned forward clasping his hands together as he spoke. "I believe there is a way for us to break the curse and restore magick in Endaria."

Silver put her chalice down and turned to look at me. I looked around the table and everyone's eyes were on me waiting.

I met Khaldon's stormy stare, and he gave me a nod. "There is a relic in the land of souls that is powerful enough to give us a chance at defeating Ravynne and since she has bound Khaldon to his land, and only someone from one of the seven royal bloodlines can wield it, I will go and retrieve the sword of Danann that contains ancient power from our ancestors, it will weaken her so the stolen power can find its way back to the mother, restoring the balance, giving us the use of our runes again."

"Mother above," Lex said loudly.

Aeden and Ruane looked to Khaldon who still had his eyes firmly on me.

"If we have the use of runes again, we can find one powerful enough to reverse the curse, giving Phoenix the chance to free herself on her own terms."

My heart warmed at his understanding.

"How would we get there?" Ireland asked.

"It's hidden beneath a veil off the northern coast of Sakaria. You would need to travel by sea," Khaldon replied.

I looked at my guard who were watching the king.

"We would need to prepare you, the land of souls was thought to be legend, where the worst souls of the living were condemned to spend eternity. It's a forgotten wasteland filled with the souls of nightmares, and you would need intense training. I also think it would be wise to go before the next full moon." His eyes found mine and I knew what he meant. Retrieve the sword before I had to endure another occurrence of my beast, which meant we had a matter of weeks to prepare.

CHAPTER 26

W E HAD BEEN TRAINING RELENTLESSLY since I agreed to retrieve the sword from the land of souls. Aeden and Ruane told us of the creatures we may encounter there, beasts called Ghosha's that were vicious hell hounds, their size rivalled my wolf and their bite meant death would quickly follow. It truly sounded like the place of nightmares and only sheer determination to break the curse stopped me from backing out and returning to my kingdom.

I had a day off from training and Khaldon had offered to take me on a tour of the city while Ireland and Silver trained with his most elite warriors. Esmeray had insisted on accompanying us and she brought Lex for reinforcements. The winter in the north was relentless and I pulled my fur cloak tighter as I struggled to keep warm. Children played in the streets wrapped in furs and the city of Sakaria bustled with people.

We walked through the city, and I noticed the way Khaldon's people looked at him. It was a mixture of fear and awe and if the stares bothered him, he didn't show it. We stopped at a stall as the winter's cold bit at my skin. The furs Khaldon had provided were ash white and I wondered which animal they had come from.

He bought two mugs of hot mint tea and I held mine with both hands, relishing the warmth that seeped into me.

We turned down a cobbled street lined with quaint shops and I stopped in my tracks as a man played the sweetest melody on a flute. He nodded his head and smiled as I stood in front of him mesmerised by the song. Khaldon turned when he realised I wasn't next to him and came and to stand beside me. The melody was one of strength and sorrow and I wondered what this man had been through for him to play such a sad tune, watching as he closed his eyes as he concentrated on the music. Khaldon bent over and dropped a few gold coins into the flute's case on the ground. The man's eyes widened as he stuttered over the notes and pulled the instrument away from his lips.

He stuttered as he bowed to Khaldon. "Thank you, Your Majesty."

I looked to Khaldon and saw regret in his eyes. I wondered how his life had been growing up under his father's rule, knowing one day he would take over the throne.

"Thanks won't be necessary," Khaldon said. "Your talent is admirable. Where in the kingdom are you from?"

The man looked like a deer caught in headlights, like he couldn't believe what was happening to him.

I looked at Khaldon, who was a picture of royalty. The way he stood commanded attention. His beauty forced you to appreciate its candour. I noticed a few people gathered whispering as they looked at their king engaging in casual conversation.

"I'm from the south of Sakaria, Your Majesty."

As I looked around, I got the impression that most of his people respected him, but it would take time for him to undo the damage his father had caused the kingdom even though it was obvious his rule would be nothing like his father's.

"The south is one of my favourite places in this kingdom, it's close to the border of Mercea," Khaldon said as he gestured towards me. I looked to the man who seemed stunned beyond words.

"You play beautifully, we won't keep you any longer," I said as I looped my arm through Khaldon's and walked past a group of women that had gathered outside of a pastry shop. The small crowd went silent as we passed followed by Lex and Esmeray.

We walked further in a comfortable silence and came to a garden tucked away in the heart of the city. Lex and Esmeray had stationed themselves at a corner of the garden while Khaldon and I sat on the bench in the centre.

"Thank you for showing me your kingdom, it's truly beautiful."

Khaldon smiled before taking a sip of his tea.

"You're more than welcome. Maybe one day I'll have the honour of seeing yours."

A small smile flashed across my face as I thought about the reality of bringing the shadow king to Mercea.

"It's a shame I couldn't bring you here under better circumstances," Khaldon said as he looked out over the gardens. Snow dusted the ground, and, in the centre, there was a large statue of a man on horseback wielding a sword."

"Who's the statue of?" I asked. I rubbed my hands together, willing some warmth into them.

He looked to the statue as he said, "That is my great-great grandfather, King Tirrell."

My winter boots crunched over the snow-covered grass as I walked over, bending down to read the engraving on the statue. I heard a whistling sound before hot pain shot across my face. The iron tipped arrow sliced through my skin, embedding itself in the ground next to me. I stumbled backwards as I raised my hand to my cheek; warmth coated my cold fingers as blood dripped onto the snow.

"Phoenix!" I turned around as the sound of thunder rumbled across the garden causing the ground to tremble. Khaldon stalked towards me surrounded by shadows, the sight of him was breath-taking. He bent down touching my arm and we were enveloped in complete darkness. There was no space or time between us.

"Khaldon?" I said into the air that surrounded us. Wind whipped around me, but my feet were firmly planted on the ground. I blinked a few times, but sight still evaded me. My hair lifted gently as the winds raged around us, as if we were in the eye of a storm.

"I'm here, Phoenix." Khaldon's deep voice travelled through the darkness, and I jolted as I felt his hand grab mine.

A few moments passed before daylight flared before my eyes. I blinked a few times to focus my vision, I looked down to where Khaldon still held my hand, his fair skin stark against the rich brown of mine.

We stepped out of the shadows, and I noticed the sweat gathered on Khaldon's brow as he stumbled slightly. I looked up and we were back outside of the palace, he had used his powers to get us out of danger. I turned in shock to look at the king. The use of his power had taxed him greatly, his skin was tinged with a grey hue, and he breathed deeply as he steadied himself.

Aeden rushed out of the palace taking in the sight before him.

"Khal, what th—"

His eyes flicked between us, and I felt the warmth dripping down my face. I reached my hand to my cheek and pulled it away, fresh blood coated my fingers as Aeden crossed the distance between us.

"Khal did you use your magick?" Aeden asked, fury emanating from him.

I looked to Khaldon who had closed his eyes, he took deep breaths as he tried to steady himself and I saw the grey hue that had tinged his skin slowly start to disappear.

Sweat had gathered on my brow and my knees buckled underneath me. Khaldon's eyes shot open, and he looked to me, his eyes going straight to the bloody wound on my face. He shrugged off his fur coat, throwing it around my shoulders where I had slumped on the ground, before ripping off one of his shirt sleeves. My gaze went straight to the muscles in his arms, and I flinched as he pressed the fabric to my face.

"Get her to the infirmary now," Khaldon bit out.

He stalked towards the palace leaving me with Aeden.

Aeden frowned as he scooped me up in his arms like I weighed nothing. My vision was blurred, but I made out the palace doors as Aeden carried me through them and took me down the main corridor to the end where a small infirmary was tucked away.

He stalked into the room where an older woman in a grey tunic and wispy white hair was busy on the far side of the infirmary folding bandages when she turned to look at us. Cots surrounded by white curtains and shelves of ointments and salves sat on the far wall but I couldn't focus on them as the woman hurried over. "Mother above, what happened?" she said as she rushed over to where Aeden was slowly lowering me onto the cot holding the makeshift bandage to my cheek. I winced as she pulled the sleeve of Khaldon's shirt away from my face.

"Who did this to you?" she asked, her brows furrowed with concern, and I tried to stop the nauseating feeling that rose in my stomach. The iron from the arrow was travelling through my blood making me feel nauseous and weak. My body was burning, I felt like my skin was on fire.

Before I could answer Khaldon stalked into the room, his face like thunder. He had changed his shirt to a sleek black one and my breath hitched at the fierceness of him.

Aeden said, "Does anyone want to tell me exactly what happened out there?"

Khaldon looked to my cheek which was starting to burn more with each passing minute. I closed my eyes as the room spun around me. It was becoming more of an effort to stay conscious.

"Taresse, it was an iron tipped arrow," he said, and I noted the hint of fear in his voice.

"I need bandages, a cleansing ointment and a healing salve." Taresse barked at Khaldon.

He rushed to gather the supplies the healer had asked for. Aeden sat on the cot facing me, still determined to get an answer from one of us.

"Khal!" he said, his voice thick with tension.

Khaldon brought the supplies to Taresse putting them on the cot next to me, he inhaled deeply before turning to Aeden. "We were attacked in the city," he said while the healer tended to my wound, the blood flow had slowed to a drip., but the pain was coursing through my veins.

I inhaled sharply as she applied the cleansing ointment to my wound, I cried out as the ointment burned the iron from my skin, then the world went dark.

CHAPTER 27

Khaldon

"DID YOU SEE THEIR FACES?" Aeden asked as his gaze flicked to mine. I turned back to Phoenix. She had passed out from the iron and probably the pain too. I had been cut with an iron blade when I was younger, I was exploring the palace dungeons with Aeden and came across weapons that had been confiscated from vigilantes, the blade had nicked my finger, and I howled the palace down in pain as the iron worked its way through my blood. It was excruciating, and my knees went weak as I looked at the princess.

I pushed her hair off her face, every brush of her skin against my fingers ignited a primal instinct inside of me that I couldn't make sense of.

"No, I didn't, we were too busy being attacked by iron tipped arrows."

"So, you used your powers to escape Khal? Even though you knew the consequences?"

"I didn't have a choice!" I shouted.

I placed the back of my hand against Phoenix's forehead. "Taresse, she's still burning up. I need a bowl of cold water and a cloth."

Taresse rushed to the back of the infirmary to gather the supplies, and my gut clenched at the thought of Phoenix in pain because of me, because of my father's legacy that caused my people to distrust my crown.

She rushed back over with the water and cloths and I went to reach for them before she put them down and grasped my hands in hers.

"Please, Your Majesty, let me heal the princess."

I nodded reluctantly as Aeden came to stand next to me. I watched helplessly as Taresse kept Phoenix's body cool and applied another healing salve to her wound.

I clenched my fists at my side, the feeling of helplessness was overwhelming, I couldn't protect my kingdom and I couldn't protect the princess.

We waited for Phoenix to wake but she lay unconscious, her silver hair spread out around her.

"She should be awake by now." I pressed.

"Taresse knows what she's doing, just give it some time," Aeden said.

I couldn't just do nothing, so I paced the infirmary as Aeden questioned me again about what happened.

"We were at my great-great grandfathers' statue in the gardens. Phoenix went over to read the engraving and an arrow was shot out of nowhere."

"Where were you when the arrow was shot?" Aeden asked.

"What do you mean?"

"I mean, if you were standing next to Phoenix then you could have been the intended target."

I thought back to the look of terror on her face as her blood dripped onto the ground.

"I was on the bench. I wasn't anywhere near her."

"So, the princess was the intended target," Aeden said grimly.

Fury boiled under my skin at the thought of anyone wanting to hurt her. It was bad enough that her own people had hunted her, but I couldn't allow her to come to harm in my kingdom.

"Taresse, she should be awake by now!" I stalked towards the back of the infirmary and pulled some smelling salts from the shelf.

"Your Majesty, the iron may have been a shock to her system, she'll come around when she's ready," Taresse said calmly.

Even though impatience was eating away at me I had to agree with her, but the not knowing if Phoenix would be okay was torture.

Aeden turned to me. "Khal, Taresse is the best in the kingdom, she'll be okay."

For all our sakes, I hoped it was true.

CHAPTER 28

Phoenix

THE SMELL OF ASH AND SMOKE infiltrated my airways and I choked as I tried to breathe fresh air into my lungs.

My eyes shot open, and I saw the healer leaning over me with a jar of salts in her hand. Nausea churned in my stomach and I retched as the healer rushed to get a bucket. The moment the bucket was in front of me I vomited a thick rust coloured substance.

I closed my eyes and took deep breaths.

"It's the iron working its way out of your system."

My gaze snapped to Khaldon, his stormy eyes already on mine.

"I feel like death," I said as I wiped my hand across my mouth. The healer passed me a damp cloth and I smiled at her gratefully.

"Being poisoned will do that to you," Aeden said as I looked to the men watching over me.

"How long was I unconscious?"

"Less than an hour," Khaldon said as he came over to the cot.

"Thank you," I breathed. "Thank you for saving me." I dreaded to think what would have happened if Khaldon hadn't got us out of there.

Aeden stepped forward, his eyes like two different jewels, shining back at me.

"I'm glad you're okay, Phoenix." He turned to look at Khaldon. "You have to be more careful and think about the consequences, Khal, this is serious."

"What consequences?" I asked. I wasn't sure who would answer but by the look of anger on Khaldon's face I assumed it would be Aeden.

"Ravynne left Khaldon with a sliver of the power he should rightfully have before she siphoned it. If he uses all of his remaining power before he forms an alliance with her, then he will die," Aeden said it with such conviction that it took me a moment to process what he had just said.

"Wha—" I was cut off by my guard bursting through the infirmary doors.

I winced as I saw the deadly look on Esmeray's face. She stalked over to me, and I noticed Aeden take a protective stance next to Khaldon.

"What the hell was that." She said through gritted teeth. "You swore nothing would happen to her!" Her voice wavered slightly as she stood tall. "She is my responsibility." She stepped closer towards us, almost nose to nose with the shadow king. "Mine."

I jumped up from the cot swaying as another wave of nausea coursed through me. "Enough," I said as I put a hand on her arm.

I could feel the anger thrumming through her body. I knew she would never forgive herself if anything happened to me.

"Esmeray, I'm okay," I said as she turned to look at me, her eyes flicked between mine frantically and once she saw the healing salve had knitted my wound back together, she took a step back.

"Khaldon, used his power to get us out of the gardens even though it could have killed him."

Lex walked into the infirmary, I hadn't even noticed she was missing until now. She held a sack in her hand and I watched as she pulled a head out of the bag, a human head.

"I believe this is one of the men responsible."

The man's grotesque head was dripping with blood onto the infirmary floor, his face was frozen in a pained expression.

Ruane walked into the infirmary and raised his eyebrows at the scene before him.

"Mother above Lex!" I couldn't control my outburst. "You can't go around cutting the heads off men!"

She put the head back into the sack. "Phoenix, I am required by law to protect you at all costs. If beheading this man who thought he could attack the crown princess of the mightiest kingdom in Endaria—" She stopped herself before nodding towards Khaldon. "No offence."

The edge of Khaldon's mouth lifted into a smile.

"Then that's what I am going to do," Lex continued.

She turned to Aeden who rubbed his hand down his face. I think Lex had rendered him speechless.

"Is there somewhere I can put this?" Lex said as she gestured to the sack in her hand, blood had started to seep through the fabric, and I watched transfixed as the ruby pool spread through the beige material.

Esmeray stepped forward. "We need to see if there is a connection between those who attacked you and the issue back home."

"What issue?" Khaldon asked.

Esmeray sighed as she looked around the infirmary. "Is there somewhere we can talk privately?"

"Aeden, show Lex where she can put the head," Khaldon said. "Phoenix, you need to rest. I'll send Serafina to your room with some refreshments."

"If you are going to be discussing traitors that want me dead, then I want to be a part of it." I looked to my guard. Lex had left with Aeden, but Silver and Ireland stood behind Esmeray.

"You should rest Phoenix," Ireland said and I could see the regret in her eyes of not being there to protect me.

"Either you include me in the meeting, or there is no meeting at all." I stood staring at them, willing one of them to defy me.

"Fine," Khaldon said. "Meet me in my study."

I watched his back as he left us in the empty infirmary.

WE MADE OUR WAY to Khaldon's study and the tension in the room pressed against my skin as I looked around at my guard and the men I had come to care for in a strange way.

Esmeray started as Lex closed the door behind her. "We have information of a group of rebels that have taken it upon themselves to turn against the Deveraux crown."

I looked to Khaldon but his face gave away nothing. I looked to Aeden and Ruane, unspoken words travelling between them.

"You knew." I spoke into the silence.

I stepped closer to Khaldon, a muscle flickered in his jaw as I got closer.

"We got wind of a rebel group while I was in your kingdom, when I came to ask you to visit Sakaria." Ruane admitted.

I turned around to look at him. "You knew this whole time and didn't think to mention anything?"

"We didn't think it would be an issue while you were in Sakaria, Phoenix."

Lex stepped forward. "What do you know of them?" She asked as her eyes scanned Ruane's face.

Ruane looked to Khaldon before turning to me. "We know that they have ancestral ties to the lost kingdom, we think they seek to overthrow your throne given its vulnerable state."

I turned to Ireland. "The forgotten shall rise, that's what the man from the hunting party said." A wave of panic coursed through me. "I'm being hunted, even without my beast."

"We won't let them harm you," Lex said, it should have brought me comfort, but it did the opposite.

"I'm not safe anywhere," I said as I ran my fingers over the wound on my cheek.

"Phoenix," Esmeray started but I cut her off as I turned to look at her.

"No, you don't understand!" I shouted as I slumped into one of the empty chairs. "The future of my kingdom is in my hands and I'm running out of options to save my crown."

Khaldon looked to Esmeray then back to me. "Then we fight."

I had seen him training with Aeden and Ruane, he was pure muscle and strength, he moved at lightning speed, and I shuddered as I thought of how powerful he would be with his power returned to him.

The king stared into my soul as he said, "Our kingdoms combined have enough resources to take on a group of rebels but first we need to take care of Ravynne."

I ran a hand through my hair pushing it back off my face. I was tired. So, so tired.

"Okay." I sighed. "We take care of Ravynne, then we deal with the rebels."

My guard filtered out of the room and Khaldon pulled my arm back. His touch was a feeling I would never get used to, it felt as though it had been made just for me, and tiny sparks jolted through me as his stormy grey eyes met mine.

He pulled me closer towards him, so we were almost chest to chest. "You will survive this Phoenix, don't underestimate how strong you are."

I looked up at him and had to stop myself from reaching up and brushing my fingers over his lips. I gave him a weak smile and dropped my head, looking at where his hand was on my arm. It took every ounce of strength I had not to lean into his touch, where I could melt into him.

Khaldon cupped his finger under my chin, lifting my face so I could look into his eyes. I closed my eyes and took a deep breath, the very sight of him stole my breath and I was trying not to fall apart.

A knock at the door interrupted the moment and Khaldon kept his eyes on mine just a little bit longer before dropping his hand, and I almost

229

choked at the absence of his touch. I cleared my throat before excusing myself and making my way to my rooms.

KHALDON ASKED FOR US to train together, without anyone else watching. He felt that I would be able to let myself go completely if it were just me and him. I had seen him training often whilst I sat in the courtyard with Khayna. He was pure muscle and strength and usually trained topless.

I braided my hair back off my face and made my way to the indoor training ring. Esmeray escorted me and stood guard outside of the hall that encompassed a huge training set up. A wall of weapons was set against the far side of the room and I flinched as I saw a lethal archery bow that had been reinforced with shadow steel. The wound from the iron tipped arrow had healed but the sight of the weapon still made me nauseous.

I looked to the centre of the training ring where Khaldon was doing one handed push ups. Sweat glistened across his skin and I wondered how long I could watch him without it being inappropriate.

I stepped into the ring and started stretching so I wasn't just there, eyeing the king aimlessly.

Khaldon rose from the floor and walked over to me, his bright white smile only made him more beautiful and I cursed my stomach for flipping at the sight of him.

"Good morning," he said as he grabbed a cloth and wiped his sweat.

"Morning," I said almost sheepishly as I tried not to stare at his chest.

I reached a hand over my head and leaned to the side, letting my muscles elongate, my shirt lifted, and I caught the flash of Khaldon's gaze dropping to my exposed midriff.

Khaldon cleared his throat. "I thought we could work on your sword strength. There is no telling what you will face in the land of souls, and I need you to be as prepared as you can."

My eyes shot to his as something tugged in my core.

"Careful shadow king," I teased. "People might get the impression that you care about me."

The king looked at me with what I could only describe as yearning in his eyes. "Caring for the future queen of Mercea is nothing to be ashamed of, princess."

Whether he was calling me princess or by my name it ignited heat throughout me, prickling the surface of my skin.

I wasn't expecting his response, so I left the ring walking over to the far wall and selected a sword from the range of weapons. I tested the weight of it in my hand before stepping back into the ring.

"Shall we?" I asked. Khaldon's mouth curved into a crooked smile, as he chose a sword for himself before joining me.

I steadied my footing expecting him to unleash himself on me, instead he cocked his head while he stared at my feet.

"Your stance is off."

"Excuse me?" I had trained relentlessly to perfect my footing.

He pointed towards my feet with the tip of his sword. "Your left leg is too far out, so when you go to thrust your sword, you overcompensate, using up your strength and energy.

I looked down at my feet as he walked over to me.

"Here," he said as he placed his left hand on my hip and moved my foot into place.

I could hear Ruane barking orders at the guard outside whilst the scent of Khaldon's sweat mixed with the scent of storms drifted into my lungs as though that was where it was meant to be. The air around us was charged with heat and I inhaled deeply through my nose.

"Thank you," I said as he walked over to his side of the ring.

He came at me suddenly and my training kicked in. His sword grazed my shirt as he thrust it towards me and my eyes widened at how close he had been to cutting me. He laughed as he whirled around, thrusting and parrying with me back and forth. I knew he was holding back, I had seen the strength of him when he trained with his men. I needed to get an advantage, so I feigned tiredness so he wouldn't suspect my move. He stepped towards me, ready to thrust the sword towards my gut when I charged at him, taking inspiration from Lex as always and swiped my legs low, taking his legs out from underneath him. I crashed on top of him as he pulled me down with him.

In one swift move he had disarmed me and flipped us so he was on top of me. His muscled arms were solid at either side of my head. His breath mingled with mine as he pinned me to the ground. "Interesting," was all he said before standing up and offering me a hand.

I stood up as I tried to make sense of what just happened. Surely, he felt it too. There was something between us that I couldn't make sense of.

He motioned to the bench, and I took a seat as he poured us some water.

We sat in silence, the air between us was heavy but neither of us seemed brave enough to speak on it.

Khaldon broke the silence first.

"When you tried to use magick on the feather in the kitchen, you said you could feel the essence of the magick there but there was a block. Once you remove that block Phoenix, there is no telling how powerful you could be."

He caught me off guard. I hadn't attempted to use magick since the incident with the fireplace, where my attempt only resulted in another nose-bleed.

"My father called a Tithe on the winter solstice."

"Your birthday you mean?" Khaldon replied.

I looked to the king, his broad shoulders were inches away from mine and I dropped my gaze to his leather trousers where a dagger was sheathed at his thigh.

I felt as though he had caught me out in my shame. "Yes, my birthday."

He didn't reply, instead waiting patiently for me to carry on.

"There was a woman that tried to break the curse. She whispered in a tongue I wasn't familiar with, and I felt my magick trying to rise to the surface, but some invisible force snapped her neck before she could finish."

"Something killed her?" Khaldon asked.

I shuddered as I remembered the sound of Quelin's neck snapping in the throne hall.

"Yes, or someone."

He reached for the dagger at his thigh, twirling it as he spoke.

"My guess is the person that triggered your curse also killed the woman that may have been able to break it."

I looked to him in confusion.

"I never told you about that."

Khaldon laughed. "You didn't need to, surely you know all of the kingdoms have eyes and ears across Endaria."

"Yes, but what of your kingdom? Outsiders haven't been able to step foot in Sakaria since my birth."

A flash of regret crossed his face. "Once we have dealt with Ravynne and restored the balance, I will be removing the wall and I intend to ally with the other kingdoms."

I couldn't fault him for trying. His hands were tied while he was essentially powerless, and it would take everything he had to restore his kingdom to greatness.

"Is there a reason you refer to your birthday only as the solstice?"

I frowned slightly at the change of subject, not wanting to strip myself bare in front of him.

"I suppose the night of my birth is also the night that claimed my mother's life, it's hard to celebrate when it's a reminder. I'm a reminder of such tragedy."

Khaldon studied me as I spoke, his grey eyes pierced through my skin as though he could see right down to my bones.

"You're coming into the world is always something to be celebrated, Phoenix."

I warmed at his kindness, it was a mystery how a man that had been raised under an iron fist could be so thoughtful and kind.

I picked up my sword, stepping back into the ring desperate to work off my feelings and levelled it at him. "Don't hold back, shadow king."

Khaldon laughed before launching himself at me. We twisted and clashed, and it wasn't long before my arms were aching, and my breathing became laboured. He pushed me to my limit and I knew my guard had trained me well, but this was on another level. Every time I felt like giving into the pain, he would push me harder, never letting me quit.

The shadow king was an ally. Nothing more, I told myself.

□

CHAPTER 29

THE DAY HAD FINALLY COME for us to leave Sakaria and sail to the land of souls. We stood looking over the northern cliffs of Reynis, it was the most northern point of Endaria and the view was breathtaking. Sakaria surprised me every day, the beauty of the north was magickal, and I stared in awe as the sun set over the horizon. Khaldon had asked me to ride with him and my back was pressed to his chest while he guided the horse. The smell of sea spray collided against my skin carried by the winter sea breeze as we rode across the lush green peaks that overlooked shores of black sand.

I leaned forward so I could get a better view. Turquoise waves lapped against the black shore, as I looked to where the sea met the sky in the distance.

"It's beautiful," I breathed, and Khaldon leaned forward so his mouth was next to my ear. He turned to face me, his mouth so close to mine his breath caressed my face.

"It's my favourite place in the world," Khaldon replied. I wanted to reach up and run my fingers through his hair while I brought his mouth to meet mine.

I looked into his smoky grey eyes and pushed the urge down, aware of my guard watching us.

"I can see why," I said as I pulled away from him, trying to put some distance between us.

Khaldon nudged the horse forward and we descended the cliff, the ship was waiting for us, anchored at the shore, its mast bearing the Trevelyan flag.

"The ship needs to be embedded with the blood of a royal bloodline." Ruane said.

I looked to Khaldon who's gaze was already on me. I went to speak but he cut me off.

"I'll do it," Khaldon said, his eyes never leaving mine.

I frowned as he spoke. I was more than capable of giving a few drops of blood.

As if he'd read my mind, he said, "If you're retrieving the sword, it's the least I can do."

Khaldon dismounted the horse before holding his hand out to help me down. We left the horse with a member of his guard and made our way onto the ship

"So how does this work?" I asked him as he pulled a dagger from his boot.

"Anything passing through the veil needs to contain the blood of one of the royal bloodlines. Whether that's a person or an object."

I looked around the deck of the ship. "So, the wood will absorb the blood then we can pass?" I asked.

"Exactly." He replied with a crooked smile.

He held the dagger over his palm and drew the steel blade over his skin. He removed the dagger and squeezed his hand into a fist while his blood dropped onto the deck. I watched as the ruby droplets seeped into the wood of the ship.

"Now what?" I asked.

He took a cloth from his pocket and wiped the blade clean.

"Now you will be able to pass through the veil."

"You make it sound so simple."

Concern clouded his face as he looked at me. "If you don't want to do this, you don't have to. We can find another way."

I gave a weak laugh. "My father scoured Endaria my entire life and came up with nothing. This might be the only way to end the curse and be rid of Ravynne for good. It's no guarantee that I will find someone to love me."

His eyes roved over my face lingering on my mouth for a second before giving me a tight smile as he sheathed the dagger back into his boot.

"Ruane and Aeden are my best men. I would trust them with my life."

"I feel the same about my guard," I said as I looked over my shoulder. Silver and Ireland were walking up the runway with the supplies we would need for the journey. Khaldon squeezed my hand. "Please be careful, Phoenix."

I nodded as his hand left mine. The way he said my name with such intent stirred feelings in me that I didn't want to acknowledge.

We sailed at dusk to the land of souls. Aeden would have to navigate the black sea in the dead of night but he was more than confident of his ability to do it.

Ruane came below deck where my guard and I were eating and picked a strip of dried meat off the plate in the centre of the table as he said, "We should arrive in the land of souls by sunrise, we need to be out by sundown."

"Why sundown?" Silver asked. Her icy blue eyes fixed onto Ruane.

"We do not want to be on those lands once the sun goes down. The very souls that have been condemned to spend eternity there are free to roam as they please. We do not want to encounter a soul of the damned."

He shook his head as if the memory of something he couldn't bring himself to talk about had crossed his mind.

The ship swayed as it rolled over the waves, The candlelight flickered, casting shadows over us as my thoughts drifted to Khaldon.

I had been in Sakaria for two months now and he had helped me in ways I could never have imagined. I hadn't encountered my beast since we arrived in the shadow kingdom and for that I was eternally grateful.

Ruane and my guard swapped battle stories as I sat back and let them talk. It was nice to not be the focus of a conversation and I watched as my guard laughed and reminisced on their times in the field, protecting the Devereaux crown.

DAWN BROKE OVER THE HORIZON as I peered over the edge of the ship, the water beneath looked as black as night. Land was approaching on the horizon, and we were almost at the land of souls. Ruane came to stand next to me and braced his hands on the ship's railing. His eyes roved over the black sea as he said, "Khaldon said the sword should be in the centre of the land but that's all he knows."

I looked up at Ruane. His jaw was chiselled, and his shoulders were broad. He stood well over six-feet tall, and he had his whole life ahead of him.

"Why would you risk your life on a fool's mission?" I asked him.

We were about to enter the land of the dead. Knights on their phantom horses guarded the lands and creatures straight from the depths of hell prowled the barren wasteland.

He choked a joyless laugh and turned to face me.

"It's the least I could do." I wanted to delve deeper, ask him what he meant but I felt I would be overstepping.

I turned to face the water and saw abandoned ships closer to the shore. As if men before us had tried to take these lands and it had swallowed them whole. Just as I was about to point out something in the water, a huge wave crashed against the ship.

Shouts rang over the deck as my guard ran towards me. I hated that everyone here valued my life above their own.

Ireland rushed over to me. Her copper hair covered in sea spray. "Phoenix, we need to get you below deck!" Her voice was drowned out by the raging black sea.

The waves were getting bigger, and the boat was rocking side to side. I couldn't help but feel that the seas were angry with us for disturbing the peace.

I gripped onto the railing as a wave crashed over our heads. I looked behind me, Ruane was strengthening the sails whilst Aeden tried to navigate us through the choppy waters.

There were jagged islands above the sea's surface, and I didn't know how we were going to make it to shore. I looked over the railing and I saw a figure just below the seas surface. Its head emerged from the water, and I couldn't look away even though the sight terrified me.

The creatures' skin was a blue grey, its hair deepest green like the weeds that grew beneath the seas surface and its eyes an endless black. Its nostrils were nothing more than two slits in its face and when it opened its mouth rows of black, pointed teeth were revealed. It shrieked a horrific sound that made me cover my ears to dull the intensity of it. My ears felt as if they were bleeding and I stumbled as the ship rocked.

"We're almost there!" Aeden shouted across the deck.

I had to hold on to something before I was thrown overboard, I wrapped my hands around a mast and tilted my head to push my ear against my shoulder to drown out the noise that was coming from the creature.

More figures appeared under the water and one by one their heads came above the surface. They were waiting for us to go overboard so they could devour us down to our bones.

We sailed through the mist that was the veil between the living and dead. I felt it as we passed through to the other side. My skin prickled as if millions of eyes were boring into me, watching our every move. My skin crawled as phantom hands roved over my body as if the dead were trying to claw their way back to the living.

The sea calmed and I looked back to where the sea spirit's heads bobbed above the water.

The ship docked at the harbour and the water lapped against the rocks. A weathered flag was blowing in the bitter wind, and I took in the sight before me. Further down the harbour an abandoned ship hung heavily on her side, her remaining sails hung beaten and torn. The emptiness of the harbour cast an eerie feel and the abandoned ships looked ready to haunt the seven seas.

We dismounted from the dock and made our way onto the waste land. A thunderous sound of hooves came from the distance, and I looked across the planes to see clouds of dust rising from the barren ground.

"The knights are coming," Aeden said.

My guard drew their swords simultaneously. Ruane's head whipped in our direction. "Put down your weapons, they will do us no harm if we don't provoke them. They are tied to the Royal bloodlines, so Phoenix is safe, but we might not be so lucky."

Esmeray hesitated, looking at me then back to Ruane. She gave a brief nod and sheathed her weapon, Lex, Silver and Ireland followed.

The knights rode to where we stood. They were ethereal beings, more shadow than flesh. Their armour was beaten as though they had fought more battles than one could imagine. There were seven knights, one for each kingdom.

I was speechless.

The front man of the knights paced his horse back and forward as if he was waiting for one of us to speak. The horse was onyx black, wearing a headdress that had a glistening obsidian stone in its centre. This had to be the horseman that was tied to my bloodline. I looked to the other horseman and their steads that varied in shades of honey gold to pure white, each horse had a jewel that represented its kingdom in the centre of its head piece.

I looked at Ruane who dropped on one knee, Aeden did the same, so I dropped to my knee, silently cursing them both.

The front horseman stopped pacing and stopped his stead in front of me. I couldn't bring myself to look up at him so I bowed my head as a sign of submission and before I could stop myself the words escaped me.

"I am princess Phoenix Devereaux of Mercea. I have come to retrieve the sword of Danann, as was left to these lands by my ancestors. We mean you no harm."

My heart was beating wildly, and I could see Silvers hand shifting slowly to the dagger at her side. I knew she would take on all seven knights if it meant keeping me safe.

The head knight seemed satisfied by what I said and motioned for us to follow him. He dismounted his horse, and we followed him through the barren land.

We walked in silence, there were no sounds except for our footsteps on the dried earth. The head knight led us through a valley that must have been a riverbed once. It was hard to imagine this land with life flowing through it. The sides of the valley were covered in rocks with the occasional dead tree emerging from the ground.

I looked up and saw a black figure slink towards the edge of the valley and grabbed Esmeray's arm as the creature crept down the valley walls. It was some sort of hybrid. Its fur was jet black, its yellow eyes glistened in the grey, overcast light and thick leathery spikes ran down its spine. Esmeray unsheathed her sword and stepped in front of me.

The head horseman put his hand up to halt us. He walked forward to the creature, his body poised to defend us. He thrust his sword forward, missing the creature by inches. The beast bared its yellow fangs and roared, starting towards the horseman, swiping its thick paws across the horseman's armour. It was a combination of a deadly wolf and some kind of sea creature with thick scaled armour that made it impenetrable. The battle of man and beast had me rooted to where we stood. My guard watched in shock as the horseman thrust his sword through the beast's underbelly, causing it to roar in pain. Its thick black blood leaked down its stomach and the horseman took off the beast's head with a lethal swipe of his sword.

Silver's voice broke the stunned silence. "What in the mother's name was that?"

Aeden grimaced, his hand braced on the hilt of his sword that was sheathed at his back. "That was a Ghosha."

CHAPTER 30

W E HAD BEEN WALKING FOR HOURS on high alert, no one daring to make a sound. My guard formed a wall around me as we followed the horseman through the barren wasteland. The air was thick and stale and although the sun wasn't anywhere to be seen my skin was covered in sweat as we suffocated under the lifeless sky.

I craved a lush forest where I could find a cool stream to drink from and wash away the feeling of death that had clung to my skin. My throat tightened and I had to tell myself that I wasn't suffocating, I stopped walking and braced my hands on my knees, there was no air or wind to cool me.

Lex turned around and saw me struggling to keep up. I was among some of the fiercest warriors in Endaria and couldn't match their stamina.

Lex asked the head horseman, "How much further will we travel?"

He turned around to face us, before pointing to a mountain range in the distance.

"Can you speak?" I panted, he hadn't made a sound or revealed his face.

The horseman stopped and turned to face me slowly, shaking his head silently. I looked towards the mountains in the distance and willed my legs to keep going.

We came to a cave after walking through the wastelands for hours.

The head horseman stopped at the cave's entrance and turned to face me, his weathered armour blowing on a phantom wind.

The mouth of the cave was deep and dark. He raised a hand and pointed toward the entrance. My stomach sank as my thoughts flicked back to Amaris. The cave you fear to enter holds the treasure you seek. I stepped around the horseman and peered into the mouth of the mountain.

Aeden spoke. "The sword is in the cave?"

The horseman stood steadfast, not giving anything away.

Ruane stalked forward walking straight towards the entrance. He went to step into the darkness when he hit an invisible wall. He tried again but he couldn't pass the threshold into the cave. Esmeray walked over to where Ruane stood banging on the invisible barrier. She cautiously lifted her hand and was met with resistance.

"It's been warded," she said. "If only a person from the royal bloodlines can wield the sword, then the same must be said for the retrieval of it."

Aeden's eyes flashed to mine. Nausea churned in my gut as I realised what I had to do. There was no way of knowing what I would encounter in the cave, and I would have to go forward without my guard.

"It has to be me," I said as I looked at the group.

I unsheathed my father's sword at my back and steadied my breathing. "No," Silver said, as she slammed her sword into the ground, dust flying around us. "There has to be another way."

I stood in front of the cave's entrance and raised my hand before me. I hoped I would meet resistance too, so I didn't have to go through it alone, but my hand slipped through the ward effortlessly. I slipped my body through the entrance as Lex banged her fist against the invisible barrier. All sound was cut off from outside the cave, I couldn't hear a thing.

"I'll be okay." I mouthed to Lex hoping she could understand what I was saying. I looked around the darkness and wished I had some light to guide me. I sheathed my father's sword as I took a deep breath and placed my back against the wall as I took small sideways steps. I thought about what was riding on this, my kingdom, my future. The mountain's surface was cool against my back. I looked to my right and the cave entrance was a small dot of grey light disappearing with each step I took.

The wall curved slightly the further I went, I could hear the faint sound of still waters and my fingertips grazed the mountain as I guided myself further into the unknown.

An instinct led me deeper into the cave, as if a thread were pulling me along as I wondered which of my ancestors gave their blood to forge the sword.

I stumbled over a rock throwing my hands out to steady myself.

That's when I heard it. A whisper. I strained my ears to hear which direction it came from.

Someone or something was here. The deeper I went into the cave the louder the whispering became. It sounded as though the walls of the cave were spilling the secrets of the spirit.

I rounded a corner and came to a temple. I looked up as grey light seeped into the cave through a hole in the belly of the mountain. There were steps leading up to an altar, which was set in front of a pool of glistening water. I slowly unsheathed my sword and the weight of it gave me some reassurance. I could almost convince myself that my ancestors were right here with me. I stalked forward slowly, not wanting to make a sound. My feet crossed the distance to the steps, and I began the climb.

I reached the top and was met by a pool of infinity. The water glistened like the stars and the magick thrummed against my skin. I looked to the far end of the pool where the altar was and I saw it, the sword of Danann. Its blade was pure steel with an intricate gold hilt with runes in gold etched into the centre.

I looked down at the pool, expecting to see my reflection looking back at me but was met with nothing. I knelt to run my hands through the water.

"Shit!" My voice echoed through the temple, as I wiped my stinging hand on my trousers. The water was so cold it burned.

Movement in the corner of my eye broke my focus and I stood as I raised my sword. A creature that wasn't man or beast slinked out of the shadows followed by another.

I stopped suddenly, assessing how I was going to escape from them. I was out in the open, completely exposed. I had to get the sword and get back to my guard. One of the creature's heads swung in my direction, and I willed my heart to beat at a normal pace. It was beating so fast it was a vibration thrumming in my chest. The creature scanned the temple, its eyes a colourless milky white. Its gaze seemed to go past me, and I wondered if it had any sight.

I took a small step to the left expecting the creature to pounce but it continued scanning the temple as if it sensed someone was here but couldn't see.

The other creature stayed back as if waiting for orders. I edged closer to the sword placed on top of a stone pillar, just a few more steps and I could reach it.

I took a step forward as a deafening screech rang in my ears. Something crashed into my side and I turned as I fell, the creature falling with me with its mouth bared as I fell into the infinity pool. My father's sword was knocked from my hand, crashing against the ground as I hit the surface with a crash and fought for air as the impact sucked me under. The creature grabbed my shoulders pushing me down into the freezing water. I tried to break free of its hold, but it had a deathly grip on me, sinking me into the darkness. I thrashed and kicked, trying to find my way back to the surface. I was going to die, and no one was going to be able to find me. I thought of my father, my guards, Khaldon, even Ruane and his mischievous grin came into my mind those moments before death.

My body started convulsing as the creature pushed me down further into the depths of what could only be hell. My lungs burned with the need to draw breath, but I knew once I opened my mouth my life would be over, my father without an heir.

My hands felt for the dagger sheathed at my thigh and I thrust it into the creature's gut. Its claws were buried in my shoulders, but it loosened its grip on me and that was all I needed. I pushed to the surface, swimming as fast as I could, my head throbbed and my heart pounded in my chest.

When my lungs felt as though they were about to burst, my head pushed through the surface of the pool. I coughed as I struggled to catch my breath, swimming to the edge of the infinity pool and lifting myself out. My skin felt raw, as if I had been burned alive. I rolled over onto my side, choking on the deathly cold water.

I pushed myself up, still gasping for air, and the creature pushed its head above the pool's surface, screeching a deafening sound. The other creature reacted, lunging across the pool towards me.

I scrambled to reach the temple, throwing my hand around the hilt of the sword. I lifted it from its resting place and the sword erupted with light. After a moment, I looked at my hand and the sword seemed to have absorbed the glow.

I stood up slowly from where I had been crouching and looked over to the edge of the pool. Both creatures had dropped to one knee and bowed before me. I looked down at the sword, an eon of ancient power residing inside of it.

The creatures made no effort to move from where they knelt. I walked over to where my father's sword lay next to the pool and sheathed it at my back, along with the sword of Danann as I slowly edged towards the steps. Never taking my eyes from the beings that had bowed before me. I walked down the steps, my heart thundering with every step. When I reached the bottom, I turned to look at the creatures, they were in the same position kneeling before the temple.

I rounded a corner and ran. I had to rely on memory to find my way out of the cave. I remembered it veering to the left on my way in, so I swung right and pounded my feet into the mountain floor as hard and fast as I could. I saw the grey light of the cave entrance further down the tunnel, just a few more steps and I would be free.

As I ran faster the light got brighter and I was almost at the entrance, I saw Aeden turn around, shock registering on his face. His sword was in front of him ready to take on whatever was behind me, but he couldn't help me if he tried. I pushed myself to my limit and burst through the entrance of the cave, falling onto the dusty ground. I was on my knees coughing trying to force air into my lungs, but no matter how much I drew breath my chest still burned.

My guard crowded around while I struggled to breathe.

"Phoenix, what happened in there!" Ireland shouted.

I looked back at the cave entrance. "Something tried to kill me."

Silver stalked over to me, looking into my eyes as she checked me over for signs of injury.

"It-it tried to kill me." I stuttered as I finally could breathe again, my throat burned with every breath.

Esmeray's eyes darkened. "You were foolish to go in the cave alone Phoenix, we could have lost you, and then what? It would have been the end of our kingdom."

Her words stung, I knew I had been reckless going in alone but no one else would have been able to come with me. I was out of options. I could take her disappointment if it meant my kingdom was safe.

We walked back to the harbour, my eyes constantly scanning the horizon wondering what else this place had to offer us. The swords I carried were a heavy presence at my back, I was so close to the curse being broken.

Lex spoke into the silence. "When we get back to Mercea, I'm retiring."

I whipped my head towards my friend, scowling at the thought of her leaving me. Ireland laughed, and my shoulders relaxed when I realised she was joking.

"You wouldn't dare," Silver said, a coy grin on her face.

"Well, I'm having some time off. I'll go to the south for a week, no, a month actually and feast on lemon shrimp and pastries, in the southern summer."

"That sounds like heaven," Ireland added.

I looked around at my guard, they gave so much for me and my crown. The horseman walking ahead of us as we trailed behind him.

"If we break this curse and all is well back home, I will ensure that my father gives you all a month's paid leave, or more if you need it."

Lex nudged me. "We couldn't leave you for that long Phoenix, a week's paid leave will do." She said as she winked at me.

Even the thought of being without my guard for a week filled me with dread. I was determined to not live in the shadows of the curse anymore and once we were back in Mercea, I promised myself I would start living.

Movement came from our left, bringing reality crashing down around us. I unsheathed my father's sword as my guard gathered around me. Before I could register what was happening, I was spun around so Lex was in front of me, and I was facing her back.

Then the creature lunged.

I heard Ireland scream as the Ghosha sunk its teeth into Lex's neck and tore a piece of her flesh out. Her blood sprayed across my face as she cried out in pain, and I flinched at the warmth that coated me.

My world slowed down to nothing. I couldn't hear, I couldn't speak. There was no air, no sound, nothing. My lungs closed in on themselves as the air was choked out of me.

I watched helplessly as Silver and Aeden managed to take the creature down with their swords and Ireland rushed to Lex's side as she fell in a heap to the ground. My legs gave way and I fell to the ground next to her.

I could feel something awaken in my blood, the pressure growing more intense with every passing second. I felt the tingle in my blood as my magick woke after a long slumber. I thought it was gone forever.

Lightning flashed across the sky as thunder rumbled in the distance.

I looked down at Lex through the tears that poured down my face.

"Please don't leave me," I begged.

When Lex opened her eyes, they were completely black. The Ghosha had infected her with death.

"Do something!" I screamed at Esmeray. I knew she didn't deserve my rage. I couldn't live with myself knowing that Lex had sacrificed herself so that I could live, I was a cursed soul anyway.

I held Lex's hand as I screamed and screamed at my guard to help her. The wound on her neck was getting bigger, spreading down to her chest, it was eating away at her flesh, it was eating her alive. I unsheathed the sword that held the ancient power within it and held it over Lex, I had no idea if it would work but I had to try. I pointed the sword at her wound and willed life into her but nothing happened, there was no power. This had all been for nothing.

I felt so helpless, all I could do was scream.

After time seemed to stand still and I had screamed until my throat was raw. I looked to Lex's neck, the size of the wound had stopped growing and I looked to where it had stopped. It had eroded her heart away so there was just a hollow hole where it should be. I knew she was gone for good, and it was all my fault.

"Phoenix," Ireland said gently.

The thunder and lightning had stopped, and the land went back to stillness, my guard closed in around me and I couldn't breathe.

"No, no, no, no, no," I said, each time getting louder. I could feel the pressure building inside of me until I couldn't hear myself think, then I exploded.

It felt like a lifetime's worth of magick had been building under the surface with no outlet, but now my hand had been forced. I screamed as the storm raged inside of me, shattering the pieces of my soul.

I threw myself over Lex's body as the force of my power erupted around us and my guard were thrown back. Aeden and Ruane dug their swords into the ground to anchor themselves.

The pain was splitting me in two, tearing me apart limb by limb, a ring of fire erupted around me and Lex, the flames so high I couldn't see past them. The fire raged around me and my friend, and I would never forgive myself for what had happened.

I buried my head in Lex's neck and cried, the sobs choked me as I lay in the cocoon of fire my magick had created. No one could reach us, and I wished I could stay here forever.

CHAPTER 31

Khaldon

I TRIED TO FOCUS ON THE REPORTS before me, but my mind kept drifting back to Phoenix. I couldn't pinpoint the moment she had gone from being a political ally to something more. My eyes roved over the papers that covered my desk, but I gave up and leaned back in my chair. I clenched my hand into a fist as I tried to convince myself that everything would work out.

A shadow rose over me, and I turned to look out of the window. The sky had darkened in a matter of seconds and thick black clouds came over my kingdom.

I stood and walked to the window unease curling in my stomach as I looked out over the grounds of my palace. Nothing but despair had consumed my life on these lands, and I often thought about giving it all up, but my sister wouldn't be able to carry the burden of the cursed crown. I stared out into the horizon as a cloak of darkness covered the sky. The edge of my grounds was surrounded by trees, I enjoyed the privacy it gave me in this palace of moonstone. No one would dare breach these grounds thanks to my father's legacy of wrath, but the unease was rising in the kingdom. My people were still cautious of me as their leader, believing me to be a tyrant like my father. I wanted to be a better ruler, a ruler whose people respected, not feared them.

I looked down to where my men gazed at the sky, puzzled by the sudden change in weather, and a flock of birds flew from the trees as if a predator was amongst them.

Then I felt it.

The world shook as a blast of wind ripped across the palace. The window to my study shattered and I dropped to the floor as I raised my arm to shield my face from the broken glass that flew across the room.

Something had happened. Something sinister. Khayna rushed into my study. Her usually warm, golden skin pale.

"What the hell was that!" she cried. Her chest heaved with rushed breaths and her eyes flicked from me to the window and back again.

"I don't know," I said as I stood up, brushing broken glass from my clothing.

Khayna stepped into my study, her eyes searching through the broken window as if she could see into the land of souls and make sure everyone was safe.

"Something terrible must have happened, I can feel it."

My eyes snapped to my sister, I didn't want to agree with her, but I couldn't deny it either. They wouldn't be returning until the morning and the not- knowing was eating away at me.

We wouldn't know until Phoenix returned. As the only one there with royal blood, I was counting on her to save us all.

CHAPTER 32

Phoenix

W HEN I FINALLY EXPENDED MY RAGE and my flames had dimmed to cinders, I opened my eyes. A ring of black ash had formed where I had burned the ground with my flames. I could feel my heart freezing over. The land of souls had taken my friend, it had taken away one of the most important people in my life. She deserved better. The only reason she was here was because of me.

Esmeray reached out to touch my shoulder and I flinched at the affection.

I leaned over and took Lex's necklace off and put it around my neck. I closed my eyes and vowed I would never take it off.

I felt exhausted. The power that came out of me was consuming and I could feel blood dripping from my nose mixing with my tears that had soaked my skin. I wiped the blood with my sleeve and rose to stand up. I looked over at the slain creature as its lifeless body lay on the burnt ground. I took the dagger that was sheathed inside my boot and calmly walked over to where it lay.

I knew it was dead, but I couldn't help myself, I needed an outlet for my anger, burning the world to ash wasn't enough. I stabbed the creature in its soft underbelly, again and again and again until my arm burned from the effort and its oily black blood had splashed across my body, but I couldn't stop, I threw my dagger to the ground and tore at the beast with my bare hands, I caught my hand on the spikes running down the length of the creature that tore into my skin but the pain just spurred me on.

I wanted to kill every Ghosha in this forsaken place. I panted as I tried to control the surge of power I could feel building again, my magick seemed to be triggered by extreme emotions.

My hands were covered in the creature's blood, I needed to get back to the shore and wash the death from my skin. I stalked off not knowing which way I was going, I heard footsteps behind me, and I whirled around to see Esmeray following me.

"Don't," I said through gritted teeth.

For the first time since I had known her, I saw Esmeray hesitate. I could see the conflict warring across her face. I just needed some space. I couldn't even look at my guard without the feeling of guilt consuming me. I couldn't breathe.

I knew I was being selfish; my pain was no more warranted than my guards. They had lost their sister, their comrade.

"Phoenix, you can't be alone, it isn't safe," Esmeray said, her voice was the softest I had heard it and I looked to my friend and saw the grief etched into every part of her.

I couldn't handle the pain, it would kill me before this curse did.

Sparks flew under my skin as my magick coursed through my body, the feeling was foreign but a comfort. Whatever mental leash had been containing it, suppressing it, had well and truly snapped. I had a fighting chance of ridding the world of Ravynne and her darkness, maybe freeing myself from the curse but at what cost? What use was it if the curse was broken but I had suffered a great loss? We all had. My heart sank as I thought about my guard, it had been the four of them for so long.

I fell to my knees and screamed and a line of fire ripped from me incinerating the lifeless beast that had killed my friend. But it didn't stop there, my flames carried on into the distance turning anything in their path into ash.

I took a deep breath and made my way back to where Lex lay. Silver had closed Lex's eyes and was kneeling over her body, sobbing quietly. She rose as she heard me approaching and I couldn't have hated myself more.

Ruane stepped forward keeping his distance. "The veil won't let us pass with someone that isn't living."

"What do you mean?" I bit out.

"The veil won't allow us to pass with Lex on board."

I looked around as the realisation hit me. We would need to bury Lex here in the land of souls.

"She'll be alone. We can't leave her here!" I screamed.

Aeden stepped forward. "There is no other way, Phoenix." His tone was serious, and his face was grim.

"It will be dark in a few hours, we need to head back to the ship." Ruane said as his eyes scanned the horizon. "We cannot be in these lands when the sun has set."

I looked around desperately, trying to find a way to bring my friend home.

"We need to bury her." I said, my voice hoarse from the screaming.

I walked over to a spot under a withered tree. I reached out and touched the dead leaves that were nothing more than skeletal, my friend deserved so much more, and I hated myself for failing her.

I sank to my knees, as I clawed at the barren ground, my bloodied hands stinging as the dirt mixed with my wounds.

Ruane and Aeden joined me, and we worked in silence as we dug Lex's grave. I couldn't bear the thought of my friend being here all alone.

We carefully placed Lex in the grave and covered her body with soil. Ireland handed me Lex's sword and I placed it on top of the mound of dirt where my friend was now buried.

I unsheathed my father's sword at my back and my guard followed, the sound of the deadly metal whispered through the wasteland.

I stood at the head of the grave looking outwards, Esmeray positioned herself at the foot and Ireland and Silver stood on either side.

The vigil of the princes was an old tradition in Mercea. When a soldier had fallen their comrades would stand guard at their grave. It was thought that while the fallen soldier's spirit was travelling to the afterlife, the body couldn't be disturbed or their soul may not make it, destined to wander between the veil of worlds for eternity.

The horsemen had returned and formed a protective circle around us while we mourned our friend as Aeden and Ruane bowed their heads.

I slammed my sword into the ground and gripped the hilt, bowing my head as I said a silent prayer. I promised the gods I would return for my friend and bury her where she belonged, then I fell apart.

CHAPTER 33

I WOKE TO THE GENTLE MOTION of the black sea rocking the ship. For a moment I forgot where I was, until the searing pain of grief crashed over me. My world had gone dark after we buried Lex. A part of me wished I had joined her in death, at least I would be at peace.

I was still in the clothes I had worn in the land of souls, and I retched at the mixture of my friend's and the Ghosha's blood that was clinging onto me.

I rinsed my hands and face in the basin of my cabin and changed into clean clothes before pulling a fur cloak around my shoulders and creeping up to the deck. Aeden stood at the helm of the ship, guiding us back and I breathed the cold sea air in deeply as I walked to the foot of the ship, the waves of the black sea crashing against the hull as I stared into the distance.

The journey back to Sakaria was calmer, the seas were still. The only motion was the Trevelyan ship cutting through the black sea, there was no sign of the sea spirits.

I sat on the deck in silence while Aeden guided the ship home. He must have felt my presence, even though I hadn't made a sound, because he turned back to look at me every now and then, but I was frozen to the spot, staring into the darkness.

A million stars lit up the moonless sky, I looked up as Lex's screams still rang in my head, and I swallowed my rage. I would never be worthy of her sacrifice.

I looked down into the murky black sea, the grey waves splashed up the sides of the ship coating me in sea spray. My hands gripped the railing, the cold metal biting into my already frozen skin. Thoughts swarmed my mind of how I was going to face everyone back home. I would have to tell Axel that his twin sister was gone. The guilt of Lex's death was eating away at me, and I didn't know how I would live with this feeling every day. I couldn't see a way out, all I could see was Lex dying in front of me while I was helpless.

The depths of the ocean were unknown, and I thought about giving myself up to the endless black sea as I stared at the waves, the pull of it luring me in like a siren's song. It could swallow me whole and relieve me from this torment.

I placed my foot onto the first railing.

"Don't do it."

A deep voice interrupted my thoughts and I turned slowly to see Aeden a few feet behind me. I gripped the railing tighter as I calculated if I could throw myself overboard before he reached me.

"The pain you feel now won't last forever," Aeden said as he took a step closer.

I looked down at his feet that had edged closer to me—he was almost within arm's reach.

"How do you know?" I asked. My voice thick with grief.

"Because the pain is making you irrational. Lex died protecting you. She died with honour."

My chest tightened at the mention of her name. My hands gripped the railing until it hurt, and my torment overcame me. I knew Aeden was right. Lex would never want me to harm myself in any way. If I died, her sacrifice would have been for nothing.

I let go of the railings and my knees gave way underneath me. Aeden was next to me in a heartbeat, pulling me up. I turned around and buried my face in his chest. and he said nothing as he held me while the pain poured out of me.

"I promise you won't feel this way forever, Phoenix."

I cried until I had nothing left. He didn't owe me anything, but he was there for me in my darkest moment. An unspoken bond was formed that night—I owed Aeden Varsano my life.

OUR SHIP DOCKED ON THE SHORE and birds flew overhead as dawn broke over the horizon. I couldn't bear the weight pressing down on me. The sword of Danann was sheathed in my cabin, and I resented the sight of it. It was the cause of my torment and my salvation. Aeden anchored the ship as I walked down the runway, my footsteps heavy like my heart. I didn't wait for my guard to follow me. I wanted to run to the ends of the earth—I wanted to run until my feet bled and I could find an escape from my grief.

My eyes scanned the shore, where Khaldon was waiting with members of his guard. He stalked over to where I stood, and I crumbled. My knees gave way as an invisible knife twisted in my chest. He crossed the distance to where I lay on the beach, the tears fell down my face, joining the sand where they would be swept out to sea. I didn't care that people were watching. I closed my eyes and wished I could disappear. The pain was consuming me as Khaldon's boots appeared in front of my eyes. He knelt and ran his knuckles over my tears.

"What happened?" He bit out as he looked towards Aeden and Ruane.

Esmeray ran to where I lay, and I gripped my hands in the sand as I tried to cling to my sanity. The loss of my friend because of my fate was a burden I could not carry.

I closed my eyes as the world spun around me.

Ruane's voice rang in my ears. "We lost Lex." His tone was grim with the reality of what we had faced in the land of souls.

I writhed in the sand as the pain devoured me. Khaldon leaned over and wiped another tear from my cheek.

"Phoenix, we have to get you back to the palace."

I could feel my magick rushing to the surface, trying to protect me from this agony. I didn't have a chance to warn anyone before my body was engulfed in white-hot flames. Khaldon jumped back, raising his hands to shield his face.

"What the fuck happened out there!" he roared at Ruane.

I could hear their voices arguing around the chaos that was my magick. I don't know how long I lay there, burning myself from the inside out. No one could get close to me, my magick was protecting me the only way it could.

I heard the splashes of water as Khaldon's men tried to put out my flames, but they burned hotter and fiercer, they might as well have battled the sun.

Eventually, the well of my magick ran dry and my flames reduced to embers. I could hear my guard pleading with me to let them in.

Pain shot across my skull as blood dripped from my nose and I wondered if I had gone too far.

I lay on the shore, my body limp and lifeless, as I felt hands scoop me up from underneath. Khaldon flinched as his skin blistered with the heat of my body, then the darkness saved me from myself.

I BLINKED AWAY THE HAZE as twilight seeped into the room. I didn't recognise my surroundings at first. The familiar room slowly sank in, I was back in my chambers. A soft breeze came in from the open window blowing the curtains. I couldn't bring myself to move. I turned to lay on my side and the scent of the sea and storms filled my senses and I realised Khaldon had been in my chambers. I pushed the quilts off, and my feet found the floor. My skin felt tender to touch as if it had been burned by the sun.

The bedroom door opened and Khaldon's silhouette appeared in the empty space.

I squinted as the light from the hallway stung my eyes. He came in bare foot, wearing a loose shirt and trousers. He placed the tray he was carrying on the table on the other side of the room and came to sit next to me on the bed. He tucked my hair behind my ear, and I tried to understand when this line had been crossed between us. I came to this kingdom to break my curse, but the feelings Khaldon stirred deep inside of me were becoming harder to ignore.

"How are you feeling?" he asked, his voice sending shivers through me as his warm breath caressed my skin.

Silver moonlight shone through the open window and his skin was illuminated. I lay my head on his shoulder, and he leaned into me as he lightly stroked my skin.

"I don't know how I'm going to live without her." My voice cracked as my eyes stung with the anticipation of tears. "I'm so tired of crying Khaldon, I'm so tired of people that I love being hurt because of me. Lex is gone. Buried alone in the land of souls because she saved me instead of saving herself. How am I supposed to live with that?"

"What happened to Lex wasn't your fault."

"Don't! Don't try and make me feel better by lying to me. She died saving my life. I'm only here because she's gone... she's gone." I clenched my fist as I fought back the tears.

A knock on the door interrupted us and Khaldon sighed as he let go of me. I immediately missed the presence of him and I pushed the feeling down.

"Sorry to disturb you, Khal." It was Ruane. "There have been reports of a breach on the shores.

I jumped up running to the door. "What do you mean a breach?"

Ruane's face was conflicted as his gaze flicked to me then back to Khaldon.

Khaldon looked down at me, his expression unreadable.

"Meet us in the dining hall," he said to Ruane.

Ruane gave a short nod and made his way down the corridor.

Esmeray stepped from where she had been standing guard and I threw my arms around her, I never wanted to let her go.

"Are you okay?" I asked as I pulled back to read her face. Her hazel eyes were bloodshot, and she set her jaw before giving a curt nod. I felt like I had been punched in the gut.

"I need to get dressed. I need to make sure everyone is ok."

I threw a fitted shirt and some trousers on and raced to Ireland's room. I burst through the door and halted as I saw her sat on the couch,

"What happened?" I asked, my voice full of panic, the red of her eyes only made the green stand out more and I knew she had been crying. "Where's Silver?" I asked as I scanned her room, I only had three guard members left, I refused to lose anymore.

"Silver is in her chambers, is everything okay?"

I breathed a sigh of relief. "Ruane said there have been reports of a breach on the shore."

I looked around her room for a weapon. Although I was in a foreign kingdom, I had a deep-rooted instinct to protect it as though it were my own.

"Where's the sword?" I asked.

"The king has it," Esmeray said as she pulled a dagger from the sheath at her thigh and handed me the blade.

We made our way to the dining hall where Khaldon stood at the head of the table, the sword lay before him. His eyes flicked up to mine and I couldn't sense what the emotion was behind them. I stood next to my guard, relieved to be close to them again.

Khaldon had his arms crossed as Aeden filled us in on the breach.

"We think when Phoenix's power erupted in the land of souls, it made cracks in the barrier."

I looked at Khaldon confused, how could my magick cause cracks in a veil that had been there for centuries.

Khaldon spoke as if he had read my mind, "There have been reports of Ghosha's along the north coast."

My eyes widened in horror as I looked at Khaldon. What had killed Lex was on these lands.

☐

CHAPTER 34

THE GROUND SHOOK as horns blared in the distance. It sounded like an army of a thousand horsemen were heading straight to the palace. Arrows flew through the grounds as I rushed to the window behind Khaldon and looked outside.

A stampede of horses in shades of ivory to onyx wearing jewelled head pieces raced towards the palace. "The horsemen," I whispered.

Ruane rushed to see what I was looking at. "Mother above."

"What does this mean? Why are they here?" Silver asked.

I grabbed the sword of Danann off the table, it's hilt alight with the ancient power and ran down the corridor. The palace door was open as Orion and the other guard members stood on the steps, and the horsemen and their phantom horses rode up to the palace. Khaldon and I stood together as the head of the knights dismounted his horse before kneeling at the foot of the steps in front of us.

In the land of souls, they had been ethereal beings but in Sakaria they were pure flesh and bone. The horseman linked to my kingdom took off his helmet and stepped towards me.

"Tynan Dubiel of the soul's guard, we are here to protect those who wield the sword, princess."

I looked in shock to the man standing before me. He reminded me of my father, his deep brown skin mirrored mine and his eyes were the deepest brown, so dark they were almost black.

I looked down at the sword he had come to protect as my grip tightened around the hilt. He led us to the sword in the land of souls, as if I were fated to wield it.

My guard, Ruane, and Aeden rushed out behind us.

"How are you here?" I questioned in disbelief.

He looked behind me at Khaldon bowing before answering.

"We swore our souls to protect the sword at all costs. After you left the land, we saw the Ghosha walking to the shore and disappearing into thin air. We have not left the land since our souls were bound there, but our instinct is to protect the sword and those who wield it."

Khaldon stepped forward and held his hand out to shake the horseman's hand.

I watched as they clasped each other in a firm grip, I reached up and touched his arm, his armour was solid steel etched with the Devereaux crest.

"The Ghosha are on their way," Tynan said.

Panic coursed through me as the consequence of what I had done bore down on me.

"How much time do we have?" Khaldon asked.

"Not much, they weren't far behind us," Tynan said. "We'll stand guard while you prepare yourselves."

Khaldon and I raced inside, followed by the others.

"We need to use the sword on the Ghosha." Khaldon said.

"What about Ravynne?" Silver asked, "it's the only thing that can kill her and we don't know how much power that will take."

I worried about how using the sword might tip the balance of nature, but time was running out.

"At the moment Ravynne is imprisoned in the cells, we need to deal with the Ghosha first, they are the immediate threat." Khaldon said.

Ireland unsheathed her sword. "Okay, what are we waiting for?"

I hesitated before speaking. "I worry that using the power will upset the balance of nature more than it already has been. We can't know the depths of the power inside the sword and I fear if we use too much there won't be enough left to defeat Ravynne."

Everyone in the room turned to look at me and I knew deep down we had no other choice, we were dealing with creatures that should never have been able to leave the land of souls. The same creatures that killed Lex. I had to make things right somehow. "Only someone from the royal bloodlines can wield the sword, so, it will have to be me or Khaldon that unleashes its power."

Ireland and Silver's eyes shot to mine, and I could see them battling internally with wanting to save me and making sure our kingdom was safe.

"I have an idea." I said as I looked to Khaldon, his eyes searching mine as he waited for me to explain myself.

"What if we use the sword on Ravynne first? We can weaken her with its power and her stolen power will find its way back to the mother where it belongs, giving us an advantage."

I watched the king as he contemplated my plan. "It's worth a shot." Khaldon said and I breathed a sigh of relief.

I walked down the steps into the cells beneath the palace. Aeden unlocked the cell door, the iron groaning as he pushed it open. I peered into the cell and Ravynne was almost unrecognisable from the night I spent in the cells. Her movements were feral and she seemed more animal than human at this point.

She hissed as we entered the cell and Khaldon took a protective stance in front of me so if she did attack, he would take the brunt of it.

"How do you want to do this Khal?" Ruane asked.

Khaldon turned to look at me taking the sword from my hand gently. "You don't go near her."

The chains holding Ravynne clashed together as she scuttled backwards. I looked to her ankle, which was raw and bloody. Dried blood had crusted on her lips and I brought my hand to my mouth as I realised what she'd done.

"Mother save us—she's tried to chew herself free," Esmeray said, a dagger in her hand should she need to use it.

Ravynne was crouched in the corner of the cell and I wondered what had led to this moment. How she had ended up here with her death moments away.

Aeden entered the confined space, and she swiped her hand towards him, her nails were sharp points, the only weapon she could use against us was herself and he jumped back to avoid her wrath.

I stepped from behind Khaldon and her eyes flicked to mine instantly. They were completely black, and a shiver crept up my spine as she stared at me.

She lunged forward desperate to reach me and Khaldon shoved me backwards until I felt Esmeray's arms wrap around me, twisting to shield me from Ravynne. I didn't know what I had done to deserve her wrath.

"We have to remove the cuffs if we want her power to leave her body," Aeden said and Ravynne started thrashing like a wild animal.

"We've got one chance Khal, we can't miss," Ruane said.

Khaldon whirled around and slammed the sword into her back, the tip of the sword sticking out of her chest as black blood poured from her mouth. Aeden unclamped the cuff from around her neck as Ruane loosened the ones around her wrists and ankles. Light erupted throughout the cell, and she choked as the sword poured that ancient power into her. I watched in horror as the sword drew her life force out of her, her veins turning black under her sallow skin, as she choked on her blood.

The blinding light in the cell was dimming and I looked to Khaldon, his teeth were bared as he took the brunt of the force. The power left her body as though it had been caged this entire time, desperate to be free.

Orion, the head guard burst into the cell, his eyes widening as he took in the scene before him. Khaldon's arms trembled with the effort of holding onto the sword, the force of Ravynne's magick was more powerful than us all, but with every passing second, I saw the balance of nature tipping. Every second that Khaldon poured our ancestors power into her, magick poured back into the world and I felt my flames dancing under my skin, desperate for a release.

Ravynne's screams rang against the walls of the cells as Orion shouted. "It's Khayna! She's been attacked by the creatures!"

I looked to Khaldon as his horrified expression clouded his beautiful face.

He loosened his grip on the sword for a moment and Ravynne slumped forward, falling to the ground as she clutched her hand over the wound in her chest. His arms slackened at his side as the sword fell to the floor. Instinct overcame me and I dove for the sword as Ruane snapped the iron cuff around her neck, putting a block on her remaining power.

Esmeray and Silver pulled me up as I gagged on the putrid blood that had smeared up my sleeve. It smelled like death itself. I kept the sword firmly gripped in my hands, it was the only thing that could free me.

Khaldon raced out of the cell and panic tore through me as I thought about Khayna.

"Get those cuffs on and restrain her now!" Esmeray barked orders at Ruane while Silver and Ireland pulled me out of the cell.

"Phoenix, we have to get you to safety," Ireland said, her voice distant although she was standing next to me. My heartbeat pounded in my head like a war drum.

"It's happening again," I whispered. "She can't die."

Lex sacrificing herself for me was already too much of a burden to bear, the thought of something happening to Khayna because of me too brought me to my knees.

My legs gave way at the thought and Silver hauled me up. "Phoenix, just hold on, we've got you."

"No," I said, adrenaline coursing through my body, and I knew what I had to do.

"We have to get you somewhere safe, away from the Ghosha, we'll leave Sakaria right now if we have to."

"No!" I shouted, "I can't leave, I can't leave them like this."

Ireland turned to look at me as we reached the doorway at the top of the stairs. My guard looked between themselves, as I heard shouts coming from the infirmary and I ran.

I gripped the sword so hard pain shot through my palm. I rushed into the infirmary and saw Khayna laid on the bed, her golden hair matted with blood and her arm had a wound so deep I could see the bone.

I covered my mouth as Ireland and Silver burst in behind me. Khaldon looked up at me from where he was leaning over Khayna. Fury was etched into every part of his face as he stalked over to me and my guard.

"Khaldon," I said softly.

His eyes met mine and a war of emotion crossed his face.

"Phoenix!" I turned around as Esmeray burst into the infirmary. "We need to leave Sakaria. Now."

I jolted at the thought of leaving Khaldon in this mess. Because of me. I shattered the barrier, and now Khayna was dying.

I took a deep breath and willed the world to stop spinning, I just needed a moment to think. The hilt of the sword warmed in my palm, and I knew what I had to do.

"I'm not leaving until I finish what I started."

I walked over to where Khayna lay on the cot, her eyes were completely black and the veins in her temple were grey under her skin, death was crawling through her.

Four of Khaldon's men had to hold her down as she thrashed in pain. I pushed her hair back off her face, the golden strands damp with sweat.

I leaned to whisper in her ear, "I'm so sorry Khayna."

I raised the sword above her arm, I willed the power inside of it to draw the death that was consuming her out and to force life back into her, it didn't work in the land of souls with Lex but I prayed that the sword would allow me to save Khayna.

I pushed the tip of the sword into the wound and she hissed, the sound animal-like. Everything I feared had come true and I couldn't lose anyone else.

Light flowed from the edge of the sword into Khayna's wound as the ancient power slowly knitted her skin back together. I whipped my head towards Khaldon who was staring at Khayna, his muscles tensed as we waited to see if it had worked.

Everyone in the room held their breath and a guard rushed into the infirmary, thick black blood had splashed up his armour and I held onto the cot as flashes of Lex in the land of souls filled my mind.

"Your Majesty, the palace is swarmed with these creatures, the horsemen are fighting them off, but we can't hold them for much longer." The guard was breathless and wiped a streak of blood from his face.

I looked down at Khayna, the black had gone from her veins and the life had come back into her face. She took a deep breath, as though she had come up from being underwater and her blue eyes were crystal clear.

"Mother above, Khayna!" I threw myself over her and wrapped her in a tight embrace.

"I'm okay," she whispered.

I reluctantly let her go and grabbed the sword. I looked to my guard, and they followed me instantly.

Esmeray pulled my arm and I sighed. "Ez we don't have time, only me or Khaldon can wield this sword and kill the Ghosha."

Her eyes flicked between mine as she set her jaw.

"Fine, but we surround you at all times," she said as she looked to Silver and Ireland. "Silver, you take the left flank, I'll take the right, and Ireland you guard her back."

We reached the infirmary doors before I halted as I heard Khaldon call my name.

"Phoenix, wait."

I turned around to face the king, I gripped the sword tighter, he couldn't stop me if he tried.

"I'm coming with you."

I raised my eyebrows as he stalked towards me. I had expected a speech about how I should stay indoors, and it wouldn't be safe. He turned around and shouted into the infirmary. "Ruane, you're with me, Aeden do not leave her side." He barked as he looked at his sister one last time.

I looked to Aeden, his jewelled eyes glinted with sheer determination as he pulled a sword from the sheath at his back.

I followed Khaldon as he stopped outside of a door on the corridor and opened it to reveal an arsenal of weapons.

"Take whatever you need," he said as he strapped daggers and a sword onto a weapons harness.

We stepped outside into the battle of man against beast. I froze as I looked to the guards on the ground that had been slain by the Ghosha, black blood had splashed up the moonstone bricks of the palace and lay in murky pools on the ground.

"Phoenix!"

I snapped my head to the right as Esmeray pushed me out of the way and swiped her sword along the length of a Ghosha.

Khaldon was ahead of us, cutting through the beasts like it was nothing as he enveloped them in shadows, the return of some of his power giving him the advantage. We had only released some of Ravynne's power back into the earth and I watched terrified as Khaldon used the last remnants of his magick. As royals our magick was naturally stronger but Ravynne had bound him to her will and until the balance had fully been restored using his power could kill him.

I felt blood splash across my back as I whirled around to see Ireland cut the head off one of the beasts.

"Why are they surrounding Phoenix?" Silver shouted as she launched a dagger that embedded itself in a Ghosha's eye before a horseman stepped forward and gutted it.

"It's the sword," he said. "It's their instinct to stop anyone from wielding it."

I looked to Esmeray. "They don't want me to have it."

She looked ahead, her eyes fixing on something in the distance.

"Incoming!" she bellowed as her voice travelled across the grounds.

Khaldon's head snapped up and he ran towards the incoming threat with no hesitation. The horsemen surrounded Khaldon as he charged at the beasts.

"Let them come," I said. "I have the sword, let them come closer. I can kill them all."

"Phoenix," Esmeray panted.

"You have to trust me."

"We need to tell the king," She said and I ran to Ruane who was on our right defending the palace.

"Ruane, I need you to get to Khaldon, tell him I'm going to kill them."

He panted as he wiped the thick black blood of a Ghosha from his sword across his leg. He looked to the sword before opening his mouth to object.

I held up my hand cutting him off. "I don't have time to explain, tell Khaldon to let the Ghosha come to me."

"As you wish." He said reluctantly before running to Khaldon who was cutting the beasts down like stalks of wheat.

"Tell the guards to get back," I said as Esmeray barked orders to the guards that were still standing. It had been too late to save the ones that had been bitten but we could still save the ones that hadn't.

I edged towards a clearing on the grounds, it was the perfect place to destroy the Ghosha with no harm coming to Khaldon or his men. I looked to the distance where Ruane was telling Khaldon the plan and his head snapped towards me as I held the sword of Danann above me. Spring was coming, and daylight glinted off the steel as the yellow eyes of the Ghosha followed it to where I stood.

"Get back," I said to my guard as they cautiously stepped away from me.

I willed a wall of white-hot flames to surround me as the beasts charged towards the sword. I prayed to the mother as the hilt of the sword warmed in my hand, if this didn't work at least I had tried. I had fought for my kingdom until the bitter end.

"Now, Phoenix!"

Silver screamed as I slammed the sword into the ground and light erupted. The force of the sword's power threw me backwards and I slammed to the ground. My ears rang as pain coursed through me. I lay on the ground, disorientated, as I tried to lift my head and groaned as a sharp pain shot up my neck.

The sword stood solid in the ground and there was no Ghosha in sight, flecks of grey dust floated through the air as if they had just turned into mist, and I sank back into the ground as I breathed a sigh of relief.

CHAPTER 35

MY RELIEF WAS SHORT-LIVED as the sound of chains slinking across the floor of the place entrance snapped my attention to the doorway.

My guard took a protective stance in front of me and Ravynne slinked out of the palace dragging her foot behind her. Fresh putrid blood covered her mouth and I grimaced. "How has she escaped?" I breathed as fear coated my tongue. I couldn't see a way out.

Khaldon was in front of me in a flash, the sound of thunder cracked so close I covered my ears and he grabbed the sword from where it stood in the ground, disappearing into the shadows and reappearing behind Ravynne before she had the chance to escape.

He thrust the sword through her back again before ripping off the iron cuffs with his bare hands. The sword glowed as the last of Ravynne's power found its way back to the earth the weaker she became, there would be no more suffering because of her wrath.

She threw her head back, smashing into Khaldon's face and blood poured from his nose as he loosened his grip on the sword.

"Khaldon!" I screamed as panic surged through me, the sword hadn't weakened her enough. She whirled around as phantom claws struck him across his chest and I could see the whites of his flesh as his shirt became soaked with his blood.

I screamed again as he fell to the ground. I couldn't let Ravynne get the sword, it was the only thing that could kill her.

A dagger whistled through the air and those phantom talons of hers sliced it in two, the blade falling to the ground, separated from the hilt.

I threw a barrage of flames at her as I shouted to my guard, "Get the sword!"

We had to get Khaldon to the infirmary and keep the sword out of Ravynne's hands.

"You are no match for me Deveraux," Ravynne spat, her voice a thing of nightmares.

I blasted her with fire that only stopped her for a moment, but it was all I needed. I threw my flames at her over and over until I had forced her away from the sword.

With every step she took, I edged closer to Khaldon. My guard and Ruane tried to come at Ravynne from every angle, but every thrust of their blades was met with an invisible force working against them.

I crept closer to Khaldon until I was in front of him and I shoved a wall of flames around us. Ravynne battled to get through but couldn't penetrate the barrier I had created. I didn't feel a thing, but the flames burned so hot they were blue.

Ravynne's face was a look of death. I knew she wanted to kill me and she wanted to keep her power to seek revenge for her slain sisters. I couldn't let that happen. She threw her phantom claws at my wall of flames as I reached to grab the sword.

Esmeray launched another dagger, and it embedded in Ravynne's shoulder as she laughed, the sound haunting. She pulled the dagger free from her arm like it was nothing more than a rose's thorn.

I looked over to where Khaldon lay, the blood pooling around him on the ground. "Khaldon please" I begged. "Please stay with me." The flames roared and crackled around me. I needed to help him. I needed a reprieve. I was using everything in my power to keep myself encased in the wall of flames. Khaldon groaned as his eyes flickered. The wounds were so deep I knew he wouldn't make it if I didn't help him now. Ravynne looked to where Khaldon lay a smirk appearing on her lips. That was all I needed. I opened a gap in the barrier I had created and threw my flames into her, she shrieked as the first blast hit her and stumbled back as she tried to shield herself.

I had caught her off guard and that was all I needed. I took a step forward and pushed my hands out, the flames danced around us as I encased us both in a prison of fire. I blasted my flames at her hands and she roared in pain, satisfaction crept over me as her skin blistered.

I pushed forward and plunged the sword into her chest. Light pulsed through it as it drew her power from her, I had to finish what we had started so we could all be free. I pulled the flames back slightly so my guard could reach her with their weapons.

Blood dripped from my nose as I felt myself weakening, I couldn't hold on for much longer, but I clenched my jaw as the last drops of Ravynne's power found their way back to the mother.

The force of the transfer pushed me back, and I dug my heels into the ground to steady myself. I couldn't fail, I had lost too much already.

My arms ached from the weight of the sword, and I screamed from the depths of my soul as I willed the strength to finish this. The light diminished as a final blast of power left Ravynne's body, ripping winds around us. The enchantress choked, gripping onto her neck as she struggled for breath and I shoved my flames down her throat. A lifetime's worth of rage escaped me, and I screamed as sweat dripped down my back as she gasped for air, gargling as her body melted from the inside out.

I heard muffled voices behind me, but I couldn't make sense of the words, as though I were under water suffocating from my own power. I stepped closer as Ravynne's body turned to ash in front me. Her bones lay in a pile on the floor, but I didn't stop. I reached inside the depths of me and drew on the last drops of my power, I wanted the world rid of her for good. I blasted the bones with the deepest, strongest part of me until there was nothing left.

"Phoenix!" Esmeray's eyes were wide as she took in the sight before her. I could feel my nose bleeding and I was damp with sweat. She held up her hands to shield herself from the flames as they retreated, pulling themselves back into me as I fell to the floor. A tear escaped my eyes as I lay lifeless on the ground.

"She's gone," I whispered and fear flooded me as I watched Ruane kneeling over Khaldon. "Please don't let him die."

He picked Khaldon up, his blood staining the front of Ruane's shirt. "Get to the infirmary now!" His voice bellowed across the grounds.

I WAS DYING. I could feel my heartbeat slowing with every moment I lay in the infirmary. Shadows swirled around me as I thought about being reunited with my mother.

Ravynne was gone and my father didn't have to fear anymore. Khaldon's kingdom was safe.

The world was slipping away. I blinked as tears fell onto the pillow underneath me. I thought about the people I would be leaving behind. Mistiness clouded my vision, and I felt myself sinking. I didn't feel afraid, I felt tired, as though my soul had done what it was destined to do.

"She can't die." Khaldon said through gritted teeth.

I felt as if I was being pulled underwater, and I knew I wouldn't be tethered to this world much longer.

"Someone do something!" Silver shouted. I could see Khaldon wince in pain as I struggled to keep my eyes open. I just wanted to rest. Just for a moment. The creaking of the infirmary bed and a scuffle made me open my eyes and I could see Khaldon trying to sit up as Aeden and Ruane struggled to hold him down. Then darkness fell, consuming me. I felt calm and content as if I were falling into a deep sleep. The darkness pulled me deeper into its embrace and I gave up fighting it.

"She can't die, because I love her." Khaldon groaned. I felt something snap in my soul, the bonds of the curse unravelling from around my heart as my last breath left my lungs.

☐

CHAPTER 36

Khaldon

I COULD FEEL MY POWER returning to me as it knitted my wounds back together. My shadows enclosed me in darkness, but I could hear everything. Esmeray was screaming at Taresse to help Phoenix. I was helpless until my power had fully returned but I could feel it building under the surface. Phoenix was dying. I could feel it in my bones and I couldn't lose her.

Ireland screamed as I heard Phoenix take her last breath. My wounds hadn't healed but I couldn't let her die. I pushed myself off the cot as one of the wounds ripped back open, hot pain shot through my chest, but I found my feet and pushed to stand up.

"Khaldon, you need to let your power finish healing you!" Aeden shouted as he raced to my side pushing a bandage to my chest. I looked at Phoenix lay on the bed next to me, blood had crusted around her nose and her silver hair was spread out on the pillow behind her. If it weren't for the blood on her face, she would look peaceful, as if she were just dreaming.

I stumbled over to her bed and grabbed her hand. "Phoenix stay with me—stay with me!"

I pressed my ear to her mouth and couldn't feel the dance of her breath across my skin and panic flashed through me.

"Pass me the sword!" I roared at Ruane. It was filled with the ancient magick that was powerful enough to defeat Ravynne, it had to bring her back. My shirt filled with warmth as my blood soaked through the fabric. My magick was fighting a losing battle trying to heal me, but I had to try for her. Ruane came rushing back into the infirmary. "NOW!" I bellowed. He thrust the sword into my hand, the moment I touched it, a bright light glowed from within the blade. The handle warmed in my palm as I held the sword with both hands, feeling the power under the surface.

"Her tunic, I need it open!" I shouted as Esmeray rushed over and ripped Phoenix's tunic open revealing her under garments and the smooth brown skin of her chest.

My heart thundered in my chest. I had no idea if this would work. I was following an instinct, a primal part of me that knew I had to keep Phoenix alive. I raised my arms to position the sword above Phoenix's chest, pulling another wound open. I hissed as the pain spread through my skin like fire. I prayed to every god there was as I slammed the blade into the centre of her chest, right through her heart. Light erupted through the room as my shadows enclosed us in a cocoon of darkness. They swirled around us as a glow appeared under her skin. The ancient magick worked its way through her blood, as if she had absorbed all that ancient power. I held my breath for what felt like eternity and as I fell to my knees clutching my chest, her eyes flickered open to meet mine.

CHAPTER 37

Phoenix

MY BODY FELT HEAVY. As if the force that kept me tethered to this world was pulling me down, like I had gained another soul. Echoes of my guard and Khaldon screaming rang in my ears. Lights flashed across my eyes as I blinked slowly. I looked down at my hands, a soft glow was dancing beneath my skin. I turned to look at my guard, I could hear their hearts beating so loudly. Aeden had placed Khaldon on the cot next to me and my heart sank as I saw him covered in blood. I tried to push myself up, but my strength was non-existent.

"Is he dead?" I asked no one in particular. The tension was heavy throughout the infirmary.

"Is he dead!" I shouted. I was helpless as I lay there, and not knowing whether he had survived was torture. I heard him before I took my last breath. He'd said he loved me. I couldn't bear losing another person I cared about because they were trying to save me.

"What happened?" I demanded, my breathing quickening as I looked back to Khaldon. Aeden stepped forward eyeing me warily. "You died Phoenix, so Khal put the sword of Danann into your heart."

I looked down to see my tunic had been ripped open, a faint scar on my chest glowing with every heartbeat.

"How am I here?" I looked around frantically, everyone in the room looked at me as if they had seen a ghost. As though I were a spirit from the land of souls among them.

"We don't know Phoenix, the power from the sword must have given you life," Silver said, her voice hoarse.

Tears pricked at my eyes. "But I died, I felt it."

Khaldon coughed, blood sprayed from his mouth and my heart dropped to my stomach.

"No, no, no, no." I rolled onto my side as I slid off the cot. I stumbled over to Khaldon running my hands down his face. "Khaldon, I'm right here."

His breathing was shallow, his chest rattled as blood filled his lungs and bile burned in my throat at the thought of losing him.

"I need the sword!" I shouted as my feet swayed, it was an effort to stand upright, my fear was turning into panic, I knew I wouldn't survive another loss.

Esmeray grabbed the sword from the other side of my cot and placed it in my hands, I looked down waiting for the handle to light up like it had anytime me or Khaldon had touched it.

I looked to Aeden and Ruane, "Why isn't it lighting up? Where is the power?"

Ruane's eyes flicked to the scar on my chest that was pulsing with light.

My hands went slack as the sword dropped to the floor, the steel clashing against the cold stone.

"You're the sword, Phoenix," Ireland said in disbelief.

I shook my head refusing to believe what Ireland had said. The power of the ancestors had transferred to me.

Aeden approached me cautiously. "The mother chose you to retrieve the sword Phoenix, the mother trusted you with this power."

If that was true, then only I could save Khaldon.

I leaned over the king as I thought about my ancestors standing with me. The curse was broken and I had saved my bloodline. A warm light emitted from my hands, and I held the glow over Khaldon's chest. He had worn himself out trying to save me and himself at the same time. His power should have healed his wounds by now, but his chest was soaked with blood. I willed the light to heal him. I willed the light to bring him from the cusp of death. The ancient magick that had brought me back from the dead was now flowing through my veins and I prayed to the mother to help me save him.

I leaned to whisper in Khaldon's ear. "Please come back to me. I love you too."

The warmth seeped into his skin, and I watched as the magick glowed under his skin. Ruane came to stand next to me as I heard Khaldon's heartbeat getting stronger.

"It's working!"

The entire infirmary held its breath as we waited to see if the healing would be enough.

"Ez." I turned to Esmeray and held my hand out, "I need a dagger please."

She passed me a blade, and I ripped through his shirt to reveal his fair skin coated in blood, the pulse of his heartbeat getting stronger was the only sound.

I knelt on the ground as I placed my hand over his heart. Moments passed with nothing but silence. Then I heard the smooth deep voice of the king.

"The woman I love shall never bow before me."

I choked a sob as I jumped up and threw my arms around him. I looked into his stormy grey eyes and thanked the mother that it had worked.

My hand weaved through his hair as all restraint disappeared, and my lips crashed onto his mouth. After almost losing him, I wasn't wasting another moment. I was aware of everyone watching us but after cheating death, I wasn't willing to hold back anymore.

"I love you, Khaldon," The taste of him wrapped around my tongue as he pulled me back towards him so his mouth could devour mine.

"I thought I had lost you." I said as I held on to him as his arms wrapped around my waist, I didn't know why the mother had chosen to bring me back to life, all I could think about now was the man I loved and getting back to my kingdom.

"Not even death could keep me from you Phoenix, I would crawl through the depths of hell on my knees to find your heart again."

I lost control and sobbed, my tears a mixture of pain and pure bliss. Khaldon nuzzled into my neck, and I promised myself I would never let him go.

CHAPTER 38

I COULDN'T WAIT TO GET HOME to my father. Now that the curse had been broken, I hoped that we could forge some semblance of a normal relationship. I had sent word before the land of souls that all was well. Now I had to go back to my kingdom and face Lex's family. I had been in Sakaria for three months and spring was starting to break through the hard shell of winter.

Just the thought of Khaldon brought me so much comfort, it made me realise how starved I had been of love.

I fingered Lex's necklace as we approached the palace. I thought about my friend and how I was about to break her twin brother's heart. I scanned the crowd and saw Axel towering above the other palace members as I pulled the horse to a stop before the gates.

"I can't do this." I couldn't face the guilt of facing Axel when I felt responsible for Lex's death. If it weren't for me, she would still be alive.

"Phoenix, we'll do this together," Esmeray said, and I noticed the faint sheen of tears in her eyes.

A lump formed in my throat as I nodded and turned to face my home. I dismounted my horse as we approached the palace steps and looked for my father in the crowd that had gathered. I noticed the guard had their mourning uniform on. I dreaded to think of how many casualties my kingdom had suffered from the Ghosha. I wondered if they realised I was the one that shattered the veil between the living and the dead.

I walked towards the members of the guard and staff that had gathered in front of the steps. Axel dropped to his knee in front of me, and the guard followed. I looked to where Isaac stood in the crowd that had gathered, and he placed his hand over his heart before taking a knee.

I ran my gaze over the crowd again, still unable to see my father.

"Where's my father?" I asked.

Axel stood towering over me as he said, "The king has passed on to the other side—Your Majesty."

"My father's gone?" I whispered. This was too much to bear, I felt my flames rushing to the surface to shield me from the devastating pain I felt.

I whirled around to look at my guard who had also taken a knee.

"Esmeray what are you doing?"

I grabbed Lex's necklace as panic surged through me. Axel noticed my movement and his eyes flicked to the necklace then behind me to my guard. He went to step forward, then thought better of it. I dropped my hand as I closed the distance between us.

"Axel, I'm so sorry." My voice cracked as I said the thing I had been dreading the entire journey back to Mercea.

A muscle feathered in his jaw as he fought back tears, and I couldn't have hated myself more.

"It was my fault, it's my fault she's gone. I'm so sorry." I didn't deserve his forgiveness even if he could find it in him. I would never forgive myself.

Esmeray stepped forward. "Phoenix, that is not your burden to bear."

My blood pounded in my ears as my chest tightened.

"What happened to the king?" Esmeray asked.

Axel stood taller, quickly falling back into his role as the general of Mercea's armies.

"We were overrun by creatures from the seas and they infiltrated our land. The king was with us in battle, and we lost him."

My father and friend were both gone and the crown had passed to me. I was now the Queen of Mercea, and I was in love with the King of Shadows.

ACKNOWLEDGEMENTS

First and foremost, I wanted to thank you—the reader, your support means the world and I really hope you enjoyed the first part of Phoenix's story.

I wanted to thank the amazing Tommy's research team at St Mary's hospital, for your endless support and encouragement, especially while I was sat on the reception desk dreaming of being a writer.

A special shout out to Faye, for helping me choose my book cover.

I wanted to thank my friends and loved ones for supporting me on this journey.

Thank you to my Beta reader Kristin, your input helped me so much and for that I am forever grateful!

Thank you to the cover designer Gabriella Regina, and my editor Jade Church for helping me make this book the best it could be.

☐

ABOUT THE AUTHOR

A. J. Ford is an emerging fantasy author, currently working on her next novel. An avid reader, she loves anything that isn't set in the real world, preferring to escape into magic filled fantasies. A Crown of Souls is the first book in her Cursebreaker trilogy.

If you enjoyed this book, please consider keeping in touch with A. J. Ford on social media, she would love to hear from you!

Printed in Great Britain
by Amazon

27268228R00172